AF615277

The FLYING CIRCUS

The FLYING CIRCUS

Emily Trafford Berges

WILLIAM MORROW AND COMPANY, INC.
New York

Library of Congress Cataloging in Publication Data

Berges, Emily Trafford.
The flying circus.

I. Title.
PS3552.E7192F55 1985 813'.54 84-1112
ISBN 0-688-02989-2

Printed in the United States of America

2 3 4 5 6 7 8 9 10

BOOK DESIGN BY PATRICE FODERO

For my mother and
my father

I don't call it pluck, I call it joy.

—Tiny Broadwick
Aerial Stuntwoman
(1897–1978)

It's going to get me someday. It's sooner or later going to get us all.

—Ralph Johnstone
Exhibition Pilot
(1886–1910)

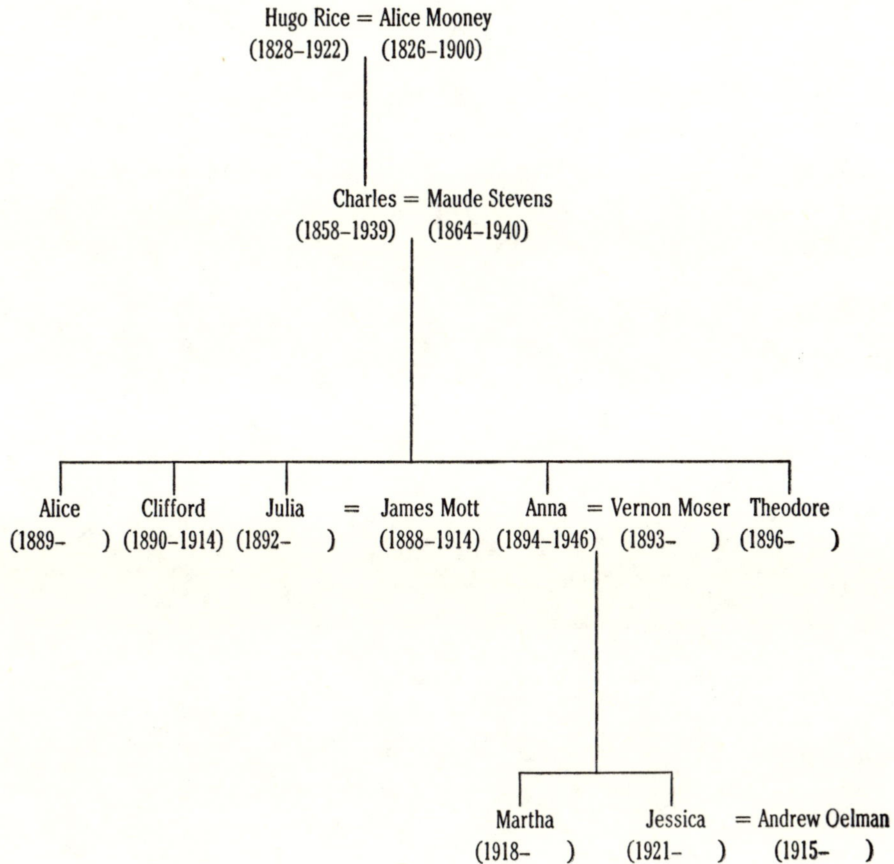
Hugo Rice = Alice Mooney
(1828–1922) (1826–1900)
Charles = Maude Stevens
(1858–1939) (1864–1940)
Alice (1889–)
Clifford (1890–1914)
Julia (1892–) = James Mott (1888–1914)
Anna (1894–1946) = Vernon Moser (1893–)
Theodore (1896–)
Martha (1918–)
Jessica (1921–) = Andrew Oelman (1915–)

July 4, 1952

i

ALICE

It wasn't exactly your perfect day for flying, a little too heavy and hazy for that, but cool up here anyhow. The struts on the Jenny were humming like crazy as we hit her top speed and her little engine was clacketing away, and then, bitten by some devil, I buzzed that damned construction site, skimmed right on by at about two hundred feet. Hoped I scared the bejesus out of somebody, even just the watchman and his cat.

I wondered how Buddy was taking this little caper, which wasn't part of the original deal. Far as I could tell from his back he wasn't screaming bloody murder or anything, not that I could've heard him with the racket of the engine and the roar of the slipstream and that twanging in the struts. Funny thing, here's Buddy, who had Rices flying over his backyard every day of his life, all of a sudden sits up and takes notice, decides to try it himself. Saw that *Flying Leathernecks* out to the drive-in this week, I bet, whatshisface Wayne; usual bunch of claptrap'll do it every time.

Buddy wasn't the only customer I'd had today, of course. I must've taken up close to fifty other folks too. Not bad at three-fifty a head. Might have made a whole lot more if we'd done our regular holiday air show, but that wasn't *my* fault, Teddy acting so persnickety about everything. . . . I rolled out nice and easy and considered how I might just buzz that old site again, for the pure and simple hell of it. Used to be a racetrack, and I did hate to think what was going to happen, any day now, that pretty brown and green oval, the flowerbeds and grandstand, all flattened down into, what did they call it? . . . a shopping *mall*. Row-de-dow. Bunch of stores and a parking lot. When we got so rich after the First War we bought the track ourselves (along with a lot of other fool stuff—it's fun to be rich, I won't kid you). Hung on to it more than thirty good years, till Martha had to sell it off to the developers last fall to pay the tax bill. Pretty soon probably be selling off some more of the old Rice land, losing it piece by piece, dying a little at a time; sad way to go.

Right down there was where I saw my very first airplane, way back in 1911; a little traveling air circus, two teams of fliers, Wright versus Curtiss, that big rivalry who on earth remembers today. I wasn't but twenty years old, a scrawny tomboy who didn't want to grow up, and I got so bug-eyed by the whole thing, I took myself off the very next day for the flying school down to Dayton. Sat me in one of those big cloth and wire contraptions; four hours later I was flying the damn thing, wind in my ears, sweat on my hands, tears in my eyes, but only because I didn't have my goggles yet. I'm not a sentimental type.

A couple of days later I came back home and taught my little brothers and sisters everything I learned down there. We bought ourselves a couple of airplanes, and before you knew it we were out on the exhibition circuit with all the other airstruck kids. The Fabulous Flying Rices, that was us, and we were just as famous as the Stinsons or the Moisants or the Wright Brothers themselves. You could read about us in any of those books about the old days, "Pioneers of the Skies," and such. Nowadays people thought we were dead probably, if they thought about us at all. The great days of aviation were over; anybody would tell you that.

Buddy was pointing down at the ground, and I looked out to see what he was pointing at. A baseball field with some kids playing. I guess he wanted me to buzz them too. I was starting to hear that little gag and miss in the engine. This one was a finicky old airplane and couldn't be trusted when she overheated. But then I figured, what the hell. I signaled him he should hold on tight. He was harnessed in so it didn't really matter, but I knew he'd enjoy himself a lot more hanging on for dear life.

As I rolled into a 180 over the diamond I could see, off to port, all slanted from the steep bank, our old rickety hangars, the fancy signs on the roofs faded to shadows now: RICE . . . RICE . . . RICE . . . FABULOUS FLYING CIRCUS . . . SCHOOL OF AVIATION (Accredited)

. . . DELUXE CHARTER AIRLINE All Points Service. Beyond the hangars and the row of sugar maples were the house and yard, the picnic table with its fluttering paper cloth, the familiar little figures of my sister Julia and my baby brother Teddy, my nieces Jessie and Martha and their men. All that was left of the Fabulous Flying Rices now. Back in the old days we'd been the stars of the Fourth of July parade every year—five of us throwing loops and rolls with red, white and blue smoke flares. Big crowds yelling and cheering to beat the band. But that was way, way back.

I did a nice little show for Buddy's pals, a big lazy S, a couple of snap rolls, and then went down to about two hundred again so Buddy could wave or make faces or whatever it was he wanted to do. Then I headed back to the strip. Enough was enough. I was ready to put my feet up and pour myself a stiff drink. I'd done a good day's work, a double day's work if you wanted to look at it that way. But I didn't want to look at it that way. We all pulled together in our family. . . .

Usually we gave a real snappy little performance along with the rides—funny costumes and dramatic action and laughs. Teddy dressed up like the villain in a black helmet and scarf and I'd be the hero in an old World War I uniform, and the two of us would do a lot of tricks that looked like a dogfight. Teddy used to use a real Fokker triplane, the authentic article, bought like the old track when we were so flush right after the war. But that old Fokker gave up the ghost a couple of years ago. Even Dennis couldn't save it, had to leave it rusting away in bits and pieces in a corner of the old Circus hangar. A pity. But he had his hands full just keeping the business airplanes together. That was bread and butter for us still. Never mind history.

Oh, and one other piece of action we gave them sometimes was to have me dress up as an old lady—well, I am an old lady, but I mean a little old lady with a lavender flowered dress and a little hat and button-up shoes. I'd go strolling out onto the field like I didn't know where I was at and climb into an airplane and sort of accidentally take off. I'd fly around doing all kinds of nutty stunts. Everybody always loved that part of the show. I got the idea when I saw Lincoln Beachey do it at a county fair in Nebraska back in '13, a couple of years before he got himself killed in that crazy accident out in San Francisco. But nobody remembers him today either.

I was pretty darn sure there wasn't anything wrong with the other

Jenny, but poor old Teddy, he was doing an awful lot of malingering and dawdling around these days. And Lord, he was six years younger than me. But, except for my white hair, which I'd had when I was thirty anyhow, probably nobody would ever guess. I almost dyed my hair last year when I saw one of those Tintair ads on the TV. People never did like the idea of flying with a lady, especially an old gray-headed one. But I wasn't like my sister at least, worrying how did I look and checking in the mirror every two seconds. (Julia practically took a whole vanity table with her in the cockpit. Never stopped her from flying the pants off everybody, me included, I have to admit.)

I was just bringing us in when I noticed that mean little twinge in my right hand again, pretended not to. Darned engine was really starting to cough and spit now. I blipped the ignition a couple of times to cut our speed. Not much on fancy controls, these old girls, but you could set 'em down at thirty-five. The whine in the struts simmered down to a hum and a whisper as I let her roll to a stop at the end of the strip and watched the propeller whop itself down and quiver and stand still. Then it got real quiet all of a sudden, the way it always did, and you could feel what a hot day it was, sticky waves of Ohio heat closing in on you all over again. I jumped out and reached up to help Buddy. "Those friends of yours down there?"

"Yeah," he said. "My brother and some kids. He was the pitcher."

"We put on a show for 'em, didn't we?" I tied the airplane down and we started to walk back, but then I saw Dennis coming toward us on his crutches, waving for us to stop. So we stood there in the hot sun and waited for him to catch up with us. Bugs were jumping and humming in the long grass and I had to keep swatting them off my face. "What's the matter?" I said when he got up even with us.

"Nothing. Want to push her inside so's I can work on her later. Didn't like the way she sounded just then."

Buddy was hopping along, trying to keep up with Dennis, who could swing along pretty fast on those crutches by now. The two of them were a funny pair to watch together, like a comedy team where the wrong sizes were part of the joke. Buddy must have been about a foot shorter than Dennis, with a perfect little man shape, even if it wasn't but five feet two inches high. He was already seventeen, so there wasn't much chance of him growing any bigger. "Hey, Denny," he said, leaping along sideways ahead of us, still full of pep in spite of the heat, "my brother was down to Chillicothe that day, and he said it looked like you was getting killed."

"Nah," Dennis said. "Could've been a lot worse, believe me."

"Was your bike *wrecked*?" Buddy had the kind of grin on his face that made you think he hoped it was. Kids always seemed to love the idea of a good wreck.

"Uh-uh. Bent a little, like me. Come on, kiddo, let's get these doors open and push her in." He turned to me, pivoting neatly on one crutch. "Alice, why don't you go on back? Buddy and me can take care of this. You already done your share today."

"Well, okay." To tell the truth I was kind of beat, just as happy to leave them to it, so I headed off along the road to the house. Got to daydreaming and almost walked right into Martha coming around the corner of the garage with a big plateful of deviled eggs.

"Oh, Auntie Alice, you scared me!" She had that same breathless way of talking her mother'd had, a sort of wide-eyed, kidlike quality that Anna lost too early, but Martha must've been way past thirty now. She really loved these big holiday do's and always went a little overboard in my estimation. Four kinds of salad, three kinds of dessert, hot dogs and hamburgers and chicken too. Way too much for me. But I didn't want to be ungrateful, after all. "I have time for a bath before we eat?"

"Oh, sure you do. The charcoal's not even started yet."

"You better take this." I pulled a handful of crumpled bills out of my pocket. Sometimes we let Jessie sit out there and collect the fares, but she'd been having a bad day so I'd done it myself. "And guess what? Little Buddy says he wants to take some lessons. I thought maybe we could give him a half-rate, what do you think?" Martha wasn't as soft as she looked, not about money, not about anything. She had to try to keep us solvent, and that wasn't always so easy. "Uh, he's a good kid, you know."

"Where's he going to get the money?"

"He's saving it up from after school. Doesn't want his dad to know, of course." Buddy's father, Otto Dapple, was tough as a nut and never had much truck with any of us but Dennis.

"I guess it's okay. Can't be real choosy, can we?" She gave me that gentle smile made you think she was harmless, shy as a lamb. Just a little bit of a thing, Martha, but round everywhere. Probably look just like Julia when she got to be our age. "Where'd Dennis go, I wonder?"

"He's out back with Buddy. Thought the Jenny sounded bad."

"Oh, it always does, and he's supposed to be staying off his feet today. Honestly! . . . Well, never mind, you run on up now and get your bath. I'll call you when it's time."

I watched the water slowly filling the old clawfoot tub, kept clenching and unclenching my right hand, trying to ease away those little needle twinges. I'd been flying for five solid hours, after all. . . . But in the back of my mind I recalled my sister Julia and all the excuses she used to make when her eyes went bad on her back in '40, before she finally had to ground herself. A smutty windscreen, a dust storm (over someplace like Seattle), a swarm of locusts, a pea-soup fog the U.S. Weather Service never heard of. Truth was she was nearly blind as a bat, but it took months before anybody could get her to admit it. I didn't want to be like that.

I took the bottle of Jack Daniel's out of the medicine chest and stood it by the tub. I wasn't what you'd call a boozer, but at the end of a long day I did like my sour mash whiskey, and I liked it neat. Good for your aches and pains. Good for the blues. I'd been flying close to forty-three years and didn't know what in the world I'd find to do with myself if I ever had to stop. Scared me silly even thinking about it. But the arthritis had got to my mom when she was about my age.

The window was open and voices came floating up to me from the yard, Martha's, and Julia's, and then Andrew's, along with some charcoal smoke from the grill. I must have dozed off a little, because the next thing I heard was a tap on the bathroom door. My sister's knock, I'd recognize it anywhere, tactful but irritating all the same; I don't know how she managed it. You could bet she was right outside listening, nosy old thing, thinking poor Alice must have drifted off in here.

"I'll be out in a minute."

"All right, dear. I was afraid you might have drifted off in there." I heard her quick light footsteps—she still walked like a feather for all the weight she'd put on—moving away across the bare floor of my room. In this house it didn't do much good having a private bathroom. People respected that only up to a point.

I fumbled around in my closet, trying to decide what to wear. I'd never been much good at clothes, except for the old khaki trousers and shirts I'd had for years that were comfortable as my skin. Of course I'd never exactly been a beauty. My brothers and sisters got all the looks in our family; that was a fact I'd faced up to early on. Never let it bother me too much, though. Some men liked homely women better anyway. And when you thought about what poor Anna'd done to her life, pretty or not —sure made you think twice.

Finally I yanked on the only dress I owned, a blue shirtwaist thing with a Peter Pan collar and a white plastic belt Martha bought me a couple of years ago. Surprised myself in the mirror, looking like an organ grinder's monkey with my round brown face sticking out of that baby blue collar. Now shoes. That was the trouble with dressing up. I had my work shoes, old-fashioned clodhopper things, I had some black suede Enna Jetticks circa 1948 and I had some white gym shoes with high tops. Lord knows where they came from. I took another quick snort of bourbon and put on the gym shoes. It wasn't a damn banquet, after all, just an old family picnic.

When I came downstairs and across the front hall I heard gunshots and galloping horses and a couple of drawling voices, a good guy's and a villain's. We only got but two television channels around here, and the reception wasn't real good on one of them. I peeked into the den and there was Teddy, slumped down in the big wing chair watching some darn western on the bad channel. He had the shades all pulled down tight, but you still couldn't see much more than snow.

"Hey, Teddy, what are you doing in here all alone? We're going to be eating soon."

He turned around and kind of glared at me, like he was waking up. Teddy had a boyish look still, though he'd puffed up some around the middle. His hair was the same color it'd been when he was a baby. He and Cliff had had the same reddish-brown mops and long handsome horsey faces, but Teddy was a big fellow and Cliff had been your true Rice, little and fine-boned, with soft high-colored skin. My brother Clifford was killed at an air show off in Kansas a long time ago, so he was still a boy in my mind's eye. I could tell Teddy was embarrassed being caught watching a cowboy show, but not embarrassed enough to make an excuse, like this happened to come on after the ball game or something. Too dejected to bother maybe. I couldn't figure out what was the matter with him these days.

My brother used to be the liveliest guy you'd ever meet, always full of the devil, always planning something crazy to make you laugh.

Like once when he was flying for a little two-bit airline out of San Diego, must've been 1930 or so, he borrowed a blind guy's dog and cane and some dark glasses and walked through the airplane with them right before takeoff. It was one of those cute old jobs, a Bellanca maybe, with a seat on each side and the little drapes at the windows. The passengers were already strapped in and everything and here's the pilot, see, tap-tapping up the aisle. A couple of them were guys in the business who knew Teddy and laughed themselves silly over it. But the rest, your usual nervous Nellie types, didn't think it was so funny, and don't you know old Ted was out on his ear the next day. Not that he had to worry about finding another job. He was a first-rate pilot, strictly business in the air, for all his nuttiness on the ground. Now it seemed like he'd lost that old spark.

I scuffed over to him in my white high-tops, which could have made a cat laugh, but he didn't even notice. He was already scrunched back down staring at the screen. I almost wished I'd brought down my bottle so we could have a snort, cheer him up, but I always left it up there in the bathroom. I didn't want to turn into a regular drinker. Bad habits were like chains around your ankles, my mother always used to say, and she was right.

Right at that moment Andrew stuck his head in the door behind me. "Anybody seen Jessie?"

Teddy jerked his thumb toward the chair in the corner. Jessie was so quiet sometimes you'd hardly know she was there.

"Golly, Ted, it's dark as a tomb in here." Andrew went over and pulled up some shades and the sun slanted in on us real bright all of a sudden. Jessie put one of her thin little arms across her face and sat there perfectly still, like she was playing statues, with that arm up stiff like that.

"Come on, Jess," Andrew said to her, real quiet, the way you talk to a cat or a dog. Then he lifted her out of the chair, untwisted her arm and started walking her across the room. The sunlight kind of blanched out her face, but as soon as she was in the shadow again I could see how bad she looked. Some days you wouldn't know anything was wrong with her, except she acted a little childish and of course she didn't talk at all, but today her eyes had that look they sometimes got, blank and dull, as if she was grieving about something, only nobody had ever been able to figure out what.

The two of them went out into the hall toward the lavatory under the stairs. You could tell Jessie to wash up for dinner, and she'd do it for you nice as you please. But Andrew liked to take a lot of trouble combing her hair or washing her hands and face for her sometimes. I guess that was about all he had left he could do to be nice to her. It'd been years since she'd let him touch her any other way.

Teddy leaned forward and turned off the set when "Republic Pictures The End" came on the screen with the big eagle flapping its wings. "Good picture," he said. "Kermit Maynard. Saw it when it first came out." He stood up and shook himself a bit to settle his shirt around his little roll of stomach. "Let's go, sis. Guess you're all I got left. I'm a lonely old fellow these days." He said it slow and drawn out, in one of his comedy voices, but I could tell it wasn't a joke. He was really feeling that sorry for himself.

"That's sure a stupid damn thing to say, with seven people living on top of each other in this house. Lonely is the last thing you can be."

"Eh, what?" he said in the creaky voice, scuttling along all bent over beside me, bobbing his head and snapping his mouth like he'd lost all his teeth.

I couldn't help laughing, though. "Oh, quit it, Ted." I swatted at his behind the way I used to when he was about three, and scooted him out the door ahead of me.

ii

JULIA

I scooped up a pile of macaroni salad and a pile of chicken salad and a pile of tuna salad. Then I took two deviled eggs and a slice of ham. I caught my sister Alice's disapproving eye and resolutely ignored it. She thought I ate too much, had let myself go completely to pot, and of course she was right. But why shouldn't I? I had no one to please but myself these days. Now, Alice could eat twelve large meals a day and never gain an ounce. Yet she'd have felt wicked, positively depraved, if she ate twelve meals a day. Nature is so unfair. Alice had been provided with those thin genes by our father's side of the family. I took after my mother, who began spilling over her corsets when she was twenty-nine. But at least, like her, I'd held on to the rest of my looks. Poor Alice with her leather wrinkles and gray frizz. Given a choice, I'd take flesh over gristle any day.

Down at the end of the table Martha was loading up a platter with hamburgers off the grill. I hadn't seen her sit down once yet. She glanced at me and smiled, her face flushed and content. You'd presume a normal girl would resent slaving away her youth in a house full of crotchety middle-aged relatives. Not Martha. Why, when she was in college she'd drive home every weekend to put up casseroles and roasts for us to eat during the week. The whole family was perfectly spoiled by now. It was fortunate for us all that she enjoyed being our pillar of strength, wasn't one of those resentful, martyrish women. No, our Martha positively glowed. Men found her irresistible, I might add. All that domestic energy seemed to excite them enormously. Out of the corner of my eye I caught Andrew peeking slyly at her. Martha never noticed, of course. A charming thing, Andrew, a woman's man going to waste, yearning and yearning, but not Martha's type at all. I suppose if I'd been a little younger I might have taken him on myself. But he was my, my what, my nephew-in-law, and that might have been a trifle complicated, even for me.

Middle-aged I said we were. Actually we were almost old. *Old.* I wasn't afraid of that word. We came of long-lived stock, on both sides. My mother always said if it didn't get the TB and die at twenty, a Rice could live forever. Poor Anna, she was only the exception that proved the rule. She was forty-six, not twenty, and hoped she had the real thing at last, romantic old consumption—she didn't like being called a hypochondriac, who does?—but it turned out to be only a shoddy fungus, though *rare,* at least, and *fatal,* so she could save face. Histo-something. My brother Clifford doesn't count, because he died of violence, crushed to death in the wreck of his Wright B airplane in the summer of 1914, two months before my husband Jimmy died the same way.

The sun, round as an orange, was sinking behind the maple trees. The air was sweet and heavy and still hot as blazes. My plate was empty, so I helped myself to another deviled egg, the last one. It wasn't mere gluttony. I was trying to distract myself, and food would sometimes work. I rolled a bit of egg around in my mouth, concentrating, trying to ignore the old familiar signals, the tightness in my chest and blurring around the edges of things. . . .

They call what happens to me sometimes a "gift," but it's not a very nice one, certainly nothing you'd choose for yourself. More like one of those fairy-tale boons, capricious and ironic. (You're given three wishes and fritter them all away in insults, you have to dance your ass off in those damned red shoes; you know the kind of thing.) When I was eight I saw my grandmother pacing up and down in the dust of the road, dressed in a traveling suit, looking very annoyed and at the same time rather sad. When I spoke of it I was promptly sent to my room for fibbing because everyone knew she lay flat on her back in a hospital room twenty miles away. Later they found out I'd seen what I'd seen at the precise moment she'd died in that room, and I hadn't exactly been lying after all. But they couldn't unpunish me, could they? As a child, that was what mattered to me. I was innocent and they made me suffer. Hardly the last time I was to suffer for what I knew.

The day my husband died I saw his airplane suddenly go all black and gray, wavering before my eyes like a negative in solution. Just that one split second, and then it casually resumed its color. I blinked and shuddered, broke out in a cold sweat. Ten minutes later there was Jimmy, scrabbling at his control stick, bobbing and kicking, as the stalled airplane plummeted with him to earth. Oh, I'd babbled, I'd pleaded, and he'd stood there and listened with that maddening patronizing smile on his face, the sun flashing across his hair; such a pretty man, always. There was yet another lesson. It doesn't pay to tell what you know. It doesn't pay to know what you know.

I used the gift to help strangers—locating poor molested babies, tracing lost corpses, so many hapless victims of passion—but I preferred not to let it touch those I loved. I wanted their catastrophes to catch me unawares, merciful bolts from the blue. And I'd taught myself to resist, up to a point. Sometimes nothing would happen for months, or years even, then there'd be rumblings and bubblings in that mud pit, and I'd be taken again, filled with knowledge against my will.

* * *

The sun had disappeared. A thick greenish summer evening settled down around us. Rain tomorrow, probably. I could feel it. Bad flying weather. Off in the distance we could hear the first subdued booms of the town fireworks and see their first white glimmers above the trees. A few late fireflies were lighting up in the long grass beside the airstrip. Teddy puffed on a new cigar, and its smoke mixed with the charcoal smoke and floated gently above the table. Martha came up behind me and put her arms around my neck. I could smell her lavender soap. "Did you have enough to eat, Aunt Julia? There are nice hot coals for marshmallows, and there's a surprise. I bought Hershey's and graham crackers. We can have some-mores, remember them?"

Teddy heaved a lugubrious sigh. "Well, yes, you could marsh me a mallow, sweetie. Would you do that for your old uncle? I don't want the chocolate and crap. Just a plain old burned-up marshmallow on a green stick, the way we used to cook 'em when we were kids. . . ." He really was very tedious when he got in one of these moods.

A marshmallow blazed up on its fork and Martha lifted it off the grill, blowing at it, the glow illuminating her sweaty, pretty face. Vern loomed up out of the shadows, bobbing his head apologetically like some wretched serf barging in on the lord's revels. "Oh, poor Daddy," Martha cried. "You must be starved! Did the parade go on forever? Sit right down and I'll make you a hamburger. Dennis, get Daddy a beer."

Martha's father owned a small hardware store in town and belonged to the Chamber of Commerce. He always managed to get himself elected to the worst drudge jobs, cleanup committee or garbage patrol, made sure he never had any of the fun. He squeezed in beside Andrew and sat waiting for his supper like a good little child, his hands meekly folded in front of him, his bald head bowed.

I'd never for the life of me been able to understand what Anna had seen in Vern, except that he'd do anything on earth to please her. The only time he ever turned the tables . . . complete disaster. Of course, Vern's mother was at the root of all that. No doubt she expected Anna to refuse to make that ridiculous promise so she could have Vern all to herself again. But Anna didn't refuse, to spite the old dragon, I suppose. Poor Anna, so very . . . obdurate. I myself found promises to be the worst kind of sentimental nonsense—*love . . . obey . . . I'll never . . . I'll always*—and I'm sure I never kept one in my life. But, except for Jimmy, and that was over soon enough, I was never properly romantic, or serious, or *nice.*

Vern nibbled at his hamburger, in that tentative rabbity way he did everything (imagine him in bed, ugh), and Martha came across the lawn bearing an enormous triple-layer chocolate cake inscribed with flags and exploding fireworks in colored sugar. Alice groaned, "Oh, no . . ." Teddy picked up a knife and made a little show of carving the cake, precariously serving himself not the tiny triangle he'd cut but the hulk of the rest of the cake. Alice chuckled heartily, trying, apparently, to encourage this feeble horseplay, to cheer the poor old thing up, I supposed. "*Really,* Teddy," I said. "If you dump that thing in my lap I'll strangle you." I was about to cut myself a slice when I heard the telephone, our ring, two long, one short.

"Auntie Julia, it's for you, long distance. . . ."

"I'm real sorry to bother you on a holiday and all, Miz Mott"—Timmy Driscoll, one of my nicest policemen—"but we've got a little girl missing down here. I think we're going to need some help. If you could oblige," he added in his soft West Virginia voice. "Could you come first thing in the morning? Parents are real worried . . ."

After I'd hung up, I stood there for a few minutes by the open window, observing them all, my beloved and despised family. The feeling was pressing in on me again, humming in my ears, tingling my fingers. I was glad Timmy had called. Sorry about the little girl, of couse, but not sorry I'd have to concentrate on her instead. I looked up at the deep night sky, listening to the distant thumps and sizzles of fireworks, wondering where I might have been on this night if my life had been different. Somewhere. Nowhere. Foolishness. Here I was.

iii

MARTHA

A long fan of moonlight spread out through the trees, just grazing the edge of the airstrip, and showing up all the pocks and cracks in its tired old macadam. I couldn't imagine where we'd find the money to have it resurfaced in the spring, or where we'd find the money for six hundred other things we needed or to pay the scads of bills I'd been squirreling away and trying to forget about. But I didn't want to deal with any of that tonight. I was too happy in that simpleminded after-dinner way. Reggie Van Gleason was rubbing and rubbing against my legs, twitching his swaggery black tail (like the TV Reggie and his cape), hoping for a handout. Through some quirk of cat chemistry he adored tomatoes and had his eye on two leftover slices I was just wrapping up in waxed paper. "No you don't, Reg." I opened the screen door and scooted him out.

By now I had my family so well trained they never offered to help me anymore, so I had the big old kitchen all to myself, and that was the way I liked it. I could gaze out the window at the sun setting or the moon rising, watch my own shadow moving on the grass outside the window, and think, or dream, or plan, or worry, really let myself go. I sank my hands into the tepid water in the sink, feeling around for last lost pieces of silverware. I was almost ready to go upstairs when I spied the candlesticks full of dried wax and couldn't resist peeling it all out. Then I polished the silver cake server, absolutely the final thing.

I yawned and turned out the kitchen light. On my way upstairs I found poor Uncle Teddy in the den, fast asleep in front of the test pattern. I shook his shoulder gently, and he sat up, rubbing his hand across his face. ". . . wha' . . . what time z'it?"

"Oh, past one. Did Daddy go up already?"

"He went back to town I think, dearie."

"Oh . . ." I didn't know whether to be sad or furious. My father had a room behind his store where he could sleep, a cramped smelly awful place with only a cot in it. When I was a child he would slink off there plenty of nights, to get away from my mother. Now, lately, he'd taken it into his head that he didn't have the right to sleep under this roof at all. It was so silly. But my father did love to bedevil himself and cause himself unnecessary grief. It was a streak that ran very deep in his character, or why would he have married my mother in the first place? Still, I did feel sorry for him, sleeping in that old storeroom all by himself.

The upstairs hall was dark and quiet, except for a sliver of light under one door. Poor Andrew, reading late again, I guess. But I was never too pleased by the idea of him lying there sort of listening, you know. Not that I was so modest; it was the principle of the thing, a crowd of people living together trying to preserve the illusion of privacy at least. The Japanese, for instance, had all these complicated ways of pretending not to hear or see each other, crammed into those flimsy houses, imagine . . . where did I read that? . . . Well, let him listen, if it made him feel better. He didn't have an easy life.

I closed the bedroom door quietly and stood waiting for my eyes to get used to the dark. There was Dennis on the bed, a long pale shape, his cast blue white against the white-white sheet. I tiptoed over, stepping around the piles of clothes he'd left strewn everywhere. "You awake . . . ?" No, I'd spent too long downstairs. Sigh. I unbuttoned my dress and let it slide down over my knees. A hand reached up suddenly out of the darkness and clamped around my wrist. "Oh, you . . ." I laughed.

"You took your old time." He hauled me down onto the bed.

"Well, I had a lot to do." I was worming my way out of the rest of my clothes. "My work is never done." I slid over to him.

". . . watch it . . . Jesus . . ." We had to be careful to keep the weight off his bad leg. It was still so hot, even with the breeze from the window, and the sticky sheets were all pleated up around us before we were finished. He sank back finally with a last little surprised grunt of pain, and I disentangled myself cautiously, limb by limb.

"Not bad . . ."

He gave a snort. Well, it hadn't been three weeks since he'd tried to drift across a bad turn and his big Harley skidded out from under him, tumbled around with him awhile, then landed smack down on his left ankle. Most of the bruises had faded away by now, but he'd probably have to wear this cast till the middle of August. Dennis wasn't exactly foolhardy, but he never did give himself much of a margin for error. He liked flat-track motorcycle racing better than anything else in the world. It was the fastest, most dangerous kind of racing there was, and he was a glutton for speed and danger, as stubborn as they come.

". . . is it hurting a lot? . . . I'll get you an aspirin."

"Uh-uh. Don't. Itches like a sonofabitch . . . s'worse . . ." His voice was already thick and drowsy. He could always sleep, no matter what happened to him. Lucky Dennis.

Of course we'd had plenty of practice, making love around all kinds of obstacles and devices attached to his battered body, cloth and plaster, miles and miles of adhesive tape. That was the way it was with motorcycle racers. I could practically write a *Kama Sutra* of my own by now. Two summers ago, when he broke both arms at once, was the worst. He couldn't do any work, which always drove him wild, and we'd had to hire the dim-witted boy from the Sohio station to tune the precious engines. Dennis loomed over the poor creature, glowering, eagle-eyed, two huge white plaster arms stuck out in front of him like a statue's. As a further indignity I'd had to cut up all his food and feed him, which he absolutely hated. And then, in bed, he was completely at my mercy, which he didn't hate as much as he'd expected to, to be honest. But when I first knew him Dennis was very conservative about sex, truly believed there was only one way you ought to do it.

That was back in 1949, when our A & E, our aviation mechanic, took to drink. We kept finding the poor thing out cold on the hangar floor, some kind of problem with a woman. Then one day my uncle Teddy took off on a charter to Chicago with a loose elevator cable, and we all knew something had to be done. I asked around for days until finally a man at a truck stop scratched his head and said, "Well, you got Denny Hewitt, best there is . . . be over to your track this weekend . . . one of them motorcycle boys. . . ."

I was covered with dust and half deaf from the roar of a hundred Harley 750s by the time I found him, quite a picture in those black racing leathers that fit him like a second skin—an enormous beautiful snake, or some mutant dropped in from outer space. (He had a silly metal plate strapped to the bottom of one boot, for squashing revolting overgrown mutant insects? No, to protect his pivoting foot at those ridiculous speeds, what else?)

"Are you Denny?" I practically had to shout above the din.

"Yeah . . . Dennis," he replied in his flat Michigan voice.

He took off his helmet and there was this crest of only slightly greasy brown hair, a wide shark mouth, a bold nose. The men standing around began bawdily joshing at him, muttering and laughing behind me, and I wanted to sink into the earth. But he quelled them instantly with a mean look across my head, fixed his narrow brown eyes down on my face, not blinking or smiling or staring even, taking me all in. Naturally I thought he was marvelous. Oh, I could see he must be years younger than me, but I wasn't going to let a little detail like that stop me. He was twenty-six that summer and I was almost thirty-one.

People always tended to underestimate Dennis, of course, figuring a person who did the kind of work he did and had no discernible conversation must not be very bright. But everyone had to admit where machinery was concerned he was a genius, a wizard, a poet. He could make anything from a twin-engine airplane to a Mixmaster run better than it ever had before in its life—all he had to do was lay one of his huge hands on it, or listen to it.

Sometimes he didn't even have to listen. When I was driving over to my college reunion last year, the car started making this funny hissing noise and then sort of gritted itself down to ant speed and stuck there. I crawled into three gas stations where the men stood around like ninnies, fiddling with wires and stroking their chins, clearly mystified though they wouldn't admit it. Then I called Dennis up, and before I could finish describing the symptoms he said, "You got a pinhole leak in your radiator." The man at the next gas station was very impressed, thinking I'd diagnosed this problem all by my little self. . . .

Now you might consider it shocking that, whatever his profession, here I was sleeping with a man I wasn't married to, right under my own roof. But there'd never been any hypocrisy about sex in the Rice family, not ever. In fact, it was my Aunt Julia who took me up to Akron to get my first diaphragm when I was nineteen and starting to sleep with boys. (The doctor was an old beau of hers. She had old beaux in all walks of life, in every major city; very convenient.) But all of the Rice women—my mother and my aunts, my grandmother, my *great*-grandmother—had been breaking the rules way before me, tossing off their corsets, putting on trousers, going where only men were supposed to go, doing what only men were supposed to do.

There was a picture on the wall in the den, Mother and Julia, two pretty teenagers standing by a plane. (Was any Rice ever in a picture without a plane? Any Rice but me?) They were flanked by half a dozen fierce proud fellows in uniform, their *pupils*. They taught so many boys how to fly for that war, but then when all three sisters tried to enlist themselves, the army wouldn't have them. No, indeed. Alice finally did go over to France with the ambulance corps, which was okay for women because it was like being a nurse. Julia was too disgusted, so she ended up in Hollywood doing stunts in the movies instead, and my mother got married to my father and started me.

She, my mother, made some sacred vow never to fly again if she got pregnant, but she took me up with her once, holding me on her lap in the front seat of a Jenny with Alice in back doing the flying. I must have been about six. I was struck dumb with terror, my little fingernails digging into her arms, the wind blinding me, sucking the breath right out of my mouth and grabbing at my clothes like a live thing. And then the dreadful slow heaving up of the wing as we banked, the horrid blue expanse of space, the huge emptiness of the sky, with clouds and birds and little houses and people far far below . . . I hated high places of every kind now. Even climbing a stepladder made my palms sweat and my heart beat too fast. So I'd turned out to be the only earthbound Rice. That was my fate.

But fortunately my sister adored flying. She was a natural, everybody said. She crowed and chuckled and grinned out of the cockpit at me as they taxied in after her first flight. And she was littler than I'd been, only about four, when Mother took her up. You might think I'd be envious of all the praise and scrutiny my mother lavished on Jessie after that, but I was, honestly, only relieved. I merely had to recall the horror of that one flight, and every other emotion would melt away to nothing beside the power of that memory.

And then, in the end, Jessie had to suffer so much, pay so dearly for her courage and her skill, and it began to look as if I'd been luckier all along. I'd followed my instincts, even when they seemed defiant or perverse, and managed to save myself without ever noticing that's what I was doing. I couldn't save poor Jessie, though. I'd never thought she needed saving. You can be so wrong about those things, so wrong.

I kept moving around in the bed, trying to find a sleep-inducing position. The moon had climbed up over the trees and was shining right in our window. The luminous dial of Dennis' clock read quarter to three. I eased my way out of bed, put on my robe and crept downstairs. All the books about insomnia say it's best to get up and occupy yourself with constructive work instead of tossing and turning all night, and that's what I usually tried to do.

I went down to the basement and put in a huge load of laundry. I sorted and folded yesterday's load. I ironed a dress and some shirts.

(It was cool in the basement, perfect for ironing.) I came back up to the kitchen and boiled some eggs for egg salad for lunch. I made out my shopping list and cleaned out the refrigerator. Then I went into the den, sat myself down at the desk and took all the unpaid bills out of the top drawer. It was an enormous wad held together with rubber bands. I took the rubber bands off and started sorting them into three stacks: PAY NOW!, WAIT-A-MONTH and WAIT.

By the time I got through the whole lot of them and added up the figures, it was close to dawn. Birds were already chirping in the trees near the house, an incongruously peaceful and cheerful sound, since I didn't feel the slightest bit peaceful and cheerful. I stood up and tried to stretch the tension out of my weary body and then dragged myself back into the kitchen in a daze. I began going through the familiar morning routine, taking down cereal bowls and cups, measuring coffee, opening the breadbox, but my mind was reeling.

Everything was so much worse than I'd thought. I didn't see how we were going to survive the next few months without raising cash. Getting rid of the old racetrack had been hard enough. Selling off even one acre of the original Hugo Rice land would surely be greeted with horror and alarm. I loved my uncle and my aunts, and I knew they'd never understand. When we'd still had stocks, I could always sell a few of them on the sly. Now the stocks were long gone . . . everybody talked about the terrible slump in private aviation, and everybody said it couldn't last. Maybe things would get better, if we could only hang on a little longer. How, though, *how*?

I made myself a cup of tea and was slumped down over it at the kitchen table when Julia appeared, stepping softly into the kitchen in the pearly dawn light, wrapped in a blue silk robe, auburn hair curling gently around her face, blue eyes peering sleepily at me through her thick glasses. Her skin looked smooth and ivory-pink even though she'd just rolled out of bed. She was still a beauty, no question about it. I certainly hoped I could look that sexy when, and if, I ever got to be sixty. The way I felt right now, I doubted I'd make it.

"I told you not to bother to get up for me," she said huskily, blinking at me. I could tell she was secretly pleased.

"I was up anyway." I avoided her eye, poured some of Jessie's Sioux Bee honey spread into my tea; I'd sunk that low, thinking some sugar in my system might help. "I couldn't sleep . . . you know me." Aunt Julia was sharp in her way, but I knew better than to tell her what it was that was preying on my mind so. She did not consider money a fit topic for civilized discourse. Well, and she was right. "Why don't you go wake Teddy and get dressed and everything, and when you come down I'll have breakfast all ready for you. . . ."

I ended up making them omelets, toast, pancakes, the works, and sending them off with sandwiches and a big Thermos of coffee, which was silly since Julia always got lunch free, courtesy of the Moundsville P.D., and Teddy never ate when he drove. The sandwiches would come back soggy and inedible, and I'd have to dump out the stale coffee and wash the smelly Thermos with ammonia. But I couldn't help myself. I craved tasks to ward off the dismal futile buzzing of figures in my brain. Such ridiculous amounts of money, the Fabulous Rices, deadbeats . . .

I stood in the driveway in the fresh summer morning air, watching the station wagon disappear around the curve in the road, feeling forlorn the way you always do seeing people off early in the morning. Then I trudged on back to bed and lay there staring at the sun dazzles on the ceiling till the alarm went off, wondering, did I dream all that, did I sleep and dream. . . ? But I knew I hadn't dreamed those bills, and the day of reckoning was bound to arrive sooner or later. It was up to me, as usual, to decide what to do.

AUGUST 15

i

MARTHA

It was going to be one of those awful muggy days. The air was closing in like a soggy old blanket already, and the sky was a thick hazy no-color, with a few low clouds scudding along here and there, so the kitchen was bright one minute and gloomy the next. I snatched two pieces of bread out of the toaster with one hand and slapped them onto a plate for Alice. With the other hand I was stirring Julia's eggs. I was wearing my best summer outfit, a yellow piqué suit, and trying not to spill anything on it. I'd told them all I was going to the dentist. I felt nervous, though, wicked, as if I were going to town to rob the bank or elope with the butcher. I couldn't reveal to any of them what I was really going to do. I couldn't tell a soul, except maybe Andrew. I had my reasons.

"You know, I could drive you in to Dr. Cram's, Martha," Andrew said. He was leaning back against the sink, drinking his coffee, his jacket over his arm. Andrew was the type who wore a jacket even in this kind of weather. "I could run you back during lunch period."

"Oh, thanks, but I'll be finished way before that."

Julia's toast popped up, and I flung a piece down next to her eggs and handed the plate across. She stared at it suspiciously for a minute, as if she were looking for bugs, then finally took it. Aunt Julia rarely got up early unless she was traveling, but these days she wasn't sleeping well and came down at eight along with everyone else, always in a very bad humor. Today I was glad to see her, no matter how cranky she was. I needed her to keep an eye on Jessie for me while I went to town. Alice would be out with Buddy's lesson and my uncle might not come down for ages, and besides, he wasn't very reliable right now. (What luxury, to have the time to be depressed. Maybe I'd try it sometime.) We never liked to leave Jessie all by herself in the house.

"Where's my good jam?" Julia said, her voice getting high and tinny the way it always did when she was on the verge of an outburst. Alice gave her the jar of Kraft marmalade. "No, no, *no.* The good jam. Not this supermarket shit."

At that I almost lost *my* temper, something I hardly ever did. (Having the coolest head in the room always gave you the advantage, I knew for a fact. Living with my mother taught me that.) I yanked open the cupboard and found the jar of English preserves, whacked it down and skimmed it at Julia, real fast. She didn't turn a hair, opened the jar and dug in.

Jessie put down her spoon and sat stock-still, listening, all big-eyed. She could pick up all those little flutters and tensions in a room faster than anybody, even when you thought she was far far away. I fussed with her collar and blew on her neck to reassure her. She'd sunk a pool of milk in the middle of her oatmeal and was making her spoon dive in and swim across for each bite. She had all kinds of games she played with her food. One doctor told us she might need to act childish for a while, so she could grow up all over again and turn into an un-crazy adult. That was one of the more hopeful theories, years back.

Andrew picked up his briefcase and went off to school and everyone else was busy eating, so I could slip up the back stairs for my hat and bag. I was strolling across the lawn to the car when I saw Dennis coming around the corner of the garage with a very determined look in his eye. He'd been up since the crack of dawn, getting his machine ready for a big race on Labor Day. I leaned my chin against the open door of the station wagon, looking him over critically as he limped toward me. He'd lost weight, dragging casts around for two months, and there hadn't been that much of him to begin with. Dennis was built like an overgrown jockey, with those wide flat shoulders and the rest of him as scraggy and leggy as some weed by the road. "Well, what do *you* want? I'm in kind of a hurry, you know."

"Look, do me a favor and take my car, huh? Can't exactly, uh . . ." He shrugged, embarrassed.

"Oh, right, of course." Naturally he couldn't work a clutch in his condition, and my station wagon had the automatic shift. But I really hated to drive Dennis' car. Today of all days . . . rumbling mufflerless up Main Street, parking in front of the lawyer's office in a thing that had one purple fender and a door tied on with clothesline. "You probably shouldn't be driving at all." Fat chance he'd fall for that.

"I got two feet, remember? Listen, I could take you in, pick you up on my way back, if it'll help any. Otto's combine's down again. Got his workers all standing around. Told him I'd take a look at it."

"No, never mind." I handed him my keys with a sigh. You didn't need keys to his car; you jammed some wires together to start it. I eased my way gingerly across the tattered upholstery of his front seat, avoiding the bare springs.

"May need gas," he said, nudging the door shut on me.

I gave him a look. "Wonderful . . ."

He gave me a look back. "Okay, when was I supposed to get it? . . . Kind of dressed up, aren't you, for the dentist?"

He didn't miss much, my Dennis, I had to give him that. "No, I'm not. It's an old suit." He couldn't touch me, being all over grease to the elbow, so I slid my hand around behind his neck and kissed him nicely, to show I wasn't really mad and because I was feeling guilty sitting there smiling with a little lie between us. To him, a lie was a lie. He wasn't exactly what you'd call flexible that way.

"You going to be okay?"

"Yes, fine. But don't stand there watching me, please." I took the two stripped wires from under the dashboard, pressed them together like a magician and felt the powerful engine shudder to life under my feet. The car jumped backward, quick as a rabbit. Dennis stood there watching and grinning like a big idiot, really getting his money's worth out of the spectacle of me at the wheel of his devilish car.

I drove cautiously along the narrow county road, trying not to let the car leap away under me like an Indianapolis racer. When I stopped at the junction with the four-lane, waiting for a big eighteen-wheeler to go by, the driver gaped and leered and gave me a comical bellow on his airhorn. I merely touched the accelerator, and the car peeled out behind him. Then two hoody high-school boys tried to drag with me at the next light.

I parked in the Kroger's lot, where I drew quite a few more stares as

I emerged from the jalopy in my yellow suit and white straw hat. But there were always strange families shopping in town these days, interlopers from the housing developments that had sprung up at the other end of town, new people who worked in the brewery or the machine-parts factory over in New Philadelphia. Not that anything was wrong with them, really, except that they didn't have roots like the rest of us. Fancy stores with glamorous window displays had opened up to please them, replacing the messy cluttered friendly stores like my father's, where people had been shopping for years and years. (Today my father's window contained the same pair of dusty boots, size fourteen, the same blue cotton work shirt on a wire dummy, the same set of glass doorknobs and rack of grimy paint samples as when I was in high school.) Probably when the new shopping center opened in the spring, the fancy stores in town would start closing up too, replaced by even fancier ones out there.

Of course there'd been a time when *we'd* been the interlopers, the new people. My great-grandfather Hugo made a large suspicious fortune during the Civil War and came out to Ohio because he liked the pretty countryside. He built a big house in the style they called Steamboat Gothic smack in the middle of the rolling farmlands, he didn't care. Then he settled down quite happily to experiment with airships and balloons and strap-on wings and other flying contraptions, now that he had the money to do it. He was what you'd call a visionary, or an out-and-out crackpot, depending on your point of view. The natives considered him the latter, fortunately, and bore with him, grinning, shaking their heads, lifting their eyes to heaven. They bore with tornadoes the same way, or Dutch elm blight or spring floods or hailstorms that came out of nowhere and ruined a year's crops. Well, but they owed us something too. In every blizzard and flood since Hugo, some Rice or other had flown out to stranded families and livestock, dropping supplies or making a daring rescue. Around here, people were clannish, but they respected their obligations and helped you out in return when they could, no matter what they thought of you personally. And my mother and my sister ended up marrying town boys, after all.

I cut through the back alley because if anyone caught sight of me going in through the front, it would be all over town in ten minutes. The people who'd nod and smile at me in the street and want to know all my business felt they had that right. Some of them could remember Jessie and me as little girls clinging to our mother's skirts, or even my mother clinging to her mother's skirts. (It didn't look as if there'd be a next generation of little Rices clinging to anybody's skirts, not mine if I could help it, not Jessie's.)

I pushed open the heavy oak door of the lawyer's office with its old-fashioned beveled glass panels and gilt lettering. Soon, thanks to me, another one of those sad little developments would appear, boxy houses in tiny straggly yards, bare new roads with silly made-up names: Harlequin Court or Jewel Terrace or Sunset Lane. . . . But I was only doing what I had to do, a matter of survival pure and simple, a matter of duty, too, sigh, because I had control of it all whether I liked it or not.

Of course my mother had been very sick when she made out her will, not quite herself (People had been saying that as long as I could remember: "Anna's not quite herself today. . . ." What was she like when she *was* herself? I wanted to ask. What had I missed, or driven away, being so wicked?), and she passed over my sister, her favorite, for me. Jessie wasn't crazy then, so that wasn't it. She might have figured I was the stable homebody, and could be trusted to keep the old place together. That was what her own mother had done to her. More likely it was merely to spite me, never mind tradition.

Mr. Hutchens was a jaunty man with a round bald head like Jiminy Cricket. He knew how nervous I was and kept smiling gravely to reassure me. I didn't like the looks of Mr. Smythe, the developer person, one bit. He had a crewcut so short you could hardly tell if he had any hair at all, a teeny necktie, a strange skimpy suit of olive green. I supposed that was all the rage in New York or Cleveland or wherever he came from. Well, Mr. Hutchens was wearing a gray suit made of plenty of good thick cloth, designed for a man with a normal human shape. We were two dowdy middlewesterners, out of date as dinosaurs—you could see that from the skeptical way Mr. Smythe let his eyes wander over us. He didn't look at me as if I was a woman at all, and he wasn't more than twenty-five years old to be so full of himself. . . . Oh, I wished I were a thousand miles away; no, just eight miles, at home opening up the mailbox and finding a big fat check from a contest I'd forgotten I'd entered.

"Now, Martha, before you initial those pages . . ." Mr. Hutchens was terribly conscientious, and I knew he'd think he ought to read the whole damned thing to me. I didn't care what it said. I just wanted to close my eyes and sign on the dotted line and forget all about horrible *money* for a while.

ii

JULIA

Teddy was still leaning against the counter with his eyes half closed. He hadn't even had a cup of coffee yet. "You'd better get a move on with this weather." He probably wanted to mooch about in his pajamas all morning, watching cartoons with Jessie, what he indeed would have done if this job hadn't turned up. "Well, you must shave at least. We can't have you looking like some boozy old bush pilot. Go on, now." He mumbled something and trudged away.

I spread some of my jam on a piece of toast and gave it to Jessie, feeling a bit contrite about the way I'd behaved earlier. A harpy. You see, I was being driven round the bend because they hadn't found my little girl yet. Usually I managed to finish these cases quickly, in a day or two, but this one had been dragging on for six whole weeks. I could be bold enough in the blaze of a moment, certainly. My famous sangfroid. However, over the long haul my nerves failed, simply raveled away like the sleeves of a cheap sweater.

When I'd arrived in Moundsville back in July, Timmy showed me the missing child's things, a little coat and some shoes and a doll, and I knew right away she was dead. I didn't always work well that way, "reading" objects, but on the very first try I received a series of intense, powerful images. She'd been murdered, strangled probably, by a man close to her, whose name began with an *M* or *N*. I saw, kept seeing, a strange landscape, luridly green, chaotic and splattered, like a child's painting; a solemn Indian profile, with feathers, like the one on the coin; a huge number "44" scrawled in black on some shiny gray surface.

Now, the child—her name was Lynnie Gates—lived on Indian

Point Road in a hilly suburban area, two doors down from number 4400, at which address lived a man called Morris Nordhoff. Everything seemed to click into place . . . until I'd been shown poor Morris and knew right away he wasn't the one. He was a perfect suspect for that type of crime, a tall old thing with wispy hair and a dribbly mouth, most certainly a genuine half-wit, who looked extraordinarily depraved in newspaper photos. He wasn't depraved, merely scared to death, but everybody wanted a monster to blame. It was always the same when pretty children were murdered. However, poor Morris was fortunate enough to have an alibi.

Then it dawned on us, *Indians, Indians,* so Timmy rounded up some volunteers and we all trooped over to the big Indian mound at the state park. I received a strong repeat picture of the landscape and the Indian's face. I was strolling through the brush with Timmy and some of the men when suddenly, Timmy told me later, I started clutching at my throat, writhing and struggling and turning blue. (Charming.) All I could remember was a dreadful sucking in my chest, as if the breath were draining out of me like blood. Timmy'd worked with me before, so he wasn't put off, but the other men shied away from me like poison after that. Timmy took me back to his car, while the rest of them searched the very spot. They found an old flashlight battery, rusted and leaking, and three used prophylactics, equally ancient.

So Timmy decided he'd better send me home for a while. He hadn't given up on me. He was a good young man, very shrewd and determined under the conservative red-neck surface. His mother had what she called The Sight, and it had skipped Timmy's generation the way mine had skipped Martha's and Jessie's. He could remember his childish thrill of terror as he watched his great-grandmother, a feeble ninety-year-old, extending a gnarled finger to point at a shape in the fire. I could remember my own grandmother calmly tatting by the fire, an innocuous figure, but a portrait from her youth haunted me, one of those fanatic black Celt faces, blade of nose and fierce eyes. Timmy and I had that bond. After I'd rested a week or so I'd go back and we'd try again. If only the whole thing were over and done with, so I could get some sleep.

Quacking cartoon voices filled the room. "Turn it down a little, Jessie, there's a good girl." I leaned back in my chair and took off my glasses. I'd hoped writing a few letters I owed might help me relax and keep my mind off the other thing. But I'd been sitting for twenty minutes before a blank sheet of paper. A pile of Martha's library books lay at my elbow and I flipped one open, a mystery, but the very first page, the first word, put me off. Face it, it was going to be one of those aimless days. I closed the book, doodled on the blotter, straightened a picture on the wall above the desk. Once I'd straightened that one, the rest looked crooked, of course. Another cloud passed over the sun, and the room became murky and dim.

Visitors, especially the nonflying kind, were usually quite impressed by our wall of pictures, our rogues' gallery, our family album. It was as good as a miniature history of American aviation. You could start by the door with my grandfather, bearded and bespectacled, wearing a correct gray suit and a pair of dragonfly wings. He tried to get the damn things to fly all his long life. Next to him, on a postcard from the nineties, my mother, arrayed in discreet tights, arms folded across her large bosom, leaning seductively from the wicker car of a striped gas balloon. (A banner sweeping across the top of the card read "Arabella the Aeronaut," but she was really plain Maude Stevens Rice.) Then: my sister Anna in a famous photo from 1913, wings aslant at thirty feet, racing an old Chevrolet around the track and beating it too; Teddy upside down in a Jenny, his partner dangling from an upper wing; Anna and I as girls, surrounded by dashing young aviators; myself, a black dot with wings, zipping under the Brooklyn Bridge (someone dared me); Alice and Cliff standing beside the Blériot he'd bought when he went to France for the International Exhibition; Jessie and six other WASPs striding across a Texas airfield toward a row of beat-up Helldivers; Teddy leaning jauntily against the wing of his old Ryan mailplane; Teddy and John Duffy in dark glasses and pilot uniforms, sitting with girls in some California bar; and so forth and so on, all the way around the room.

Yes, people were charmed and amused by this display, the way they were by old yearbooks. However, there were one or two items up there that definitely offended the squeamish. You see, we'd collected calamities and fiascos along with triumphs, and we flaunted . . . everything. Me weeping after my aborted transatlantic flight; Teddy's ditched Ryan, nose-down in a Dakota cornfield. And all the grisly headlines: "CLIFFORD RICE PLUNGES TO DEATH Famed Aviator,

24, Dies Instantly! Souvenir Hunters Tear Clothes from Mangled Corpse . . ." "JAMES MOTT DEAD! ANOTHER MARTYR OF THE AIR! Young Wife Watches In Horror, Then Sets Own Altitude Record . . ." "BEACHEY DIES AS WINGS SHEER OFF! Freak Accident On Coast!"

So many . . . friends, lovers, rivals, kin. Harriet Quimby, beautiful and silly in her purple satin suit, dragged up out of the mud of Boston Harbor like a broken doll. I saw it from the air, the very first exhibition I ever flew, my hands shaking on the control stick, that body flying out of the airplane so suddenly, so inexplicably. Cal Rodgers, crossing the continent, then killing himself in a truly witless prank. Charlie Hamilton—"nothing is left of the original Hamilton"—trying like mad to die in an airplane before his lungs gave out, breaking a dozen bones before he was through. Well, there they all were on our wall in their peculiar glory, and who was to say it was morbid or grisly or callous to keep them there? It was hard to explain only to anyone to whom it had to be explained, the same as why I went up and set my record the day Jimmy died. Nothing monstrous, no wonder; it was the most natural thing in the world to do. . . .

What was truly a wonder was that even three of us were left alive today. We'd been as mad for the risks as the rest of them. And people paid great sums to come and see us at it, most of them hoping we'd fail, of course. It's only normal to yearn for a good look at a demolished body not one's own. We made a small fortune on that rather unsavory aspect of human nature, so it would be hypocritical to complain. What else did we get out of it? What that might last beyond the single heady moment? Well . . . forty-odd years later, I could still remember, still *feel*—in every nerve, every pore—the splendid rush of energy and fear, wind splashing into my face like cold water, snapping at my tied-down skirts, roaring in my ears, that day over Boston Harbor. . . . And how I missed it all, missed it more than youth and beauty, more than easy money, more than sex. . . .

I could smell a storm coming on in the heavy sodden air, see it in the rapidly descending ceiling, two glowering dark brows of cloud on the horizon. With any luck Teddy would be halfway to Buffalo before the weather closed down here. I caught a glimpse of him plodding disconsolately along the road to the strip. He'd be all right once he got off the ground. The front was moving south, not north. (I still possessed a vestigial internal barometer, like every other washed-up pilot I knew.)

Behind me Jessie laughed out loud, a happy little spurt of sound that startled me so much I dropped my pen. I turned and stared, but there was nothing on the screen more remarkable than two talking crows. Once in a great while some completely normal sound would come out of her, a chuckle or gasp of wonder, even, once, a crude (but appropriate) Bronx cheer. Invariably unnerving, those phantom sounds, particularly the laugh, so like her mother's.

You could say that Jessie represented another of my temporary failures, like Lynnie, the Moundsville child. And in my present mood, hearing that Jessie/Anna laugh made me think about their story, that bit of not-so-ancient history, all over again.

November of 1946 it was. Anna had already been moved out of the house and into the hospital in town. She was terribly thin, racked by high fevers and fits of coughing like tearing cloth. Still, she hung on grimly, obstinate to the last. Jessie and Martha were taking turns visiting her, though Martha usually found some excuse to let Jessie go in her place.

I was upstairs one day, collecting some makeup and hair things for Anna, when I saw Jessie crossing the lawn to the car in her short blue coat and the conical hat that matched—such odd clothes we wore that year. Suddenly I had one of those split seconds of otherness: stunned helpless pleasure first, then the most awful plummeting feeling, as if the ground had simply dropped away beneath my feet and toppled me into some vile dark hole. Anna's powderbox fell from my hand, and powder spilled across the mirrored top of her dresser. I still remember the way it looked, a double pile of thick ugly pink stuff, the color of fevered skin . . . I ran downstairs to Martha. "Don't let her go!" Naturally, it was too late. Jessie was at that very instant roaring away down the road.

Martha called her boyfriend of the time, a nice man called Dave who kept a stable of jumping horses. She thought he could, oh, leap on one of them, perhaps, and head Jessie off. Of course the damned party line was tied up and she never did get through. The two of us spent the afternoon crouched over the kitchen table drinking whiskey-laced tea, preparing ourselves for the worst. At four-thirty Jessie waltzed in humming "Seanie O'Shea," absolutely unscathed.

Martha was kind and made excuses for me. I was, we all were, so raw and edgy, waiting for Anna to die. The strain had been too much. That bad feeling, something awful about to happen, was still looming in my mind. But what more could I say, having made such a fool of myself already?

A day or two later Jessie went off to town to do some errands tor Martha. After an hour the car came careening back up the driveway, bumping over the lawn, lurching to a stop in the middle of the rhododendrons. Jessie was sitting bolt upright, motionless as a statue, behind the wheel. When Martha opened the car door a little (we'd all run out to see) she shrank away, her eyes open very wide, startled and dark like those of an animal disturbed in its hole. She wouldn't speak, or couldn't, and she hadn't said an intelligible word since. Anna died the following Tuesday at about four in the morning. Nobody was with her because she'd sent us all away. She never knew about Jessie.

I sat there twiddling with a corner of my writing paper, and Jessie sat there watching Heckle and Jeckle, as opaque and mysterious as she'd been six years ago, locked in her shell with her secret still, if there was a secret. And I was bedeviled still, wondering what had really happened that day. *What really happened,* always a bit of a joke concept. Would it serve me to know? I doubted it. But I wanted to, all the same. . . .

"Julia? Uh, Julia . . . ?" Dennis was leaning into the room, one hand on the doorknob, the other nervously jingling the car keys. "Listen, you want anything from town? Christ, you were far away. . . ."

"Umm, yes I was. I don't think so, thanks. Should you be driving yet, by the way?"

"Yeah. Why not?" A faint polite edge of exasperation in his voice. *Lot of women worrying at him, pain in the ass.* Martha must have protested too.

"I was thinking of the car, Dennis," I said kindly. "Further damage to your person is your own affair."

He half smiled at that, not really put out. Actually, if he'd told me he planned to drive with both his ankles encased in plaster I'd not have doubted for a minute he could. Martha always chose the same type, these terribly physical men, quite ridiculously competent around cars or horses, class VI rockfaces or white-water canoes, magnificently stupid about everything else, most of them. (I must admit I'd cherished a weakness for such men myself long ago.) As it happened, Dennis was not particularly stupid and had managed to last longer than many. Oh, plain as a picket fence, yes; nevertheless, quite a nice boy in his way. "Did Teddy get off all right?" I inquired casually. I was dying to ask if he'd made himself presentable first, but I knew I'd receive a shrug and a blank look. The men always stuck together, didn't they?

"Far as I know. Look, I got to be going. See you later." He stumped off noisily down the hall, let the screen door slam mightily behind him. A moment later, Sylvester, the moth-eaten gray cat, crept anxiously into the room and slid under Jessie's chair. He was waiting for me to turn around so he could jump into her lap. He was the shyest creature I'd ever seen.

Jessie kept flipping the channels back and forth, deciding what to watch next, election news or a snowy western: Adlai shaking hands with teamsters in Minneapolis; men playing cards in a saloon; Ike, ugh, kissing an old lady in St. Augustine; close-up of an ace up a sleeve . . . all at once I saw a familiar face. I peered at the screen. Yes. *Bob Steele.* My God. I'd done stunts on a Bob Steele picture once. But Jessie ruthlessly turned the dial again and settled back to watch the news.

iii

MARTHA

I got the key from Miss Horn, the secretary, and went off down the hall to the pink-papered ladies' room that smelled of her old-lady powder. A tiny electric fan was sitting on a special shelf, turning this way and that in a birdlike frenzy, doing no good at all. My face was covered with sweat. I stared at myself in the mirror and thought, *traitoress.* Of course what I'd signed wasn't irrevocable, merely an option, till January. Or had I been signing away for good the back forty acres of Hugo Rice's land, the grass strip, the old circus hangar, eighty years of history? . . . Oh, well, we'd know in six months. I fluffed out my hair and put on some new lipstick.

I decided to go over to school and see if Andrew wanted to have lunch at the drugstore with me. I had to tell somebody what I'd done. Andrew was an official family member, but he didn't have any of those sentimental ties to everything. Besides, I knew how annoyed Dennis would be if I told him something he wasn't allowed to tell anybody else. (Not that he couldn't be closemouthed to a fault when it pleased him, as silent as a stone.) No, I needed a person who loved secrets and was very good at keeping them. It had to be Andrew.

As I climbed the tall brick steps of the Consolidated Township High School I was filled with sweet nostalgia and guilt, thinking of all the afternoons Jessie and I had slouched together there, hugging loads of books to our chests and flirting with all the boys. Everything I saw touched some soft melancholy nerve: the big plaque in the entrance hall listing the names of boys who'd died overseas, the trophy case filled with those sad useless cups and plates and foolish towers with little baseball players or bowlers stuck up on top. All the rooms I passed were empty and gave off the special smell of schools in the summer. Summer school was always supposed to be the worst possible fate, of course, until my senior year. By then a lot of the boys actually wanted to go to summer school, so they could be finished, ready to enlist and fight the big war everybody knew was coming. Now the names of some of those eager-beaver boys were written on the plaque downstairs. . . .

Andrew's room was on the second floor, and I stood outside, waiting for the lunch bell, watching all the soft bored young faces, eyes fixed resignedly on the blackboard or up at the ceiling or out the open windows. When the bell rang, all those kids swarmed to their feet in a big flooding river of noise, shoving and jostling, hooting with joy. I had to step back fast as they burst out past me, making me feel about a hundred and nine years old and invisible.

I stepped quietly into the room past the last straggling kids. Andrew was standing behind his desk, shaking together a pile of compositions. I remembered back when Andrew first started teaching at our school, not too long after he'd graduated himself. All the girls had been wild about him, because he'd lived in New York City for a while and was therefore sophisticated and dangerous. And because of the way he looked, of course.

"Hi, Andrew," I said, and his head shot up and his eyes opened wide in surprise. He took a deep breath and smiled at me.

"Martha! Well, great . . . I mean . . ."

Andrew had a very nice smile, a perfect curve of lips with no teeth showing. He also had a lot of thick wavy blond hair (you could be sure he'd never get a crewcut, no matter what). He stared at me for a minute, his eyes big like an owl's, a sort of pale grayish-blue, with very thick short blond lashes that made him look younger than he was. He had the tiniest lines now at the corners of his eyes, but so far they had a sea-captain or lifeguard look, those lines, not an old look. He was an indoor person with outdoor eyes. He was medium tall and stocky, beginning to get a little thicker around the middle than he'd been years ago when he'd been courting my sister.

He kept on staring at me, looking very pleased to see me, maybe too pleased to see me, now that the surprise had worn off. I stammered out, "I wondered if you wanted to go down to Brewer's and have lunch with me." I was beginning to feel very nervous and silly. I'd never bothered to consider what Andrew might imagine I was up to, walking in on him like this, asking him out to lunch. I never ate lunch out, not even with Dennis.

"Why, how nice of you," he said. "I'd like nothing better."

"I have to talk to you about something. . . ."

"We'll have to hurry. Those monsters you saw escaping will be back in less than an hour." He put his hand on my shoulder and pushed me gently ahead of him out into the corridor.

iv

ALICE

"Brakes . . . contact!" Buddy shouted out at me, in an extra-deep, grown-up-sounding voice. He liked the starting routine with the J-3 a whole lot better than I did, because it was like what he'd seen in the movies, I guess. Our little trainer was a beat-up prewar Cub that didn't have such a thing as an electric starter. The first couple of times I got Teddy or Dennis to come help me. But I could see Buddy had the right instincts, and I'd had enough dealings with scared kids in airplanes to tell you pretty quick which ones it was safe to trust. I gave the prop a big yank, jumped back out of the way and like a charm her little engine rumbled to life.

I scrambled into the forward seat and closed the doors. With the weather so chancy today I wanted to get us up right away. Buddy was holding the nose centered perfectly down the middle of the strip, a good smooth takeoff roll. He let her yaw to port a little, but before I could give him a signal he caught it himself. Like I said, good instincts. I let him climb out to about 3,000 and level off so I could take a look around.

Sure enough, a long mean-looking pile of thunderheads off to the west, lightning forking out of them here and there. A couple of the cells had those little greenish edges, too, heavy rain or hail. Always a pretty scary sight, but kind of splendid too. Long as you were all fueled up and safe over your home field, you could maybe sit back for a second or two, give a thought to the wonders of nature. But if you got too cocky, let your mind wander off on you, they'd chew you up, spit you out, never let you see the light of day again. Big towers of blackish cotton, ten, twelve miles high, some of them. Buddy tapped my shoulder and made a face to show he was impressed. Smart enough to be scared, scared enough to be smart; best way to make sure you got old, we always used to say.

But in the five minutes we'd been up there the clear part of the sky had already shrunk by half. That big old line squall had picked itself up and started moving in around us. We hit some nasty little pockets and took a powerful buffet or two. Airplane dropped down like the bottom fell out of something, bounced up again. I thought I'd better take over till we bulled our way out. "I've got it!" I shouted over the racket. All the plans I had, stall and recovery lesson, maybe a spin demonstration, went right out the window.

When we came into the clear at about eight hundred I let him take her in, and he did fine; perfect forty-five-degree entry, nice smooth glide and gentle flare-out. He set the J-3 down like a pro, as pretty as you please. I unhitched my belt and swiveled around so I could look at him. "You're picking it up awful fast, you know. How'd it feel?"

"Real good, mostly. Except for a minute back there I forgot to, uh, lay on right rudder, but then I remembered."

"I know." I laughed. "I could *feel* you remembering." I unlatched the doors and weaseled my way out. A J-3 wasn't designed for human beings, but for white mice and midgets. "Don't know if I can charge you for this, though."

"No, I'll pay you." He was one of those mulish types about who owes what, like Dennis.

"I've got an idea, Bud. I have to go to town this afternoon to see Dr. Bodenweber. How about if I throw my bike in the back of your truck and let you drive me in? Save me some legwork. I'd call that even for such a little lesson."

"Sure, I can do that. But it don't mean I'm not going to pay you. Are you sick, going to the doctor?"

"No, it's a regular visit." Didn't I wish that were true. I tied down the J-3 and latched her doors, and the two of us walked down the road, which was all dry now so our feet sent up big clouds of dust. I could hear locusts starting to sing in the trees with the noonday heat, that chee-chee-chee. I always liked the sound and missed it whenever I'd had to spend a summer some other place.

"Denny not around today?"

"He had to go over to Dover for something. Think he was going to stop by at your dad's and take a look at that combine's been causing so much trouble."

"Oh, yeah. He musta been up till three in the morning swearing at it, my dad I mean. Happens every year."

"He have his own or use the co-op?"

"The co-op. He says next year he's going to buy us our own. Says that every year too. Probably won't never get enough money together. . . ." He went silent kind of fast, looking down at his shoes scuffing through the dust. I wanted to tell him the little bit of money he was paying me wouldn't help his dad much, even if his dad would take it from him, which I doubted. But I thought I'd better let him work that out for himself.

He threw my old Schwinn into the back of his pickup, and we headed off down the county road toward town. When he was slowing down to pull in by the Medical Building, I caught sight of Martha and

Andrew strolling along Main Street in front of the school. I was going to wave but got the idea a minute too late. Guess I was more nervous than I liked to admit about seeing the doc.

"Here ya go, Miz Rice. I'll see ya next week on Thursday, if that's okay." He set the bike out on the pavement for me, put the truck in gear and roared away. I had to stand there a minute in front of the building, getting my mind calmed down to the idea of going in.

V

ANDREW

I leaped up the stairs two at a time, capering like Jerry Lewis and Crazylegs Hirsch, then turned and sauntered sedately down the corridor. The kids were already waiting by the door, chattering and grabbing at each other like a pack of monkeys, grooming, dominating, submitting; the works. I elbowed my way through. "Be with you in a minute."

I unlocked the door and closed it firmly behind me, shot over to the window and leaned out. I couldn't see her whole body through the trees, only tantalizing bits and pieces: pretty bare arms swinging, narrow brown ankles, little feet in white pumps, the tip of her little white hat jouncing along on top of her wondrous hair, curly golden wires like some Elizabethan lady's. . . . *Like to Diana in her Sommer weede* . . . Oh, God. Here I go again. There was a distant rumble of thunder.

I could hear shufflings of feet and outraged murmurs outside the door, but I stayed at the window for another few minutes, hoping to see her drive by in Dennis' dreadful vehicle with its magenta fender and tied-on back door. The idea of her riding in that disreputable junk heap was exactly like the idea of her sleeping with its owner, hateful but at the same time kind of exciting, much as I hated to admit it. The brute and the angel. King Kong and Fay Wray. No, not quite. Not an *ape* . . . Dennis wasn't hairy enough. A luscious fantasy began to materialize . . . Martha carried off by hideous space creatures, very hairy. They looked like yaks (did I mean *yaks* or *llamas*?) . . . she struggles in her bonds . . . screams as the first one approaches her, leering and slobbering . . . then I appear . . .

There was a heavy, accusing thump against the door. "Oh Christ, all right."

I opened the door and the kids streamed in, girls flouncing and swaying in their long skirts and tight cotton blouses, slopping along in their ballet slippers, boys strutting in that tightass adolescent way. "Hey, what were ya doing in here, Mr. O?"

"Composing myself," I replied. Someone in the back row snuffled obscenely. I aimed an evil look at that part of the room. "You think it's easy dealing with the likes of you? I need all the composing I can get. . . . Okay, let's have a little quiet now . . . that's better. . ."

The trees near the window heaved and rustled and showed their white undersides. There was definitely going to be a storm. I wondered if I could get away with letting them out early on that account. No fear the kids would object. Still, I didn't want Purvis walking by my empty room at 2:15 . . . oh, what the hell. I went to the board and picked up the chalk, hesitated, racking my brains, then scrawled, "Composition Topic: Unrequited Love." My little joke on myself. Sometimes I amused myelf by turning the kids into a sort of callow collective unconscious, snapping my own obsessions back at me, flattened out and given weird new perspective.

A groan went up as soon as they realized they'd have to spend another period writing. They'd had a composition during the morning session too. I held up my hand for silence. "You'll do two comps today and none the rest of the week, I promise. We're going to have one of those very loud thunderstorms any minute . . ." There was a convenient growl of thunder. ". . . so we'll save our discussion of the poems you read till tomorrow. When you've finished your five hundred words—that's two pages at least, remember, and when you've carefully proofread what you've written—you'll be free to go." The mutters and groans changed instantly to stifled cheers, giggles, whistles. "*But* . . . listen up now . . . no one may leave until . . ." I checked the clock over the door. ". . . Two o'clock. All right?" There was a drill-team flash of white as twenty-three hands spread twenty-three sheets of looseleaf paper out across twenty-three desks.

I leaned back against the blackboard and folded my arms. I wanted to start thinking about Martha again, but didn't dare. Kids that age were like raw wires, unbelievably sensitive to the tone of your fantasies, alert to anything that had to do with sex, and once they got onto you you'd lose your grip on them completely.

The sky was unnaturally dark, the room filled with eerie greenish light. There was a jagged white flash and an enormous bang of thunder. Huge raindrops slammed against the window, and the trees began whipping around like mad things, leaves flying, branches groaning and bending and scraping against each other. There was another earsplitting crack like the end of the world. Papers skittered along my desk in a sudden gust. I weighted them with my briefcase and went over to close the windows, catching the bold brown eye of Cathy Ann Strawser observing me over the top of her pencil from the back row. I worked my way down the row of windows till I was standing close behind her. She leaned back elaborately in her chair, letting me see the pointed white bra shape through her thin pink sweater. Wicked Cathy Ann. She edged her little shoulder against my thigh as I moved away between the rows of desks. The hand of the clock clicked forward once, twice, on its way toward two o'clock.

The storm subsided; the sky lightened to gray; thunder still growled sullenly, farther away. The minutes clicked slowly by on the clock. I thought about Jessie at Cathy Ann's age, crouched over a paper, chewing nervously on a pencil, staring up at me with worried blue eyes. Never one of those knowing little girls, Jessie, not at all like Cathy Ann. They had no wiles, these Rice women; that was why they were so devastating. Martha. *Martha.* The hand of the clock clicked forward. One forty-seven. The clouds broke and watery sunlight oozed through. At precisely two on the dot half the kids in the room stood up, hoisted books, slapped papers on my desk and sped out the door, laughing and scuffling, voices diminishing down the hall. By 2:10 five were left, two bright kids who always had a lot to say, one sadass worrywart with pushy parents who always wrote too much, one little goody-goody, showing off; the fifth was Cathy Ann, biding her time. But her boyfriend was out in the hall, casting a canny and suspicious eye in on her, fortunately. I wasn't up to Cathy Ann today. "Come on, Cath," he said finally. "I'm gonna wait for ya right here." She tucked away her pencil and slouched to her feet.

* * *

I threw my briefcase and jacket into the car. The air was clean and fresh after the rain. I felt like tap-dancing off down the sidewalk, stamping into puddles like Gene Kelly. . . . Christ, who could explain these things? I mean, I'd known the girl since she'd been in kindergarten practically. I'd eaten breakfast with her for more than five years. One minute, nothing—well, almost nothing—the next . . . All she had to do was walk into my room today, so flustered and shy, wearing that ridiculous little white hat and I was . . . *smitten* (a great word) . . . thinking about her in a hundred delicious ways: adorable oversized breasts . . . incredible ass, sloping down and down, tipping up so sweetly at the last minute. . . . I wallowed in envy of every lucky man or boy who'd ever touched her, all the way back to that cretin Harold Stolley in the seventh grade. I'd challenge them all. Swords! Pistols at dawn! A masked avenger sweeping her off to my hideaway . . . cut to fireworks, train roaring through tunnel . . .

A drop of rain fell on my neck, another on my face, two more on my outstretched hand. I started to run. The sidewalk was already covered with wet petals and leaves and blown-down branches. I must've run for twenty blocks, laughing to myself—strange sound in my ears above the roar of the rain—then I spun on my heel and ran all the way back, my hair dripping down into my face, my shirt and socks and trousers flapping against me. What an idiot.

I fell against the side of the car, holding my side. Out of shape, mister. Definitely out of shape. I dragged my wet hand out of my sopping pocket with the car keys, shook myself off like a dog and climbed into the stuffy car, sloshing water all over the seat and floor. *Ishkibibble,* as my mother used to say. I slid the key into the ignition and started to sing "I Hear a Rhapsody."

vi

ALICE

Ray sat there staring at those darned X-rays, his forehead all squeezed up in a frown, tapping his pencil against his teeth, the way he used to drive me crazy back in study hall when we were kids. We sure did go far back, the two of us. "You know," he said, looking at me over his glasses, kind of clearing his throat, "there's an outside chance you might get off with nothing worse than this mild stiffness and discomfort. But . . . hate to say this to you, Alice, I really do . . . it's much more likely the deterioration will continue, and, uh, worsen. You probably won't ever lose the full use of the hand, but for small motor activities, for fine coordination, it'll get harder and harder and . . . I'm real sorry . . ."

I didn't say anything for a minute. I was looking down at the hand where it was lying in my lap and thinking how strange it was he could take a picture of what was under that tan crinkled old skin. Seemed like magic still.

"Thought you flew by the seat of your pants anyway." He lifted his eyebrows at me and I could see he wanted me to laugh, so I did, too hard probably, cackling like a fool, in fact, from nerves.

"Yeah," I blurted out. "And you can't get arthritis in your backside, can you? What you get there's probably a whole lot worse."

He went red, and I remembered all of a sudden he'd always been like that, not a prude, a guy it was easy to embarrass. Here he'd been a doctor all these years, run through two wives, eight kids, and he got flustered when he heard a dirty story. Granted, that wasn't my usual type of joke either.

"Well, now, Alice. How about if I give you something, in case you ever have any bad discomfort?" ('Course, doctors never would say *pain* or *hurts* right out, would they?) He pulled open a drawer and stuck a couple of little bottles in my hand. "There you go . . ."

When I got on the elevator on the way out, there was Cora Horn, Dr. Cram's nurse. To be sociable I said, "Lucky you, got to see two Rices in one day." She gave me a kind of fishy look. "Martha was in to see you this morning, I hear."

"Not today she wasn't." She gave me the fishy look again, the one she probably saved for old ladies who were losing their marbles. Well, I'd seen Martha leave the house in her good clothes with my own two eyes, hadn't I? Cora stepped out of the elevator ahead of me, rustling off in her starched white dress. Smartypants. Always like that, nurses. I was still kind of numb the way you get, waiting for everything Ray'd said to sink in, trying to decide if I wanted to tell Vern about it or not. Didn't have much female vanity, that was for sure, but I hated the idea of me with this *old person's* disease.

The little bell over the door jangled, and Vern looked up past Mildred Stillwagon's head and gave me his nice smile. He was showing her some paintbrushes. The ball game was on the radio, Indians playing the Yanks and not doing too well. I puttered up and down the aisles a couple of times, then said, kind of loud, for Mildred's benefit, "Think I'll go out back and take a look at your used bike tires, Vern." That was our special signal. Not bike tires, the back room. I made up a different reason for going out there every time, if a customer was hanging around, trying to make Vern laugh if I could.

"Be with you in a minute, Alice," he said and smiled at me again.

The back room was dark and narrow, with only one little window set up high. There was a cot against one wall where he slept when he didn't come out to the house, a little stack of magazines, a pipe and some tobacco all jumbled together on the floor with some old clothes.The room had a real nice smell, I always thought, turpentine and pine oil and clean new canvas, citronella candles and maybe those old sulphur camp matches. I couldn't really put my finger on it, but I liked it, because it reminded me of him, Vern.

It shouldn't've been any great marvel that the two of us got together. Vern was only fifty-two when Anna died, and I was fifty-six, two beat-up middle-aged folks, living in a small town, sometimes in the same house. Who else would've wanted us? Vern had a lot of sweetness in him still, in spite of Anna and what she'd done to him. So it was a whole lot more than convenient, let me tell you, a big fat happy late surprise for both of us.

Turned out to be a nice enough afternoon to make love, rain pounding on the roof and all, stopping later so's we could talk a little. I almost ended up telling him everything, vanity be damned. The first flush of relief had passed, that it wasn't as bad as it could be, and I was all of a sudden struck by how bad it really was. Then I wished like hell I'd never said a word about the whole business, because he didn't catch on. Worse, he thought I was hinting around about something, trying to say I *wanted* to stop flying. You never know, do you, how even people you're that close to can get you so bollixed up in their minds.

"We'll find a little house," he said, "a place to hide away, and I'll take care of you and you'll take care of me. . . ."

"No, that's not . . . what'd you think I'd find to do all day?" Then I felt bad for snapping at him like that. I sure didn't like the idea of hiding away with him. Wanted to live out in the open, so everybody could see I had a man of my own at last. And it wasn't as simple as what would I *do* with myself, sit in a chair or stand on my head or keep his house for him—though that would be a laugh and a half, me keeping house for anybody. No, it was more complicated than I could say to him; more like what would I *be,* what would I turn into, some stranger.

He picked up my hand, the right one, all unknowing, and kissed it, palm and then the fingers one by one. I pulled it away as gently as I could and spread it out like a star, wondering how long before I wouldn't be able to stretch it like that. Then I put it down flat on his chest, almost hiding it in all the stiff gray hair. "I guess I better go. . . . Don't want to get caught if it rains again, do I? You coming out to dinner tonight?" He shook his head, avoiding my eyes, and I knew better than to try to talk him into it when he was in one of his hermit moods.

vii

ANDREW

Plumes of water churned up off the shoulder and collapsed onto the roof of the car with satisfying hollow roars. I was driving too fast for the weather, but I didn't care. I still felt wonderful, giddy, half drunk. The old routine. A yellow shape slid by the porthole. Alice Rice in her slicker, pedaling sturdily along through the downpour. Should have stopped to offer her a lift. Too late now.

I pulled into the driveway and parked beside Dennis' jalopy. The rain eased off to a drizzle and the sun began slanting out again, greenish egg yolk behind the clouds. It was that kind of day. Martha was standing on the porch, leaning against the railing. She'd changed into white shorts and a green blouse. (Okay, she'd only needed a confidant. A wise older man with no grease under his fingernails. So what.)

I stood beside her on the top step for a minute. "Maybe we'll have a rainbow," I said, but she didn't look up.

"Umm, maybe. I hope Dennis is all right, driving in all this. Did you pass him on the road?"

"Uh-uh . . . oops . . ." I went past her into the cool dark front hall, screen door snapping at my heels. Very suave.

"Jess is out back," she called after me.

"Okay." I checked the pile of mail on the table—nothing for me—and went upstairs.

They gave me this room when Jessie first got sick and wouldn't let me near her, a pleasant enough place, filled with crabby-looking dark furniture that had probably belonged to good old Hugo Rice. A big mirrored wardrobe, a rolltop desk, glass-covered cabinets for my books. Plus a decent modern twin bed, tactful for a new celibate. I'd been here five years now, maybe a little more, maybe a little less. It depressed me to deal with the actual numbers.

Sometimes I felt as if I were in a time warp, lying in the narrow bed with my radio turned down low, reading adventure stories far into the night. All I needed was my father opening the door, whispering in his gentle voice, trying to sound stern, "Turn off that light now, Andy."

But the pictures beside the bed reminded me where I was and why. Blown-up snapshot in a silver frame. Backhand scrawl of faded blue ink along the bottom: "Hi, Mom, here I am in my new *Mustang*!" And there was Jess, wearing those awful surplus men's clothes they gave the women pilots— big-ass khaki trousers, clumsy black flight jacket —climbing into the cockpit of a vicious little fighter plane. She sent that picture to her mother in the spring of 1944, and her mother passed it on to me. Mustangs were supposed to be hot shit then, before jets. How many times did I hear Jessie say, to anyone who'd listen, "The men were so scared, they had us girls fly 'em first.

Then they told the men, 'If some dumb little broad can do it, so can you.'" Of course Jessie and her girl friends got those rotten planes cold, untested, straight from the factory, and had to ferry them thousands of miles; little fighters, designed for short fast trips, not cross-country marathons. A couple of them crashed, too. Then it was, *Well, dames, whaddaya expect?* It always made my blood boil hearing Jessie talk about all that stuff. But she'd never tell me much about her own accident, or almost-accident. She'd never talk to me much about flying at all. I think it embarrassed her in some obscure way, and I never did quite catch on to all the pilots' slang.

Another picture. Studio portrait, circa 1925: a woman and two pretty little girls, three heads of thick bobbed hair, one brown, two blond; three heart-shaped faces; three sets of blue button eyes and straight brows; three stubborn down-turned mouths. I picked up the picture in its heavy wooden frame and scrutinized those three faces yet again. . . . Well, did Martha or Jessie look more like her mother? Did either of the girls bear the slightest resemblance to her father? (Answer to number one: Martha around the eyes and Jessie around the mouth. Answer to number two: No. Except for the blond hair, neither, fortunately, favored poor wan chinless Vern.) Jessie must have been about two when the photo was taken and had a plump, soft, puppyish quality still, but Martha already looked tougher, staring level-eyed into the camera, prying Anna's encircling arm from her waist with busy little sausage fingers.

I kept my journals on a shelf along the top of the bed with the books I was reading, noble tomes on literature, philosophy, politics; trash, a lot of trash. (*Journals,* fancy name for the dime-store spirals where I wrote regularly each year: ten times in January, four times in February, twice in March, maybe once during the other nine months.) I pulled one down and riffled through it until I found this passage:

How did it happen? (I had written) How do these things ever happen? I don't know. It was as if I had been given some insidious mystery to solve (I cringed, rereading), not the ordinary mystery of one woman, but the mystery of two, in the sharing of their genes a further mystery, a further possibility of enlightenment. The odd similarities I discovered, revealed like sudden shafts of light in a mirror (light, in a mirror???), that heady feeling of playing with a double-faced image, one single opalescent jewel (Oh sweet suffering Christ), a jewel whose colors shifted under my . . .

I closed the book in disgust. The date of the entry was March 18, 1946. My thirty-first birthday. I'd been married for six months. I picked up the book by thumb and forefinger, held it over the wastebasket, then changed my mind. Once in an earlier fit of revulsion, I'd actually thrown the whole pile of them out, had to dig through a slimy heap of garbage to retrieve them.

The room was musty and hot. Someone had closed the window during the storm. Martha? Martha gliding through my room in her little white shorts, lifting her naked arms to the window, turning to regard my disordered bed . . . I went over and heaved the window open, letting in the sweet damp air. The station wagon was just pulling into the driveway. Dennis and Alice climbed out. She was still wearing her slicker, but he was soaking wet, T-shirt and jeans plastered to his skinny body. He dragged the shirt up over his head and slapped it down across one shoulder. Martha said something I couldn't hear, and he balled it up and tossed it at her. Smartass. He and Alice started to take the bike out of the car.

I unbuttoned my shirt, dropped my damp trousers onto the floor and kicked off my shoes. All my high spirits, my MGM tap-dancing fervor, had drained away, and now I felt torpid and listless and foolish and bleak. I put on "after school" clothes and lay down on the bed again, back in the time warp. Thirty-seven years old and horny as hell, worse than I'd ever been at seventeen.

The thing was, I never felt the slightest bit guilty about Jessie when she was seventeen. That's how old she'd been, too, the first time. There'd been such a beautiful innocence about her, and she was always so direct about what she wanted. She and Martha were both like that when they were girls. Martha preferred to have a man around because it was pleasant and convenient. She never wasted her passion on anybody. But Jessie was more romantic. She thought she should be in love with the people she slept with. Then after a while she'd stop being in love, and it would be over and she'd move on to the next. That was the way she was when she was a young girl, and she made things very easy for a man. You could have the beautiful experience and none of the ugliness. We were a lot alike then, Jess and I. I could never make myself choose, one over the other, one for life.

When she came back to me six years later, I could see right away how much she had changed. The war had changed everyone, after all, even me, though my own experiences had been somewhat less than sensational. You lost so much: youth, friends, illusions about yourself you never knew you had. Or maybe Jessie'd always been different from the way I'd imagined her, and I was just getting around to noticing that. She was a pretty woman still, only pathetic somehow, depleted, a shade too eager to please. But when she turned to me, clung to me, I was flattered. Needy women brought out the best in me (brought out the worst in me). I was weak that way, fat greedy ego making trouble for me over and over again.

I didn't see any harm in marrying Jessie either. I was almost thirty. What was I going to do with the rest of my life anyway? Shack up here and there till I was too old to make the effort? And I did love her, in some fashion. She was gentle, passionate, guileless, and yet so bright and funny in her wry, sad way. I didn't have to think twice. I never expected . . . I never wanted what happened to happen.

It was tragic, Anna dying when she did. A young woman still. Jessie had always been so attached to her mother. A little frightened of her as well. Anna possessed a kind of nobility, along with a harsh and ruthless streak, as I had good reason to know. We'd only been married a year. We were married in November of 1945, and Anna died in November of 1946.

I took my wet clothes into the bathroom and draped them over the shower rail to dry. I stared into the mirror at myself, examining the new wrinkles around my eyes and mouth. I was getting old. I'd be forty soon. I looked every hour of forty now. Well, maybe not quite. But thirty-eight, easily. At least I was keeping my hair. I combed it and brushed my teeth to get the afternoon-nap taste out of my mouth.

Jessie was sitting in the old glider on the back porch, hulling peas from a paper sack into a bowl she held between her knees. She was wearing an old shirt of mine over her blue Bermuda shorts, and with her hair held back by a tortoise band she looked awfully young, more like twenty-one than thirty-one. Going in opposite directions, the two of us: she sliding back into the past, shrinking, diminishing; me swarming ahead, old beyond my years; star-crossed lovers out of some science-fiction time fantasy. Oh, stuff it . . . save it for your diary, Bub. . . .

I bent over her, smoothed her soft hair, kissed her temple. She kept at it, dropping peas into the bowl, ping, ping, ping. I sat beside her, moving the glider back and forth with my toe. The smell of something baking, cookies or a pie, slid through the kitchen window, along with the pleasant clanking evening sounds of Martha busy in there. "Here, Jessie." I popped a pea into her soft little mouth. Sometimes I could provoke the faintest of smiles, but not today. She accepted the pea the way a bird takes a seed, tested it against her teeth and swallowed it down.

October 10

i

JULIA

Normally I hated to appear in daylight downstairs in my nightclothes, too slatternly and depressing, but I was eager for company today. I found Alice and Vern and Jessie sitting around the kitchen table eating identical tuna fish sandwiches and drinking milk from assorted Howdy Doody glasses (acquired free with peanut butter, ugh). A looking-glass family, slightly askew, Mom and Pop and an extra-large child. Poor Jessie, my goddaughter; after all this time she could still catch me unawares, appall me. Vern and Alice looked up in unison as I came in. Jessie ignored me, urgently picking through her sandwich, rearranging celery bits.

"You're up at last," Alice said.

"As you see." I was not going to let her irritate me today.

"We thought we'd let you sleep in," Vern said.

"Dennis said you conked out the minute you got off the bus. You look a little better today."

"You found the little girl . . ."

"In the park . . ." They were beginning to get on my nerves, two parrots, taking turns like that.

"We heard it on the news."

"Yes. We did find her." I didn't want to talk about all that yet. "Where is everybody this morning? It seems so quiet."

"This afternoon, you mean. Teddy took the Stinson to Chicago. Mrs. Lah-Di-Dah and her sister went to some wedding."

"Mrs. Ladida?"

"You know . . ."

"Oh, her."

". . . and Andrew's still sleeping. He beat even you. Dennis ran Martha over to Millersburg. To the antiques fair. She has her heart set on buying herself a rocking chair."

"I notice he took her over on the motorcycle," Vern put in drily. "It's kind of hard to carry a rocking chair on a motorcycle." The only time Vern was ever sarcastic was about Martha's boyfriends, and only when they were twenty or thirty miles out of earshot.

I sighed, a bit let down. Alice and Vern finished their sandwiches and began stacking plates and glasses in the sink with an annoyingly purposeful and bustling air, putting away the milk as if I might not need it for my coffee, snapping waxed paper over the bowl of tuna salad. It looked as if I'd have to make my own breakfast and eat it in solitude, with no one to sit with me and listen to my story. "Where are you all going in such a hurry?"

"Over to New Philadelphia to look for new shoes for Jessie."

I felt absurdly forlorn seeing them all go off together, tempted to call after them, "Wait, I need new shoes too. Let me go with you." But I knew an afternoon of shopping with Alice would have me grinding my teeth in no time.

I turned on the radio and opened the fridge, hoping to find some unexpected treat. The radio was silent, warming up, then blared out raucously. I twirled the dial to find some news, and it surprised me, coming softly out over the Cleveland station. ". . . skeletal remains of little Lynnie Gates, six, were unearthed yesterday in Grave Creek Mound Park, near Moundsville, West Virginia, just three months and seven days after she was reported missing. Police were aided in their search by psychic Julia Mott. Mrs. Mott had predicted . . ." All of a sudden I didn't want to hear any more. I snapped the radio off. It was simple enough. She'd been stuffed into a drainpipe that had been hidden under kudzu during the summer. The pipe was embossed with an Indian-head trademark and had the number forty-four scrawled across it, some cryptic workman's sign apparently. The "M/N" of my vision turned out to be the child's gentle cousin Mark, a librarian, vestryman of his church, collector of porcelain dogs, not the drooling nightmare figure for which everyone had hoped. . . . Oh, dear, I really didn't want to eat breakfast alone today.

* * *

Andrew's room was dark as a rabbit hole. I could just make out the line of his body under a tangled heap of blankets, a shapely naked foot and blue pajama cuff piped in maroon peeping out. I touched the foot lightly. No response. Then a tremendous thrashing and heaving about, as if some huge fish had been disturbed in its pool. His eyes flew open. "My God," he said, staring at me. "My God . . . oh . . . Julia."

"I'm sorry, dear. I didn't mean to frighten you. I was going to make breakfast and thought I'd see if you wanted some too."

"You're sweet, Julia. Shit, is it really that late? The whole day is . . . how come you . . . I mean, where's Martha?"

"Off to Millersburg with Dennis, on the motorcycle."

He sat on the edge of the bed, his head in his hands, mumbling. ". . . end up breaking both their necks someday. . . ." He lifted his head and smiled. "Listen, don't mind me, I'm just in my usual snit." He ruffled his hands back through his hair and yawned. My, but he was a handsome creature, even disheveled and puffy-eyed from too much sleep.

"You need some fresh air," I said briskly, patting his shoulder. "We'll go for a walk later. Now hurry up and get dressed." I closed the door on him and went back downstairs.

Of course what he really needed was obvious, some complaisant, understanding woman, an earthy waitress or factory girl perhaps, a young widow with children. Let's be practical. To do without sex gracefully at his age required a host of other obsessions: food and drink, work you adored, a mad scheme of vengeance. But Andrew wasn't like that. The poor boy had some soft romantic streak that set him mooning over the big sister of the woman he'd once loved. Oh yes, nature and her inequities.

I squeezed oranges and broke eggs into a bowl and grated cheese for omelets. It took forever. However did Martha do it? An inspiration struck me, and I went out to the front porch to see if it was warm enough to eat out there. The last chance this year. I tried to remember where Martha kept the big tray she used for outdoor meals. I looked under the sink and in the pantry and then in the utility closet under the back stairs, a long cavernous mouse-smelling place. I'd just caught sight of the shiny blue enamel of the tray, behind a lone galosh and a pair of Dennis' racing gauntlets, when I saw, floating against the dark back wall, the wavering shimmering outline of a strange edifice, a sort of distorted cathedral, blackened like charcoal in the center, gleaming with white diamond points along its edges. An inferno blast of heat against my face; my back, icy cold; violence all around me; terror, pain, ugly death. I cried out, but my voice was muffled by the small space so filled with soft discarded objects. The shape slid apart, disintegrated. I leaned back against the door, my hand over my eyes.

Everybody's stuff was crammed in there: Alice's yellow poncho, Vern's old windbreaker, my father's fishing creel, Andrew's Irish hat, Martha's ratty plaid fringed scarf, that anonymous black galosh, Dennis' gloves, Jessie's angora beret, my own blue suede jacket. My heart was pounding still. I backed out of the closet and into the kitchen and sank into a chair.

Andrew finally came down. Probably not more than five minutes had passed. "I'm here for the breakfast I ordered. . . . Hey, Julia, are you all right?"

"Yes, dear, I'm fine." I picked up the skillet and the bowl of eggs. Most unfair, really. Just when I was beginning to feel like a normal person again.

ii

MARTHA

The road to Millersburg wandered among rolling hills and fields, all of them turning pretty fall colors, brown and tan, rust and gold, bronze and olive. The sky was huge above us, that bright hard autumn blue. My skirt was snapping and billowing against my ankles in the terrific roaring wind. I kept my arms locked around Dennis' waist, my face pressed tight against his leather back, and I could feel his every muscle exulting, forcing the bike to sway so gracefully, never faltering, through every turn and hollow of the road. We were going close to eighty, fast enough for me, thank you; nothing at all, just a country drive, for Dennis. We soared to the top of a hill, and there smack in front of us was an old Amish wagon, solemn spotted horse, black-bearded man holding the reins. Then it was gone, lost behind us. I lifted my head to say something to Dennis, but the wind took my breath right out of my mouth.

At the turnoff to the lake, Dennis' shoulder blade shifted a quarter inch under my cheek, the bike heeled over an instant and we plunged down into the steep dank shade. I smiled to myself. Dennis could still surprise me sometimes. The lake had been one of our old places, years back, a gravelly beach and ramshackle dock, a special old tree. Dennis was acting very nonchalant, whistling while he kicked the bike onto its stand, but the look on his face was priceless, half sly, half abashed. He wasn't often caught planning a romantic interlude.

We walked along the lake, holding hands sometimes even. The water was a clear cold brown-green now that we were close to it, and had a powerful fecund smell. Everything was rotting, going to seed, getting ready for winter. Water lapped at the bleached white pebbles on the beach, sliding up into the cattails. Dennis picked up a handful of stones and skipped one out across the surface of the lake. It landed with a plink-plunk, and he tossed out another, leaning sideways, frowning, flipping his wrist expertly to make the stone hop. "Place always reminds me of my dad's about now," he said. "Nicest this time of year." Dennis' father had a little fishing camp on the upper peninsula near Escanaba. His whole huge family lived up there, dozens of brothers and sisters and cousins married and reproducing, toiling at the lake every summer, slaving in factories in the winters. Dennis was the only one who'd escaped, if you could call living in Ohio instead of Michigan escaping. He'd tried other places after the war, Colorado and Texas and Tennessee, then sort of drifted back to Ohio and got stuck here. Because of me, I supposed, not that it gave me any great feeling of power. No, it scared me instead.

I picked up a flat gray stone with a strip of yellow running across it like a streak of lightning. "Look, how pretty." I held it out, dripping, in my hand.

"Yeah," he said. "Let me see, huh." He grabbed it and backed away, holding it up out of my reach, pretending he was going to skip it out with the others.

"No, don't. Give it back, please. . . ." I leaped around him like a little dog. "Oh, please." It was our old game, from back when we first knew each other and didn't want to, you know, just sort of flop down right away. I didn't care really, but Dennis was very seemly about those things because he thought I was a nice girl. Don't ask me what he was like with the not-nice ones, probably the same. That was the way he was about women.

"Dry it off, be a plain old rock . . . ooof . . . all right, all right. . . ." I grabbed at his wrist, punched at his stomach. He put the stone into my hand and closed my fingers around it. "Come on, anyhow." The bank grew steeper and rockier around the north edge of the lake. It was a lonely, half sinister kind of place where you hardly ever saw another soul, even in summer.

He lay down beside me under the tree, an old oak with those long smooth brown roots clawing out underneath. I pulled open his jacket so I could get at the buttons on his shirt. Around us was utter silence, except for the lapping water and rustling twigs and leaves. ". . . cold hands . . ." he whispered. A leaf drifted slowly down and a bobwhite called somewhere. Everything was cold, his belt buckle sliding along my hip, our quick breath I could practically see on the air, all the excited nipples standing up. I spread my hands out under his shirt . . . Dennis' back always felt like the perfect fishbone in a cat's mouth in a cartoon, long flat spine, model ribs curving out . . . he pulled back against my hands, panting, his eyes squeezed shut. I started to come then, clutching at the small of his back. He waited just long enough and then he came too, without a word, fierce and blind and mute, like always. I twisted my fingers in his hair, gazing up through the layers of brown leaves at that snapping blue sky, listening to his harsh breathing dying away in my ear, the steady slapping of the water on the stony beach. ". . . nice, that was . . ." He lay one arm on the ground beside me, curving his hand around my head. "Yeah . . . whew . . ." I could feel the cool air seeping in, whistling along the sweaty places on my body. But I had to move finally, because something sharp, a twig or stone, was digging right into my back. He sighed and rolled off into the leaves.

When he went to zip himself up I saw the flash of crinkled white skin across his belly but had to pretend I didn't. He got that somewhere off Guadalcanal, one of those famous battles, when he was only nineteen, and after that was out of the war for good, so it was a lucky scar, I would have thought. But he hated for me to see it. Like a lot of men I'd known, he had that tiny prudish streak about his body, didn't much care for the idea of exposing it in broad daylight to the eyes of some snickering woman. Now my body, that was different.

I sat up and shook the leaves out of my hair. He slid his warm hand up under my blouse before I could tuck it in. "You wearing your little thing . . ." he said, trying to make it sound casual, like some kind of mock flat statement, a little joke between us, but I knew better. Dennis couldn't be subtle if he tried.

"Of course."

A minute later he said slowly, squinting up at my face. "You ever, uh, think about not wearing it?"

"No. Never." Whenever men so much as hinted in that direction— children, families, settling down— I squashed the idea for them fast. No, not me. That would be disaster, the end of everything. Probably I'd turn out like my aunts, alone in my twilight years, but I couldn't worry about that now. As it happened, I wasn't wearing my little thing at that very minute. But I was a perfect twenty-eight-day clock, and I always knew exactly when it was safe to skip. I sneaked a look at him to see how he was taking what I'd said. The sun had turned down in the sky now and was slanting in on us through the trees, and there was Dennis, dead to the world, asleep fast as a cat in a square of the sunlight. I watched a cloud shadow move slowly across the brown surface of the lake like an invisible ship. "Den-nis, we have to go soon. . . ." I blew across his face.

"Yeah . . . n'a minute . . ."

iii

JULIA

Andrew had picked up two perfect maple leaves and was flapping them against his cheek as we scuffed along through the piles of fallen leaves, treading on our own long autumnal shadows.

". . . Republican cloth coat," I said. "What a hoot." Andrew was a great comfort to me sometimes, my one link with the great world. He too had: smelled the ocean; ridden a subway; conversed with a Jew, a Negro, an Italian; eaten in a real Chinese restaurant (no chop suey!); and to Andrew alone could I utter the dreaded words *Adlai Stevenson.*

"Don't forget the cute pup, either. You know, um, *Checkers* . . . perfect. But wait and see . . ." he added, talking through the leaf. "Nobody ever made a fortune overestimating the . . . whatever it is. I mean, people eat that stuff up."

"I suppose you're right. Ugh, horrible man."

By the time we crossed the stream on our way back, the light was beginning to go gray and sad, and the air was turning cool. Winter. "Dark so early now . . ." I said.

"Umm . . ." He took my hand to help me across the slippery stones in the stream, perfectly polite. But he was far away, I could tell. In his own way Andrew could be as mysterious as Jessie. Any suffering always courteously concealed. His father had been the same way. Kept up appearances, as they say, after Andrew's mother died, dressed carefully, ate well, allowed himself to be comforted, never embarrassed anyone. Then simply died one day, six months later, neatly, with no fuss. Heart, they said. Of course. A tired pun. Would that happen to Andrew? I wanted him to put up more of a fight, to be more grasping and carping, like me.

"What are you thinking so hard about, dear? Feeling a bit depressed?"

"No, not especially." He gave me his opaque college boy's smile and shoved his hands down into the pockets of his jacket. "I wasn't thinking much of anything, to tell you the truth. But, I mean, if it's dark early now, wait till next week when Daylight Savings goes off. I hate that day after, it's like the end of the world. . . . Hey, listen . . . isn't that Teddy? I thought he was going to stay over."

"So did I." We stopped for a minute, straining our ears, scanning the pinkish western sky. As we came up along the cold shadow side of the Circus hangar, the Stinson passed over us and touched down, wing lights winking in that cheerful lonely way in the dusk. (A shutter flashed open in my mind, pleasant lost memory: side window of my old Lockheed, pulsing circles of light against massed clouds, nothing but empty ocean beneath, stars and empty black space above. How many years ago? Don't bother to count. . . .)

Two men climbed out of the airplane. One was distinctly Teddy, but he looked different somehow, and I couldn't figure out why until it dawned on me that he was standing up straight for the first time in months. The other shape was as tall as Teddy but bulkier and . . . obscurely familiar. Oh, my God. Duffy. I took a quick deep breath and tried to remember if I'd put makeup on before I'd left. Yes, yes. But I was wearing my old glasses, the ones that made me look like Fu Manchu. Teddy beamed at me. "Remember this old geezer?" he said, ever so pleased with himself.

"What happened to Mrs. Lah-Di-Dah?" I replied coolly.

"I dunno. Decided to stay on a couple of days. Shacking up somewhere, I guess. I dropped into the bar to have a few and was accosted by this fat fellow."

"Bumped off my flight to Pittsburgh."

"Told him he'd better come home with me."

Duffy was eyeing me eagerly but warily. I couldn't remember on precisely what kind of terms we'd parted, but I could take a good guess. "And who the hell is . . ." he said to me, rude as of old, shifting one immense shoulder in Andrew's direction, ". . . your son or something?"

Goddamn him. But then Andrew did look half his age. All right. I decided to be flattered. "No, this is Jessie's husband, Andrew Oelman."

"Oh, Jessie, my little sweetheart. Ran into her down in Texas, '43 or thereabouts. Bought her a chicken dinner. How's she doing now?"

Andrew's forehead wrinkled and he opened his mouth to say something, but before he could, Teddy had pulled Duffy off to one side. He spoke softly to him for a minute or two and I could hear Duffy's stage whisper, a loud rustle of sympathetic profanity. Andrew met my eye and smiled slightly.

Teddy said, out loud, "Let's go inside and have a taste. Alice'll have a fit when she sees you."

Andrew slid forward tactfully to walk with Teddy, leaving Duffy to me. "You bastard," I said to him under my breath. I'd just remembered a few things.

"You're looking good, Jule," he growled in my ear. "How long has it been?"

"Since *what?*" I growled back.

iv

ALICE

Jessie sat in the backseat of Vern's old Studebaker on the way home, clutching the box of new shoes in her lap like it was a box of jewels. Vern was wearing his new shoes, brown tasseled loafers I'd talked him into buying because they looked so much better than the black funeral director's kind of shoes he usually wore. He was so nervous and excited about them you would have thought he was getting himself some two-toned Florida gangster shoes instead.

"They look real natty," I said, nodding down at his long narrow foot on the accelerator.

"You don't think they might be a little too, too . . ."

"Too sexy? Well, sure they are. Just don't wear 'em in the store where any of the ladies can see 'em, you'll be safe enough, I guess." Not such a hilarious joke, but his face went red and his chest started to shake, even though no noise came out. He still had a hard time getting a laugh out, left over from the Anna years, I figured. His mother was another one. The two lady spiders. Not that I should say that about my own sister now in her grave, but it was the truth. He'd been pushed around by women all his life, until me. I was good for him, you could see that. "You going to stay out to dinner tonight? Martha left a big casserole for us."

"Have to see. Maybe I will."

"Jessie wants you to . . ." I leaned across the seat and gave her hand a little tap. ". . . don't you, Jessie?" I could feel him cringe into himself, hearing me talk to her like that, but I always thought it was a big mistake to treat her like something spooky, the way he always did. I could remember once when I was over in France there was a boy much worse off than Jessie; never moved or spoke, lay there staring day in and day out. The other women would pick him up and put him down like a plate on a table, but sometimes I'd talk to him a little, whisper a joke in his ear, stroke his face when I fed him. The rest of them all thought I was going silly over him because he was sort of nice-looking, or had been once, you could tell. Then one day, he put his hand out and touched my arm, felt heavy and stiff as a dog's paw, but it was something, showed he was still in there. So you never know. He died a little later, probably better that way. Not that Jessie was going to die on us. The doctors, whatever other fool things they had to say about her, all agreed about that. Physically she was in top shape; had that strong little Rice heart pumping away, good for another fifty years.

I said to her, poking at the shoebox in her lap, "You like your new shoes, don't you? And they're real pretty on you too."

"Don't . . ." he burst out, his face all twisted up. "Don't." He really hated it when I went against him about Jessie, but he wouldn't have it out with me; that wasn't in him at all. I knew he was going to clam up and not say another word the whole rest of the trip. I pretended I didn't notice; kept right on talking to Jessie, playing my little finger-walking game with her, and hide and seek with the shoes in the box.

At home he let me and Jessie out and then took his car way back along the hangar road to turn it around, so he'd be heading in the right direction when he wanted to leave, a typical Vern kind of move, always planning ahead for a fast getaway. As we went up the back steps I could hear a lot of commotion in the kitchen, clinking glasses and a big booming laugh that sounded familiar. I opened the door and almost dropped my teeth. "My God! Am I seeing a ghost or is that John Duffy!"

"Alice . . ." He grabbed me and gave me a big smacking kiss. I pushed Jessie forward and she let him kiss her too, sort of half smiling, though you couldn't really tell if she knew who he was or not, then I herded her on upstairs to take her nap.

John sighed a big sigh. "Oh, damn it . . . that poor kid . . ." His forehead was all puckered and his eyes were shiny. "Last time I saw her she was, what, twenty-two? Little ball of fire, practically jumping out of her skin 'cause she heard they were sending her to bomber school at Lackland. Couldn't wait to get her paws on that B-17. . . ."

"Right, and a while later they decided they needed a big girl for bombers, passed over Jessie for a pal of hers six feet tall. Nearly broke her heart. They did let her ferry Mustangs for a while. . . ."

Julia cut in on me, all hot under the collar, ready to pop off about the old woman's-rights stuff, like always. "Most of the time the wretched girl was down at Camp Davis getting shot at by half-witted ordnance recruits, towing targets in red-lined A-25s."

Teddy yawned and said to Duffy out of the corner of his mouth, "Mean airplane, that one. Used to call it the coffin."

"Yeah," Duffy whispered back. "I heard some stories. . . ." They were sort of tuning Julia out to get her goat, like a couple of kids.

"Stories? Stories? Jessie could tell you stories that would curl your hair!" Julia was all worked up, practically at the spitting stage. "It was disgraceful the way the army treated those girls, simply disgraceful. Wonderful pilots, brave as lions, wasted and broken and . . ."

"Now, now, Jule," Duffy said, patting her arm.

"Don't you now-now me . . . !"

In the nick of time the screen door slammed and everybody turned around to look. Vern came slouching in and stopped short, so fast it was comical, like a cartoon animal. When I introduced him to John he went all red, choked out a few words nobody could hear and made tracks back out the door.

I could've predicted he'd pull a trick like that. I was real embarrassed for him but I knew he hated meeting new people, especially flying people, all of them boozing and carrying on, telling jokes he didn't understand and a million war stories. Seemed like everybody'd brought in an airplane with a flak hole the size of an elephant or the rudder shot off or an engine dangling by a thread. We still had 'em, a lot of ex-students who came around to yammer at us till our eyes glazed over, never managed to put it all behind them. Then there was the other type, guys who couldn't talk about the whole business to save their souls. Dennis, for instance, had a carrier sunk under him in the Pacific, only he'd up and leave the room if you even mentioned it. My brother was the same way about what happened in France in '17, though he'd yak a blue streak about any other subject in the world. All the same, I had to grant that flying people were pretty hard to take in big doses. I couldn't entirely blame Vern for turning tail like that. Young Andrew had the same problem of course, had it ever since he took up with a lady flier; men always elbowing him, wanting him to square off. And for him it was even worse in the war-story department because he'd been stuck on a base out in Oregon teaching swimming the whole time. Didn't seem to let that stuff bother him as much as Vern, though. Better to worry about washerwoman's wrinkles on your behind than maybe getting it shot off, I heard him tell a fellow once. Always some fool contest going on with the men.

"So that's the guy your sister married," Duffy was saying, real casual, pouring scotch into his glass like it was soda pop. "Seems like kind of a twerp. Alice, you don't have a drink. What kind of place is this, lady standing here without a drink . . ."

"He looks different somehow," Julia said finally. "Duffy, I mean."

I'd expected her to go off and drink with the men. No such luck. She stayed behind in the kitchen with me, exactly where I didn't want her, looking over my shoulder and putting her two cents in. I didn't trust myself, even though Martha'd told me what to do for the dinner. I wasn't anybody's idea of a good cook.

"I thought he looked okay," I said, and dumped some torn-up lettuce into a bowl for a salad. "He always was kind of heavyset."

"It used to be hard fat, though. Now it's soft fat."

I almost said right to her face, "Talking about soft fat . . ." but I didn't have the heart. She was standing there, her eyes gone kind of dreamy, her glass up against her cheek, mooning over old Duffy, no matter what she said.

"And he seems so . . . *loud.*"

I looked over at her in surprise. *Loud* was the one thing Duffy'd always been, always would be; how come she hadn't noticed before? I never could figure out what was going on in Julia's mind about men, we were so different that way. Of course she was only twenty-two when Jimmy was killed, and she'd flat out adored him. Afterwards, you'd start to hear people say, My, Julia will sleep with *anybody,* and it was true, anybody she liked, that is. She drew the line at married men and Republicans (except that stiff-necked New England kind she called Tories instead).

I even used to admire her back then, though she'd have fainted to hear it. But I always had kind of a hard time with men, got in too deep with the wrong ones and hung on to 'em too long. Mind you, we always thought Julia might settle down finally with John. Never found out the whole story why she didn't, a big bust-up or just drifting apart.

She put her glass down on the counter with a snap, getting ready to be regular snotty Julia again, I could tell. "What have you done to that poor lettuce?" she said, peering into the bowl. "It looks so . . . dingy. You can't serve that when we have a guest. Go in the pantry and see if there isn't a can of something." And with that she took herself off to the den—we could hear them all laughing in there—and left me standing at the counter ready to wring her neck. I went into the pantry, though, took down a can of peas and threw the salad out back for the raccoons.

When I went in to call them for dinner another to-do was going on. Julia's face was all mottled, her eyes squeezed down to slits, and she was talking in that screeching angry voice of hers—you could cut through lead with it. "Oh, yes, women are unsuitable; they're emotional and unpredictable and *cute*. And besides they *bleed* every month and Jesus Christ we can't have that in an *army* airplane can we, oh my no. . . ."

"You're full of shit, Julia. That wasn't the reason." Duffy looked pretty mad himself, puffed up like a rooster. "The men needed the jobs, the women didn't. . . ."

I stepped in fast, before anybody could answer *that* one. "Hate to interrupt, folks, but . . ."

Duffy stood up, glaring at Julia. "According to you, everybody's always got it in for the women. You always were full of shit on that topic."

Teddy led Duffy away, making a face at me across his back, getting a big kick out of the whole thing, you could bet. Nothing in the world ever made Teddy that mad. "Come on, Duff, let's go clean up."

"It's true, it's *true,* and every woman knows it!" Julia screamed after them.

By the time we were all gathered around the table, they'd simmered down a little, and a lot of stories began to come back to me about Julia and Duffy in the old days, how they used to fight so much you had to figure they enjoyed it. I bowed my head and said a fast grace, even though I knew it would irritate Julia no end. I always threw it in, just in case. She called that "absurd."

"Tell me the truth now, all kidding aside," Duffy said. "How's business?" Andrew'd taken Jessie upstairs and left the four of us sitting in the den with our coffee. "Are you doing as bad as me?"

"Let me tell you something real sad," Teddy said. "Right now Alice has one student. Count 'em, one. Used to be everywhere, had to brush 'em off the airplanes like flies . . ."

"Got a few steady charters, though," I told him. I didn't want to make everything sound too sad tonight. "And we have a pretty good rep, still, you know. So people don't mind sending their families with us. And we have the Circus in the summer. Nothing like it was, though. We give 'em rides in the Jennies and . . ."

"Good God, Jennies that still fly? How can you get anybody to work on them for you?"

"Oh, we have a simply marvelous young man. Martha found him."

"You think he'd like to come out to L.A.? Just kidding. I have a hell of a time finding decent mechanics."

"Well, Dennis happens to be in love with Martha, so he's not going anywhere."

"You never know. Martha might pull something. Remember what happened with Dave."

"She wouldn't dare. Not with Dennis."

Duffy said, "Guess you don't fly anymore, do you, Jule? I heard it from Al Brody a couple of years back. Meant to write you or something."

She smiled at him, but with a pretty sharp cold gleam in her eye. "That was more than thirteen years ago, John. I'm sure you meant to write me or something, and I'm sure it slipped right out of your mind the next day, too, the way everything else does that really matters."

"Hey, now." Teddy stood up fast between them. "Let's have some drinks and talk about the good times, plenty of those."

"I'm not going to slug him, Teddy," Julia said drily. "I've said all I'm going to. Now I'd like some whiskey and ice."

Pretty soon Teddy started telling a story, about a friend of his whose mechanic accidentally welded his toolbox onto his wing. "Poor guy couldn't figure out why he couldn't keep his starboard wing up. He does his first loop anyhow, what the hell, and he sees everybody running for cover, shaking their fists at him. It was raining tools all of a sudden. He was afraid he was gonna get lynched or something."

"Is that true, Teddy? I mean, I've heard you tell it a hundred times and never said a word, but how could he weld a toolbox on the wing and not notice?"

"I swear it's true. Cross my heart."

"Sure, it's true. . . ." Duffy settled himself into the wing chair and picked up the bottle of scotch. "And I know another one even worse. Listen to this. . . ." And so we were off, one terrific story after another.

It'd been years since I'd had a night like this. "Wait a minute," I said. "Talk about your dumb mechanics. . . ."

V

MARTHA

Finally, when it was almost dark, Dennis and I found a tent completely filled with rocking chairs, like a tent full of ghosts, all of them rocking gently by themselves in the evening breeze. Halfway down one row I saw the chair I'd had my heart set on for years, cherrywood, with a high ladderback and narrow graceful arms. I sat down in it and rocked a few times, running my hand along the beautiful grain of the wood.

"Looks kind of spindly," Dennis said.

"Oh, no, it's just that Shaker style, very plain and spare." He screwed up his face at me, the educated lady. I ignored him. I was counting up sums in my head, really tempted to buy it, even though I knew business was going to be even worse in the winter, and we didn't *need* a rocking chair, no matter how pretty it was. "Well, I guess I'm ready to go now." I started to walk away. "It's nice, but it costs too much."

Dennis grabbed my arm. "Look, you want that thing, I'll get it for you."

"Oh I don't know . . ."

"Come on. I can see you want it real bad." He pulled his wallet out of his back pocket and strode over to the proprietor's stable by the tent flap. It always made me uncomfortable when men wanted to buy me things, but I knew better than to argue with him. I have to tell you Dennis was very peculiar and stubborn about money. Once he'd started sleeping with me, for instance, he'd refused to take another penny in cash salary from me. (Oh, he made a lot of other money, fixing things for people. A good mechanic will never starve.) I tried to reason with him, it wasn't me paying him but a neuter entity, the business, and certainly not for *that.* To me the lines between work and sex were perfectly clear, but naturally everything got a lot more tangled and silly inside his convoluted masculine brain. All those little cogs of pride grinding away in there where you couldn't see them. So I gave up and let him do whatever made him happy. We were hard up, after all. I could be as practical as the next person. And he was getting room and board as well as me, wasn't he?

Dennis came back, stuffing a receipt into his wallet. "He's going to send it over on the Greyhound Monday. He says you picked the best one here. You got good taste, kiddo."

I put my arm through his. "Thank you. That was sweet."

The proprietor, a little round man in a beige cashmere V-neck, was tying a SOLD tag to my chair. He kept glancing over his shoulder at Dennis and me as we strolled out of the tent. Of course Dennis was wearing his high-heeled black boots, beat-up narrow Levi's and a black leather jacket, ordinary work clothes to him, and he always wore his hair long and combed straight back. People often did gape at the two of us together. I gave the little man a juicy knowing smile, and he turned primly away. Probably he fancied Dennis' hoody and dangerous look. I'd heard some of those men did. "He's got his eye on you. . . ." I poked Dennis in the ribs. "Go on, smile at him, give him a treat."

"Hey, wait a minute." He glowered at me, embarrassed. "That guy?"

"Um-hmm. I think so . . . well, what next?" We could see the whirling and spinning and soaring shapes of every kind of amusement contraption, outlined in lights against the deep blue evening sky. "You think you're ready to take me up on the Ferris wheel again? My big brave boy . . ."

He scowled off into the distance. "Never going to let up about that, are you?"

"Probably not." I knew a secret about Dennis. He was terrified of heights, like me. I found that out the first summer we were together, when we ended up, one of those little misunderstandings that happen early on, stranded at the top of the Ferris wheel at the state fair. I bit my tongue and smiled, being brave, keeping my eyes dead level so I couldn't see the dreadful tiny shapes so far below. He was even worse off, though. His face went dead white and he said in a strangled sort of voice, ". . . sorry . . . things scare the shit outta me . . ." I could see that his hands were shaking too, and I knew I shouldn't, but I started to laugh and laugh. It struck me so funny. I mean, here was this wild man who'd take a brakeless Harley down a dusty track at a hundred and ten miles an hour, going all pale and trembly in a stodgy old Ferris wheel.

By the time we got back down he was in a total seething rage. I could see I'd pushed him too far; I always did. Even then I couldn't stop. "It *is* funny . . . *you* . . ." I choked out, practically paralyzed I was laughing so hard, wiping tears away. He told me to shut my goddamn mouth with a look that shriveled me completely. I have to admit I was relieved. Up until that moment I'd imagined him to be one of those purely good-natured men, not a mean bone in his body, and looked down on him some for it. A few days later we were crossing a street in Columbus when a seedy lolling man called out something mildly obscene—before you could say boo, Dennis grabbed him by his grubby collar and flung him up against a wall. Of course Dennis was mortified later, he always was, not that it did anybody any good. I could never resist teasing him though, even about little things; he always rose to the bait so perfectly.

"A silly little joke, why should it bother you so much?"

"Because it does, all right?" He shrugged my arm off. "Bothers me you want to get at me all the time. That make sense? You're the smart one, you tell me."

So we walked along for a while, not saying another word. I pulled the sleeves of my sweater over my hands, fairly shivering. Once the sun had gone down, it was pretty cold. Dennis was till annoyed, taking those big angry strides, so I could hardly keep up with him. Finally I stopped dead in my tracks. Let him stalk off if he was going to be that way. I watched him disappear among the crowd and lights and balloons and icky half-eaten cotton-candy spools and giant chartreuse pandas. A minute later he came ambling back, not quite looking at me.

"Up to your old tricks, I see."

"Your old tricks." I hunched my shoulders inside my sweater. "You know I can't walk that fast."

"Guess you can't. Looks like you're really freezing."

"I am. It felt like summer this morning."

"Let's head back then. But here . . ." He took off his jacket and hung it around my shoulders, a huge heavy stiff thing with a life of its own. "Wear it, and stop being such a pain in the ass."

"I think you like it when I am."

"News to me." The bike started up with a roar, and I climbed on behind him.

On the way home we stopped at Beanie's, one of those dingy little places you see by the side of any road, a kind of garage with a tipping cocktail-glass sign on the roof. Driving by, you picture knife and fist fights, women pulling hair in the ladies' room, a din of evil laughter. Actually Beanie's was a friendly and innocent sort of place.

Dennis and I sat down in a booth and had a drink to warm up. After a while we even danced a little, the way the kids danced, bodies propped together, both our arms twined around behind my back. I closed my eyes and could almost have gone to sleep right there in the middle of the floor from all the fresh air I'd breathed that day. "Want to leave?" he said into my hair.

"Um-hmm. Soon."

A few minutes later we ran into a friend of his, a wild boy from the racing circuit called Wally Biggers. (When Wally broke his ankle, he refused to wear a cast, bought boots two sizes larger and kept right on racing. He was even tougher and crazier than Dennis.) Tonight he had on a green paratrooper's uniform and his blond hair was all shorn and he didn't look tough at all, only scrawny and raw like a chicken. Leather did make a difference.

"Christ, Wally . . ." Dennis said, shocked.

"Hey there, Denny. Yeah, I know. Uncle Sam finally got me." He squeezed in next to Dennis in the tiny booth. "My last weekend around here for a while."

"Christ . . ." Dennis said again. "Where're they sending you?"

"Now, where do ya think?" He gave us a morose, resigned look. "Next month I'll be down in Seoul, probably."

"Could be Germany, you get lucky. But the Airborne . . . out of your fucking mind . . . ?"

"Didn't wanta let 'em draft me. First jump's the worst, then it's okay." He stood up and slid out of the booth, twirling his cap. "Got to go. My girl's over there. Take it easy, Denny. Glad I ran into ya."

"Better get back here, you bastard, give me a chance to knock you on your ass again."

"Bet I will," Wally said. "Any old time."

When we were outside again, crunching along the gravel of the parking lot, Dennis said, "Poor dumb sonofabitch."

It took me a minute to figure out what he meant. Typical Dennis conversation. "Are you talking about Wally? He's older than you were."

"Not by a whole lot. It's different, anyhow, line on a fuckin' map."

"But without you the Japs would've been in San Francisco, I forgot. . . ."

"Well, they might've been . . . I'm serious."

"Oh, Den . . ." But I could tease him and tease him about the war and never make a dent. He was impervious on the subject.

It was a dark starry night, and we didn't pass a single car along the county road so late. We could have been out in space, rocketing along. I was still wearing Dennis' jacket like a turtle's shell around me. I'd tried to make him put it back on. He wouldn't, of course. "Come on, I told you, I'm not cold."

It must've been close to two in the morning by the time we came to the turn for our road. Dennis stopped the motor so we could coast the rest of the way. A wasted effort. There were a million lights on downstairs, and we could hear loud voices and raucous laughter floating around the corner of the house. We crept in the back door and tried to sneak upstairs, but Teddy spotted us and called out, "There they are. Come on in here, Martha. Say hello to an old pal. You too, Dennis." Julia and Alice were there and a big bald-headed man. "Don't you remember John Duffy? He took you out once and bought you a Coke with a cherry in it when you were about six. You thought it was a grown-up drink."

Whoever it was flapped his arms around me in a bear hug. "Still a pretty little thing, isn't she?"

"Yes, I suppose I am." He roared at that. They all did. I could tell they'd been drinking and gabbing for hours, telling lies—*And there I was* . . . stories, I'd been hearing them my whole life—and talking old fliers' talk. Now they were at the stage where every little twitch of an eye was absolutely hilarious. Anything could set them off. And poor

Dennis wasn't a member of the family, entitled to be comically rude, like me. He had to behave.

"This is Dennis, the young man we've been telling you about," Julia said. She looked very flushed and merry. Then I made the connection. John Duffy, her old boyfriend.

"So, well, uh, Dennis, where'd you learn so much about airplanes?" Duffy said. "In the service, I suppose."

"Yeah, partly, sir. And I used to work on a lot of flying boats, Fairchilds mostly, up on the lake when I was a kid."

"A *kid*! What the hell are you now?" Duffy boomed out, winking at the others, and they all laughed fit to choke themselves, bending over in their chairs, snorting into their drinks. They really were impossible, like a roomful of dopey kindergarteners. Duffy kept after Dennis, just relentless, his way of being polite, I suppose. "So, in the service, you see a lot of action, or what?"

"Uh, my ship was the *Hornet*."

"Oho, that big mother. Japs got her, let's see, fall of '42 or thereabouts, correct? What do you think of that?"

"Sounds about right," Dennis said warily.

"Oh, shut up, John," Julia said. "Let me finish my story."

Dennis and I plunked ourselves down on the stiff plaid sofa against the wall, the one no one ever used. He took a sip of his drink and gave me a bland sideways look. I tried mine. It was three inches of straight bourbon, no ice, no water.

". . . and there I was," Julia was saying, ". . . point of no return, and the damn auxiliary tanks wouldn't feed. I tried every trick in the book to shake them loose, dived, rolled, sideslipped. But finally I had to give up and turn back, and I knew it was my last chance at that record. I cried the whole way, and I was having a hell of a job keeping her straight and level with all that extra fuel. My left foot was numb for days from leaning on the rudder . . . God, I was disappointed. And it turned out to be a tiny fucking valve worth about twelve cents. If it weren't for that, I'd still be famous."

Then Teddy started in. "Yeah, but listen, did I ever tell you about the time I had down in Alabama? I was in my old pusher, that'll show you how far back I'm going for this one. *I'd* lost a valve somewhere and all of a sudden oil shoots right up into my face and the engine starts coughing and I have to set down somewhere, anywhere, and damn quick. I pick this nice little field, first one I could find, cows all around, you know, looking up kinda surprised. I get down okay, and then I wipe my eyes and I see this farmer coming toward me across the field. He takes one good look at me, covered with black oil—it's Alabama, remember—and I can see him thinking, 'Well, this here's an uppity one, got his own flying machine . . .' Put me up that night, though. Cleared out the cows next day so I could take off again, once I'd fixed my damn oil line."

"Never heard that one before."

"I was trying to think, who was that other guy, you know the one I mean, a real nutty guy, drank a lot, looked like Errol Flynn?"

"Roscoe Turner, you mean, flew with the lion cub?"

"No, no, way before him. The guy I'm talking about was the one who was sitting in some bar out by the old airstrip on Long Island, and somebody asked him the time and he looks down and his watch is broken so . . ."

"I remember, I remember. Bert Acosta. That's who it was. And he ran out and jumped into an airplane and flew over to that big insurance building with the clock in New York, comes right back and goes into the bar, says, cool as you please, 'Well, gents, it's twelve-thirty, I went and checked.'"

"Are you sure that was Bert? I thought it was . . ."

Dennis set his empty glass down on the floor beside the sofa, and I hid mine under its dusty skirt. We said good night, but nobody paid the slightest bit of attention. Once we were safely out in the hall the two of us fell back against the wall, giggling and snorting. I said in a deep voice like Duffy's, "Why, he's only a kid . . ." and Dennis bent over, holding his middle. The silliness was catching, or maybe it was the whiskey. Halfway up the dark stairs I bumped into him, accidentally on purpose, and pushed him hard into the wall. "Ooops, sorry . . ."

"Oh, yeah? Are ya?" He heaved me up off my feet, so only my toes were touching the step. I hung onto him like a monkey, lifting my face, rubbing my chin against him in the dark. I could smell the outdoors in his shirt and on his hair. He was laughing, shaking against me, trying to keep his balance. ". . . asking for it, aren't ya?"

All of a sudden there was a tiny snick of sound, an arm or foot touching wood, and a shadow moved in the darkness above us.

"Jess?" I heard a door closing quietly. Dennis set me down, and we crept softly up the rest of the stairs and down the hall to our room.

"What was that?" I said when we were safely inside.

"Andy probably, went to the john."

"We must've embarrassed him . . . don't turn on that big light."

He stumbled against the chair. "Shit, did you move this?"

"No, of course not."

November 26 and 27

i

MARTHA

Back when we were little, my mother always set Jessie to me as a task, but I didn't mind. I loved it, in fact, dressing and undressing her, laying her down and picking her up like she was a big fuzzy-haired doll, better than my other dolls because she really did go "Wah!" and wet her pants. I'd lift her into her wagon and she'd let me pull her anywhere, through mud puddles and piles of dirt, up steep hills so she'd tumble back, little fat legs flying up in their corduroy overalls; then down the other side lickety-split. And she'd be hanging on for dear life, her eyes wide, her mouth scrunched up tight, never making a peep. I must have been about five then and she was close to two. I wondered where that old red wagon was now, all rusted away to nothing probably. But taking Jessie to the market these days always made me think about those other days. The same but different, you know.

I sent her off with one cart to pick out some yams and turnips while I went to look for mincemeat and pumpkin for the pies. I was going to cheat this year and use canned pumpkin. I also needed a sack of tiny marshmallows to go with the yams, pearl onions, stale bread for stuffing and about three hundred other ordinary things we were all out of.

The store was decorated for Thanksgiving with pumpkins and pilgrims and turkeys and those brown and gold twisted crepe paper streamers everywhere. All the smiling cardboard turkeys and stacks of cold white carcasses in the meat cooler made me very depressed. But that could have been merely the idea of Thanksgiving itself, always a bad-luck holiday in our family. Thanksgiving of 1942, my mother got sick. Thanksgiving of 1944, they disbanded the WASPs practically overnight and sent Jessie home all thin and burned out. Thanksgiving of 1945, Andrew and Jessie got married. Well, that was only sad in retrospect. At the time it seemed like a happy event, one more party in that giddy victory year, Jessie in yellow satin, Andrew in a nice dark civilian suit, and lots of fake champagne. Then Thanksgiving of 1946, my mother finally died and Jessie had her breakdown. So every Thanksgiving you'd have to wonder, what next?

I steered up alongside the pile of turkeys. My cart had one of those wiggly wheels, and I ended up bumping into somebody's plump rear end. Mrs. Loftus, one of the Methodist Church ladies. "Ooops, sorry." She gave me a mealymouthed smile, but I could tell she was really thinking, clumsy girl, watch where you're going. I picked out a turkey, dumped it into the cart and slid around Mrs. Loftus and on toward the baking supplies. Mincemeat. Pumpkin filling . . .

Sometimes, with all those ghostly past holidays drifting around in my mind, I'd get to brooding and wondering. Maybe if I'd been a little more sensitive, done a little more *noticing,* I could have changed things for Jessie. You can be very dense about people in your family. I'd been that way about Daddy, too, despising him for letting my mother walk all over him, never seeing the good in him. (A lot of men would have just run off, gone out, ha, ha, for a newspaper some night and hightailed it for Mexico.) It wasn't until I was older that I began to take pity on him and admit that nobody in the world was strong enough to stand up to her, well, nobody but me. That was because I'd written her off so early, absolutely made up my mind to and did. And because deep down inside me, like the thin man trying to get out of the fat man, was a perfect copy of her, my mother, Anna the bitch. . . .

When I came around the corner into the vegetable section, there was Jessie pushing a cart filled with big bulging misshapen pumpkins, the worst-looking ones I'd ever seen, a huge tower of them teetering over the top of the cart. She watched me solemnly, holding on tight to the cart, waiting to see what I'd do. Just for a split second I felt a dizzy rushing in my head, as if I'd have to grab her and shake her. But I didn't, I couldn't. Poor Jessie. Maybe I wasn't the only one with Thanksgiving jitters. The temptation was always to assume she didn't think about things at all, her pretty eyes like holes in a piece of cloth, nothing but blank blue sky behind them. But maybe she was recalling all the sad times too, in her own way.

"Come on, Jess . . . won't you help me? Dennis and Daddy are going to pick us up right at twelve-thirty, and it's already twelve-fifteen." I handed her a yam. "I want you to count out twelve of these, just this size, okay?" She let her fingers go slack so the yam fell out onto the floor and bounced cheerily away. She was still watching me with that sad, worried look on her face. I sighed and patted her hand. "Never mind, Jess, I can do it."

I worked at speed, tossing vegetables over my shoulder into the wiggly cart. Then I took Jessie down to stand in line with it at the checkout, while I did a last-minute pass through the aisles with the fast cart. I skidded to a stop in the beverage section, threw in two big cans of coffee, then snatched up one more. I always had to shop as if I were stocking a lumber camp. I hefted a case of beer onto the bottom shelf of the cart, stood up right away, pressing my hand to my stomach, thinking, maybe that was too heavy for me . . . *in my condition. . . .*

For more than two weeks I'd been hearing echoes of Aunt Julia's pruny old doctor telling me, "There is *no* safe time of the month." How I'd laughed to myself at the time. I knew my own body better than some man, doctor or no, didn't I? Now it looked like he might have the last laugh on me. On the other hand, one missed period didn't necessarity mean *that.* It could have been a lot of other things, nerves, a tumor, early menopause. I'd just have to cross my fingers a while and wait and see. I stacked a couple of bottles of Coke on top of everything else and lurched away, nearly knocking Mrs. Loftus down again. "Sorry . . ." She didn't smile back this time, horrid old frump.

I caught up with Jessie at the very instant the checker was ringing up the last item in her cart, peering around anxiously for whoever was going to pay for it all. They always tried to be nice to Jessie in Kroger's, but there were limits. "Here's the rest," I said breathlessly. "We're together." The people in line started muttering and exchanging those disgusted, fake-amazed looks as I pushed the second cart in ahead of them, but I didn't care. It was already quarter to one.

ii

JESSIE

I guess people think I'm all numb in here and don't notice what's going on or else don't care. But that's not true. I do notice and I do care. But, see, I like to pretend . . . I mean, it's like there's a big piece of glass around me or I'm living in this gigantic bottle, so I can see everybody and hear what they say but I don't have to do anything about it. I'm safe back here, trapped and safe, both at the same time. And it's okay, it really is. . . .

A long time ago in California or somewhere I went to this aquarium, a real tourist-trap kind of place, long halls full of that dark, greenish, watery kind of light and huge glass tanks instead of walls. Inside the tanks were all these weird fish swimming around real slow, just carrying on with their fish lives as if you weren't there at all. But every once in a while one of them would come up and thump on the glass, glare right out at you, some big mother with little mean eyes and those rows of jagged teeth in some kind of upside-down mouth. You'd be walking through eating popcorn or something, and all of a sudden, thump, crunch, there he is. And . . . all of a sudden . . . the glass breaks and the water flies out and the fish are piling up on the floor, gasping and flopping around and dying with all the broken glass around them. And you're still kind of watching, just curious like it's an animal show on TV . . . but maybe one of them, the biggest, leaps right at you . . . he's opening that huge mouth, showing you all those teeth . . . he's going to get back at you for putting him in there in the first place, tear right into you and the water turns red, red, and . . . chomp. That's just a dream I have sometimes. My aquarium dream. (I had a doctor once, back when they used to take me to doctors to see if I was really crazy or what. This guy kept a little stack of cards in alphabetical order of all my dreams, all his dreams, all everybody's dreams, made you write them down every morning. What a pain in the ass.) My aquarium dream. It scares the shit out of me too. Maybe it's only because I'm crazy that it scares me so much or, ha, ha, maybe it's only because I'm crazy that I have it in the first place. I can't tell anymore.

I'm used to being scared of things anyway. That's my one big talent. You'd be surprised how good you can get at it, being flat out terrified as jelly inside with nobody ever suspecting a thing.

Like the first time I ever was up in an airplane. Christ, I was scared. I hated it, I mean hated *it. My mother's hands were clamped around me tight, so tight, like she was trying to send electric currents through me or something, to make me like it, make me love it. It was horrible . . . big shadow over me from the top wing, big blade of propeller roaring up in a blur in front of me, so close, like it could lean back and chop you up in a minute. I was seven then. No, I was younger. She took my sister up once but Martha hated it too. She screamed and kicked the whole time. She scratched my mother.* What a mean little cat, *my mother said, showing her scratched-up arms where there was blood. So she filled up the tub and dropped Martha in with her clothes still on,* that's what we do with a mean little cat, *and there was water all over the bathroom floor. I was standing by the door. My father didn't see that. He was downstairs.*

Martha scratched her and made her bleed, so she had a right to be mad, didn't she? I was good. I didn't scratch or anything. I didn't cry. I laughed instead. I wanted Martha to see me laughing away. She was older and she cried the whole time. I felt bad because it wasn't her fault, but my mother was nice to me then. Sometimes she was. Nicer to me than to anyone.

I could see how much she'd changed when I came back from the WASPs. Everybody'd warned me, but I didn't believe it. I thought she'd be proud of me the way she used to be. Sick or not, dying or not, I thought she'd be nice to me like I deserved. I mean, after the hell I'd been through . . . You can get used to being scared all the time, you'd be surprised. And back then, in the war, a lot of people were scared all the time, so it wasn't so bad. And I was good, I knew that. I was the best. That was one way I got through a lot of it, the same as always laughing when I was little, laughing like a loony bird so no one could tell. I knew I was so damn good I could fly anything, any motherfucking deathtrap coffin with wings they wanted to give me. I didn't care.

There were some real bad times, though. I'd get so scared and feel so crazy and then get even scareder of how crazy I'd feel . . . God, so awful, like everything was coming loose in my head, my hands shaking and shaking, stomach like a huge empty clenching sweating ball. But I had this trick, see, once I got into the cockpit I'd act like the things I did to the airplane were things I was doing to myself, checking dials and stuff, controlling my body to get it ready too. That worked sometimes. But everybody must have had a trick to get themselves through what they had to get through, or else how come more people didn't go crazy?

I tried to make allowances because she was so sick. I tried to be nice, but you know my mother could really make you suffer if she wanted to, she could always get you where it hurt the most, scorn like acid welling up out of her and burning you like fire. She did it to me and she did it to my father and she tried to do it to Martha, but Martha was lucky. Martha could give her that fuck-you stare and never let anything touch her. Martha had a right to hate me. I'd never blame her. But she doesn't. She stuck up for me sometimes. She stuck up for my father too. Once she kicked her in the shins when he went off in the car and didn't come back till late. You made him go away, you big fat bitch. *I don't know where she heard the word bitch. She didn't hit her or anything, that wasn't her way. She liked the silent treatment the best. No matter what you did she'd pretend she couldn't see you, you know, look right through you like you were invisible and keep it up for days and days. Sometimes Martha did it back to her and that made her wild. Martha always knew how to get her going good. I never even tried. I couldn't stand it. I'd do anything to make her be nice to me again.*

I walked into her room the day I came home, going to surprise her, you know, showing up in my brand-new uniform, which was that funny blue and had the little hat that would never quite set down right on my hair. It'd cost me enough, that damn monkey suit, and I'm not talking about money. I'd sweat blood for it, if you want to know the truth, but Christ, hadn't we all. They didn't need us anymore, though, now that we finally had our fancy uniforms, because they had too many men enlisting, and the men couldn't stand having us around flying their damn airplanes so much better than they could so it was good-bye, girls, it's been nice to know you and thanks, thanks for nothing, you mean, and we all got sent home just like that, bastards. I felt bad enough about that without my mother acting so shitty. And Betty, Betty, I kept thinking about Betty. . . .

It was that close, you know, her or me, it could've been either one of us. It wasn't my fault. I got to the line first that day, only a minute before her, might just as well have been the other way around. See, the whole thing was luck, her own rotten lousy luck. I tried not to think about it, didn't do any good, 'cause it was like one of those sores that looks like it's healed, but keeps peeling open again no matter what you do, real sickening. I'd keep hearing her voice and seeing everything happen all over again. I walked into my mother's room that day and I had it in my mind like that, Betty's voice the way I'd heard her crying up to me. . . . I couldn't have heard anything, they told me, and I knew they were right, but I heard her anyway. Help me, Jessie, help me. *There was supposed to be a little latch on the canopy so you could get out in a fire, but the goddamn latch didn't work. We'd all flown that fucking piece of trash and we all knew about that tricky latch, but you had to fly it anyway and hope for the best. Say a word and it'd be,* Oh these girls, no guts . . . *And Christ there was something that didn't work on every last one of them anyway. She got the one with the tricky latch and I got the one with the loose rudder and she took off first and I saw her go down and the flames leaping and almost couldn't pull up in time to save myself and there was nothing on earth I could do for her, was there? But she wouldn't shut up in my mind, Betty wouldn't, crying up at me,* Help me, Jessie, help me, Jess. *I couldn't've heard a damn thing through the plastic canopy over the noise of the fire and my engine. I couldn't have done a damn thing to help her. . . . No, I couldn't, I mean . . . I couldn't get a word out of her, my mother, my own mother, she lay there like I was fucking invisible, like she didn't give a shit about me anymore. It even struck me funny sometimes. Here she was dying and everything and she could still make me feel like a worthless little kid again. The silent treatment same as always.*

iii

MARTHA

I patted Jessie's hair into a nicer shape and said, "Jessie, look and see if you can find Daddy and Dennis and the blue car. . . ." At that very moment the station wagon came whizzing around out of the alley and screeched to a stop on a dime in front of me. Dennis jumped out and came stalking around to us, glowering and showing off, ready to spit nickels, I could tell. Ho hum.

"Where the hell have you been?" He flipped up the tailgate and started dragging the grocery bags out of the carts and tossing them every which way into the back of the car. "Forget how to tell time or what? I must've gone around the block a hundred times."

"Watch out for the eggs," I said calmly. "And honestly, Dennis, if you didn't like waiting, why didn't you come in and help me? We'd have been out in half the time."

He slammed the tailgate down hard. "I got a hell of a lot waiting on me at home."

"Of course I don't."

"Okay," he said. "*Okay* . . . but get in and let's get going." He herded me around ahead of him into the car.

Dennis drove a car the way he rode a motorcycle, very skillfully, at maniac speeds. The station wagon roared out through the parking lot, scattering shoppers and checkout boys, peeled out onto Main Street, sailed down the four-lane and onto the narrow county road, gliding along as if it were being pushed by a happy wind, one of those fat puffed faces you see in old maps. My father was sitting up in front beside Dennis, and even from the back I could see he was just dying—he was one of those extra-slow and careful drivers. Anything over twenty-five frightened him to death, not that he'd want to let on to Dennis.

My father put Dennis into the same category as my aunts and my uncle, the demon Rices, the enemy. Even if Dennis couldn't fly a plane, he had his own daredevil credentials to flash at poor Daddy and shrivel him up inside. I guess most fathers have those half-resentful feelings toward the men who climb into their daughters' beds, especially without marrying the daughters. My father was not very "Rice" about those things. Well, and why should he be? But I couldn't remember a single boyfriend of mine that he'd ever liked, except one sweet plump boy in high school. Albert. My father'd still say to me sometimes, years after Albert had been and gone, "Now, Albert, he was nice." My father thought I was a very wicked girl, but in another part of his head I was still a virgin, his own little Martha. That was why he never could talk to me about my *relationships,* except to say, "Now, Albert, he was nice."

When we'd unloaded all the groceries, I made a quick lunch for all of them and then shooed everyone out of the kitchen so I could get down to work. Alice was still sitting there at the table when I dragged out the big enamel stuffing bowl and set it on the counter. "Are you all right?" I asked her. Holidays were always heavy business days, and she'd been working hard.

"Um-hmm," she said, as if she'd only half heard me. She was squeezing and stretching her hands and staring at them in a funny way. She came up for air finally, gazing out at me from those round sad blue eyes. "Your dad around?" Her hair was matted down on top where she'd had her hat on all day. She did look worn out, poor thing.

"He's in the garage."

"Think I'll pop out there a minute. Oh, I forgot," she said. "Tell Dennis the carb heat on the J-3's sticking again. That's from yesterday. And the port window on the Cessna's leaking. I ran into a little rain over Springfield and the Dooleys got their feet wet. That's from today."

At last I had the kitchen to myself. I'd been looking forward to that moment all day. It can be very soothing, when you have a lot on your mind, to lose yourself completely in some nice destructive kitchen tasks, slicing, chopping, shredding, tearing small helpless vegetables. Making stuffing was like that. . . . The thing was, back in the summer when I'd signed the papers with Mr. Smythe, January seemed far, far away. Now it was practically next month and I'd have to make a decision soon, one way or the other; sell the land or try to brazen our way through to better times. I felt very alone, weighed down with thinking about it all, and yet, to be fair, I had nobody to blame but myself, did I? Foolish girl, better to tell everybody everything right from the start and have some company in your misery. I was almost desperate enough to give Andrew another try, no matter what he might think. That was probably only my ego anyway. Every man in the world didn't have to fall at my feet.

No, I couldn't stand it much longer, lying awake every night, haunted by the idea of turning that nice parcel of land with its stream and woods and birds and strawberry patch, the old hangar with its smell of banana oil dope and castor oil, the whole forty precious acres, into row after row of ranch houses all the same. . . . There was a little tap on the outside door, and I turned and saw Buddy peering in at me. "Come on in, it's open."

"I was looking for Denny."

"He's way out back. Why don't you sit down and have a glass of milk first? You can reach in and get it for yourself, my hands are all sticky. In the new fridge. I suppose your mother's busy making her turkey stuffing too?"

"Nope. They're all going down to Warsaw to my aunt's. I have to stay home and feed the stock and stuff."

"Well, you come over here tomorrow if you get lonesome. You'd be welcome to eat with us, you know that. We always have plenty."

"Thanks, but, uh, I don't . . . I mean, uh, . . ." He'd gone all red and stammering, and I couldn't for the life of me figure out what I'd done to embarrass him so. "I'll be g-g-going now . . . uh, thanks for the milk . . ." He was out the door in a flash. Aren't boys that age funny, though?

I diced the celery and crumbled up some more bread, thinking and thinking and thinking . . . suppose I did finally decide to sell and then it turned out I hadn't needed to after all? A big surge in business and money in the bank again. What a waste, because there'd be no going back on what I'd done. We couldn't knock down all the little houses, say, sorry, and throw everybody out in the street and put up our old hangar again. The place would be gone forever, as if it never existed. All that history, all that, well, *life,* vanished without a trace.

I scraped the stuffing off my hands and went down to check on Jessie. I was a little worried about her. She'd been doing fine earlier in the month, but now she was getting into the sullen and weepy stage I dreaded. She was okay, though, curled up in the wing chair with Sylvester, both of them completely mesmerized by *Tom Corbett, Space Cadet.* Neither of them so much as heard me tiptoe in and out.

Back in the kitchen I caught Reggie up on the counter, lowering a languid paw into the bowl of stuffing for a giblet. I swatted at him and he hopped down, unperturbed. I was standing by the new fridge with the big bowl balanced on my hip, trying to figure out where on earth it would fit, when Dennis came in behind me, letting the door slam so the whole wall shook the way he always did. He lay his clean elbow across my shoulder and slid his filthy hand into the fridge for a bottle of beer. He was wearing his worst and favorite shirt, one sleeve ripped to shreds all the way to the shoulder. The twenty-five-pound turkey, not smiling, was squatting in there huge and pink and shiny, taking up every bit of the space.

"Put it in the old icebox then."

"Well, maybe, just for tonight. You're going to move that old thing for me, aren't you?"

"Sure, soon as Teddy gets back. Or Andy and I could do it." Reggie came skulking up to Dennis, arching along his ankles. "Yes, you're a good cat, aren't you, a gooood cat. . . ." He smoothed his grubby hand along Reggie's spine and Reggie stretched up to rub his face against Dennis' knee, glancing back at me with a clear message: Now here's a wise and generous person who knows how to appreciate a splendid animal such as myself. I looked down at Dennis' bent head. "Here," I said. "Open your mouth." I stuffed a piece of giblet in and then relented and gave a piece to Reggie too. "I told Buddy he could eat with us tomorrow if he wants, but he acted so funny about it."

"Guess he doesn't want his folks to know he comes over here so much."

"But they'll be away and they won't know."

"Yeah. That's what bothers him. He hates it, not telling his dad about the lessons and all. He was asking me, just now, what I thought he oughta do."

"Well, and what do you think he oughta do?"

"Tell him, what else, sooner the better. He'll find out sometime, bound to, and then it'll be a hell of a lot worse. I'd be mad if I was Otto, I know that . . . uh, look, when are we going to eat anyhow? I'm starved."

"I don't know. Around seven maybe. Andrew's not even home yet. . . . You can leave me that shirt. . . ." Of course he was halfway up the stairs already, pretending he didn't hear. What he'd said stayed with me, every word like a little needle pricking into my ear, "Tell . . . it'll be worse . . ." But everything was always so clear and simple to Dennis—*yes, no,* and *when do we eat?* That was the way his mind worked. What kind of advice could I expect from him? I'd have to speak to Andrew.

I plugged in the old icebox and it rattled to life, beginning to make the loud officious humming noise that had driven me to buy the expensive new Westinghouse we couldn't afford. I put the bowl of stuffing into it and took some frozen hamburgers out of the new fridge. We'd have to eat something tonight. After dinner I'd start on the fillings for the pies. The five o'clock news came on the radio, very dreary-sounding, now that it was dark at five. I began to wonder where on earth Andrew could be. Usually he was home by now. I kept looking at the clock and listening for his car.

iv

ANDREW

I couldn't get them to concentrate for more than two minutes on "La Belle Dame Sans Merci." The last period before a holiday was always the same. All I had to do was utter the fatal words "palely loitering," and they began snickering and falling about in their seats. When we got to "the squirrel's granary is full" and the even more hilarious "faery's child," the room rocked with hysteria, cackles, titters, ripples of silvery young laughter. A pencil flew into the air. Someone belched. I put down my book and tried not to smile. Apologetic eyes met mine from various convulsed red faces, but they couldn't help themselves. Only twenty minutes to freedom. And I was no better. "Granary is full" suddenly began to strike me funny too. Tough luck, Mr. Keats . . . I sighed stagily and raised my hands. "All right. I give up. You're hopeless. Go home, and enjoy your turkey." Uproar again.

"'Bye, Mr. O. Happy Thanksgiving. . . ." Slam, bang. Gone, all of them.

Once the room was empty I felt guilty and wasteful. Teachers' tic. I was supposed to be the authority figure, after all, a firm hand, not a wad of putty. And I knew how speedily those four days would pass. I'd be right back in this room on Monday, dragging myself through another performance. The idea filled me with sluggish dread.

I walked down the corridor past sober disciplined classrooms where learning was still in progress, and took the back way out, through the old elementary school. It was nearly deserted at this hour, filled with the familiar smell of chalk dust and tempera paint. The walls were covered with lurid fourth-grade daubs: cooked turkeys, walking turkeys, dancing turkeys, turkeys in sports cars, turkeys in fighter planes, Pilgrims eating turkeys, Pilgrims killing turkeys, Indians eating turkeys, Indians killing Pilgrims. I'd sat in these rooms myself once upon a time, and my own crackbrained holiday visions had hung along the same wall. Grades 1A to 6B, Miss McCue to Mrs. Dinwoody.

However, I wasn't recalling those golden kiddy years as I bopped down the empty hallway. I was thinking about college Thanksgivings, old, cold, low-ceilinged houses with uneven prerevolutionary floors, roommates' mothers with grizzled hair and bony Mayflower faces, that odd New England way of showing class, being *really kind* to the barbarian from the heartland who, however wised up to Brooks Brothers and tricked out in Oxford cloth, was still a hayseed fumbling among the silverware. I was thinking about wartime Thanksgivings, slouching into the mess hall, tin trays clattering, plates piled high with gray mystery meat and oceans of floury gravy; swapping horny jokes with doomed hoody boys from Secaucus and Joliet and Galveston. I was thinking about that one Thanksgiving in New York before the war, a sliced turkey sandwich from Gristede's beside my typewriter and a pile of dud manuscripts, my little Philco tuned to the classical station, a precisely three-minute call from my parents full of expensive, loving silence, the sudden vast emptiness of the room after I'd hung up, the long solitary walk through the windswept streets of the West Side. . . .

But how much nicer to dwell on those sweetly sad, only mildly humiliating, holidays of the past and not think about the really painful ones that came later, the grown-up suffering—desire and loss, irrevocable error. And Christ, I didn't want to think about tomorrow, Jessie writing her name in cranberry sauce and walking a drumstick around her plate, Martha with tender hands for Dennis, for Jessie, for her aunts, uncle, cats, for everyone but me . . . God, I was really wallowing in it today. I could hardly stand myself. I needed a few laughs. I needed to get laid. It wasn't as simple as that.

I got in the car and put my head down on the steering wheel. I didn't often feel this bad, about any of it. Merely a spasm, this thing. November always made you feel aimless and fraudulent, like a dot of shit in a huge bored universe. (Okay, what *kind* of shit? My old creative-writing teacher at the New School, always at me, be more specific, give us some details, what kind, what color. . . ?) Well, brown, I guess, Mr. Baggott. . . . No, make it sort of whitish-gray, birdsplat on a windshield . . . or maybe . . . now, cut it out.

I drove down Beverley Avenue past our old house. It looked different, bald and plain. Someone had cut down the azalea bushes in front. I didn't even know who was living there now; I didn't want to think about strangers in those rooms, driving out my parents' lurking shades. I doubled back onto Main again and headed out along the county road. I didn't know where the hell I was going.

I swerved right at the fork so I'd pass the old racetrack. A real masochist's delight. But when I got there it was only as ugly as I would have expected, no more, no less. Once there'd been a cozy turreted grandstand, a graceful sweep of grass and turf and white railings, decorous wooden refreshment stands, restrooms, stable rows. I'd been brought there by my parents once to see a two-bit circus, still remembered the solemn baby elephant, the yawning lion on his box, the lady in spangles flying above me like an angel. I'd been there plenty of other times, too, for county fairs and horse shows and even, yes, motorcycle races. Now it was a featureless sea of concrete with a few sinister upcroppings of cement, gray dolmens someday to come to life as squalid shoe stores, record emporia and Woolworths. Even the construction machines looked alien, hulking creatures waiting to be animated for some grade-Z horror movie. The late sun cast long strange shadows, a phantom car racing along beside me, in front of me, then disappearing under the wheels as I swung around the deserted place in slow looping circles, rat in a maze, lonely colonist on a new planet. The sun flashed down behind a cloud, and I let the car slide out onto the road again.

Radio for company: moany lugubrious voices of the Four Aces ". . . just . . ." I punched a button. ". . . ident-elect Eisenhower said today . . ." Eisenhower, Christ. ". . . go an' tell yer ma, Shredded Ralston can't be beat . . ." I turned the damn thing off. Looming up ahead in the twilight was the poison green neon of the new drive-in. The Chick-Inn. Strutting fowl in an apron hoisting a platter of its cooked brethren. What the hell.

"How to Use Magic Voicebox: Consult Menu, Make Selection, Lift Microphone into Vehicle, Press Red Button and Hold Down to Speak." I lugged the thing into the car and hunched over it, feeling like a secret agent or somebody about to make an obscene broadcast. Faint squawking, a disembodied voice, "What'll it be, mister?" How did he know I was *mister,* not *toots* or *ma'am*? Because he could see me, of course. I spied a bored-looking man in a white toque sitting with his feet up inside the hut beneath the neon chicken. Anonymity was an illusion. I cleared my throat. "Chocolate milkshake, please."

"You mean a chocolate THICK-O?"

"Er, what?"

"You want a THICK-O, right?" It sounded like some kind of silly, dirty, kids' code word. Like to put your THICK-O into that? Yuk, yuk!

I nodded, then remembered to push the button and speak. "Yes." I wondered if the THICK-O would flood through the microphone into my lap or if a long mechanical arm would extend from inside the hut. I was the only customer apparently. It was a holiday eve.

A face loomed at the window, long blond hair, little red pillbox like a bellhop's. The skin was bad, but the eyes were good, brown and friendly. "Here y'are, sir. Why, gosh, hi, Mr. O. . . . Don't ya remember me?" She was busy attaching a pronged metal tray to the door frame. "I'm Sally, Sally Price. Only now it's Sally Weddle. That's my hubby in there. We just opened the place."

"Why, Sally. Of course." One of the depressing things about being a teacher, thousands of ex-students at large in the world, aging and waiting for a chance to spring at you and make you feel like Methuselah.

"How're you doing, Mr. O? Still teaching the kids?"

"Yes, indeed."

"Well, gotta go. He don't want me talking to the customers too much. Hope you like the shake. I'll be back for the tray."

I watched her walk away, pert little ass under the tight red trousers, and tried to figure out how old she would be. About twenty-six? Sweet Sally, twirler, pep squad, prom-queen court, *twenty-six,* impossible. Actually, she looked a little older than that, poor kid. And the husband looked like a mean bastard. I remembered Sally's class, one of those magic classes that would let you get away with anything, fall off your chair, break the chalk, swear, crack up with giggles, tell horrible jokes, make impassioned speeches. They listened raptly, loved you anyway, let you do no wrong. Well, hell, I was a good teacher way back when. They'd bought Jess and me an engagement present, a silver-plated vegetable dish. Where was it now? Martha would know. Her again.

The THICK-O looked like some treacherous bog, gray and pocked with coarse bubbles. I plunged the straw in and sucked, a blockage somewhere. When I tried to drink it sans straw the whole mass sort of lurched at me, and I lost my nerve. I had to eat it with the plastic spoon. It didn't taste like food exactly, but still, not bad. The meal of the future. I finished it off without any trouble.

I'd started up the car before I remembered the tray. Sally had to come out again in her sexy bellhop uniform. She laughed at me, but kindly, softly. I did remember her nice laugh. "Here, I'll show ya." Still smiling, looking a little hard and tired under the fluorescent lights, she watched me back out. Sweet Sally. I was going to wave but saw the husband's beady simian eye upon me and thought better of it.

I sped quickly past the other new horrors on the highway—motel, car lot, motel, another drive-in called Burger Kid, motel. There were never any tourists around here, so three guesses what the motels were for. I hoped I'd never sink so low.

I went around to the back door with my eyes downcast so I wouldn't even be tempted to search for her face framed in the kitchen window. I hung up my coat on the porch, opened the back door and closed it behind me with a stealthy click. Martha came toward me, wringing her hands on her apron, a strange, half-guilty look on her face. "Oh, Andrew . . . I have to talk to you."

"Okay . . . great, sure."

"But not now," she said, glancing around meaningfully. "We'll find a time."

I could feel the sweat breaking out under my arms. Did she mean it?

V

JESSIE

A broken heart his father died of, everybody says, his parents were that close. Bullshit. You can't die of a broken heart. That's like that stupid stuff we used to read in his class, those old dumb poems, men running after women who scorned them and then the women dying or the other way around, wasting away, fainting or swooning or floating off down a river with your dress trailing behind you, as if it was that damn easy . . . that's the kind of disease she had, though. And everybody said doesn't she look beautiful and wouldn't you know Anna would manage to look beautiful on her deathbed? I heard Julia say that and Alice got real mad and said Oh hush up for once she's dying isn't she? . . . Well, beautiful is as beautiful does and I knew better.

So I walked into her room that day . . . Thanksgiving, fucking turkey smelling up everything . . . and there I was all dolled up like some goddamn Girl Scout and grinning and saluting . . . and she didn't even bother to look, turned her head away with a scowl on it like a little kid's. Two fucking years I'd been away and she'd forgotten all about me, forgot everything, how hard I'd tried to do what she wanted me to do, how good I'd been, her good daughter . . . why the hell had I bothered . . . everything turning to ashes in my mouth, all of it stupid and pointless, my whole fucking life . . . and look at stupid Martha, always went against her and hated her and look how happy she is now, blossoming out like one of those creepy southern plants, the kind with the big ugly flowers and no smell. No, that's not fair, no it isn't. Martha worked harder than she ever did to keep things nice for me . . . She said in that new voice, the one she could use with her now that she was grown up and safe and she was sick in her bed and dying, she said. . . she said, Doesn't Jessie look pretty in her uniform? *Nothing. And then out in the hall she said,* Today's a bad day, don't worry, you wait till tomorrow and it'll be better. *But it wasn't better, it wasn't ever better. She didn't give a shit about me anymore. Okay, she was dying, I knew that. She didn't give a shit about anything. I made allowances like they all told me, but I was scared like I'd never been. I didn't even know what the fuck I was scared of. See, it wasn't like I could say, Well, I'll climb into that airplane and fly the wings off the bastard and I know I can do it because I'm so goddamn good I've got flying in my goddamn blood and all that other birdshit I used to rev myself up on. No, it was this weird shapeless sort of fear, a big dead empty feeling like a fog all around me everywhere, no matter what I did I felt empty and dead and worthless and foolish, like I'd wasted my whole life. And then I'd say to myself, Why, that's silly. Christ you're only twenty-fucking-three years old, your life's not over. But it felt like it was, over and done with, dead and gone.*

Then one day I ran into Andrew in the street and he looked so good in his uniform, sexy and sad at the same time, both his parents gone one right after the other. I remembered how it had been, him and me, all those years ago. Not the first man he wasn't but the first to be nice to me like a man not a boy, nice with his body, not just all clumsy talk to fool you. He never minded being soft with a girl, or funny, or acting the way most stupid men are scared to act with girls or with anybody else, and that's what I remembered about him and that's what I thought I needed then, someone to be easy and soft with me and keep me safe. Safe. *Doesn't it make me want to laugh now, doesn't it make me want to laugh myself sick.*

vi

JULIA

Teddy and I arrived home from Chicago at about 11:30 Thanksgiving morning. As we passed over the house on final, I could see the soggy piles of leaves and long shiny strips of mud in the road from last week's rain. Nothing had changed. It was a mild but dismal November day. Teddy peered over at me once before unlatching the door, his face squinched guiltily still. "Listen, Jule, I'm really sorry I screwed up. But you know, back in October you guys seemed to be real glad to see each other. I thought it might be nice for you, like the old days."

Julia gallivanting. Weekend in Denver. Morning in St. Louis. Madcap night in Chicago. Yes, that part was quite like the old days. As for the Duffy part, I couldn't tell yet. Pleased enough I'd been to see that preposterous rhinoceros head swinging around toward us from a dark corner of the bar (an honest-to-goodness bar, not a roadhouse or some ratty beer hall). The old set of minor excitements later on, hotel-smelling sheets and street noises outside, big man's watch on the bedstand. And the rest. Remarkably good we were still, especially creaky old me, emerging from retirement. I did hate to be made a fool of, however, and had been a mite hard on poor Teddy for . . . springing Duffy on me like that. Mr. Fixit. I decided it was time to relent. "No, dear, you didn't screw up. Surprises are awkward sometimes, even good surprises."

His face cleared instantly. Teddy was about as complicated as a snail. "Well, listen, then, how do you think they're going to take to the idea of me heading out for a while, to the coast, I mean?" He attached the Cessna to its tether, and we set off along the road to the house. "I'm a little nervous what old Alice is going to say."

"For God's sake, don't bring it up today," I said with alarm. "You know how everybody gets this time of year. Wait a day or so. Wait a week."

"I promise you I'd be back by April. There's never any business in January or February, and I get so damn depressed around here in the winter. I never got depressed when I lived in L.A. The sun out all the time makes a difference."

If you're an orange, who said that? Poor Teddy. "But darling, you were depressed around here all last summer, and, I hate to say this, you were younger when you lived there last time. We all were."

"You don't want me to go."

"I was only trying to be realistic. I don't care, dear. If that's what you want to do, then do it, by all means."

"You could come with me. Duff'd like that."

"Oh God . . ." Teddy had been with positively hundreds of women over the years, but he still possessed absolutely no idea of the way the whole business worked between grown-ups, the havoc that could be wreaked. None of it ever got under his skin. But I was the soul of patience today. I said, "He might like it and then again he might not. And I'm not at all sure I'm up to it. One night is lovely . . . besides, he always has plenty of women stashed away. I'm sure that's crossed your mind, in fact." I gave his cheek a little pinch.

He looked hurt, blinking reproachfully at me, blue eyes with such long lashes. A pretty man, still, our Teddy. The change of scene might do him good, new women to chase and flatter him, He said, "No, I meant what I said, sweetie. I was thinking about you, you and him. You always used to have so much fun, remember?"

We crossed the squashy wintry grass of the yard, and I took his arm to steady myself in my tall city shoes. "Teddy, please. I can't discuss it now. You make your own decision but leave me out of it." I was comfortable in my peaceful rut, didn't want to be tempted away, did I? Remember Switzerland, Julia, the cuckoo clock, etcetera. Overrated, peace could be.

Teddy sighed, crestfallen, baby brother who still half adored, half resented being pushed around by his big sister. The aroma of roasting turkey floated around the corner of the house toward us. Sylvester was sitting on the back steps, very straight and alert, eyeing us anxiously. He even meowed once. Usually he was mute as a giraffe. I peered into the kitchen while I struggled out of my jacket and heavy sweater. Teddy was laboriously scraping mud off his shoes.

* * *

They were all in there, unnaturally still, silent and remote as an old snapshot, framed by the high square porch window: Jessie in that purple sweater that made her eyes look dark and flat as enamel; Alice peering up at Vern through her sheepdog hair; Dennis slouched back against the counter, one long leg bent storkwise, a bottle of beer dangling from one hand; Vern with his high-domed light-bulb head ducked down, laughing at something in that dreadful wheezy way he had, as if it hurt him; Andrew rising like a figurehead from behind the table, wide shoulders and soft fair hair and dreaming canny eyes. . . . Martha swung around with a dripping spoon in her hand. "Oh, no . . ."

Teddy opened the door and Sylvester streaked in. "Oh, no . . . don't let him in! That turkey is driving them wild. I already had that bad Reggie . . ." She gave me a hug. "Sorry, Auntie. What a way to say hello. . . . Happy Thanksgiving . . . Uncle Teddy . . . mmm!" She hugged him and pushed us both over to the table. "This bird's not going to be ready for hours. Have a drink."

Everybody was suddenly startled into motion, like a film unstuck in its sprockets. Dennis handed a bottle of beer across to Teddy. Vern slid his chair around so I could sit down. Andrew squeezed my elbow. "How was Chicago? You look wonderful."

"Oh, let me get my breath. . . ."

"Want a snack, anybody?"

"Nothing for me," Teddy said, winking at me ponderously. "But I bet your auntie has some kind of an appetite today." I gave him a swift kick under the table. Martha mouthed something across at Dennis.

"Oh, yeah. You gonna give me a hand, Ted? Martha wants us to move that thing out to the garage."

"The *garage*?" Alice said. "An icebox in the *garage*?"

"Right-o, sweetie, if that's what you want."

Vern started to get up too. Dennis pressed him back down. "Not you. This'll kill your back."

"I'll give you a hand," Andrew said, to my great surprise, sliding out of his chair. Usually he liked to be a bit more sly and offhand with Dennis, who either didn't notice or didn't care. *(Guy with a crazy wife, better cut him some slack,* or some such, that superstitious masculine forbearance.) I regarded the two young men, glanced over at

Martha, and a little spider-web of curiosity brushed at my mind. Andrew was lazy about his body most of the time, but he could appear extraordinarily robust and powerful when he made the effort. And here he was, taking off that ubiquitous jacket, throwing his shoulders back, sucking in his gut, making steely Dennis look rather insubstantial, frail almost, beside him. Hmm. I wondered what penny had dropped while I'd been away. Was Martha up to her old tricks? I did hope not. I was fond of them both, them all.

"Here's your wine, Aunt Julia." Oh, dear, what would it be this time? Martha was . . . unreliable about wine.

I sipped at my Gallo sauterne and watched the three men have at the old icebox, sweating and swearing and enjoying themselves immensely. They pried the thing out of its corner, now were stymied by the jutting edge of its monstrous hinged door.

Teddy stood up, red-faced. "Take the damn door off?"

"Won't help," Dennis said. "Frigging counter sticks out too far."

Teddy met Dennis' eye. "We could, uh . . . looks kinda nice where it is, don't ya think?" He cocked one eyebrow at Martha.

"Wha' . . . oh, yeah." Dennis grinned and nudged Andrew. "Hey, Andy . . . uh, leave go a minute. . . ."

Andrew stared, his fair face glowing with effort. Then he caught on, straightening up ostentatiously. "Right," he said. "Looks great here. Can't get at those cupboards, but who uses them anyhow? Just old *Martha*."

Teddy sat down with a lot of clatter. "Wheew! Glad that job's finished." They were all trying hard to catch Martha's eye. Otherwise the joke would fall flat. It was a pretty silly joke anyway. The icebox loomed in its new spot, a ludicrous old-fashioned pile of white enamel, squat-legged bottom and cylindrical grilled top.

"What's the matter with you boys, anyway?" Alice said. Teddy made a ferocious grimace at her. She shook her head, half smiling. "Act like you're all about ten."

Martha opened the oven door and bent tenderly over the turkey, gently ministering to it, oblivious of all the eyes upon her. At length she stood up, wiped her hands on her apron, frowned to herself, consulted her watch, puffed out her cheeks, pushed back a strand of hair, flicked a casual glance across the room and did a splendid double take. "What on earth . . . ?"

"Looks pretty good there, huh?" Dennis said.

"Oh honestly . . ." She spied them all watching her and smiled. "Well, thank you. Now I won't have to clean out those damn cupboards ever ever again."

"She's too damn cooperative," Andrew said.

"No fun at all."

Vern spoke up. "Maybe you should cool her off a little."

"*Dad*-dy! Now wait . . . Dennis, don't you dare . . ."

"You got the idea, Vern." He seized her around the waist, hooked his foot behind her ankles, began lugging her toward the icebox. "Stack her right in there. Get her out of our way."

Teddy was already removing the metal shelves, one by one, sadly but ceremoniously, like an executioner. Martha was struggling against Dennis, gasping and laughing. "Come on, let me go, this is . . . oh!" She tried to slap their hands away. "You won't get any turkey. . . . No, I *mean* it. . . . Come on, Andrew, leave me alone. . . . Oh, my own uncle . . . Dennis . . ." She wriggled like a fish, shrieking softly, as they swung her, feet first, toward the empty white box. Out of the corner of my eye I saw Jessie sitting very still in her chair, tears welling up and sliding down her cheeks in two long streams.

"Andrew . . ." I whispered. He turned. Jessie reached out, clamped her arms tightly around his waist, hid her face in his chest. She so rarely touched him, showed any affection or need.

". . . Oh, Jessie now . . . we were just being silly, that's all . . . don't feel bad . . ." He settled his chin down against her hair and smiled across the top of her head at me.

Martha was straightening her clothes, her face averted. The turkey crackled urgently in the oven behind us. "I'd better . . ." She began gently to disengage Jessie. ". . . she's upset, you know . . ." Andrew nodded and released her, turning quickly away, his face gone blank.

"Poor little thing," Teddy said. We could hear them slowly climbing the back stairs, two sets of footsteps, Martha murmuring to Jessie.

"All that wrestling around and acting crazy . . ." Alice said. "I could've told you somebody'd end up in tears."

"Alice, you sounded *exactly* like Mother just then." I stood up. "I believe I'll take a nap too. I'm absolutely exhausted." I shot Teddy a warning glance: no more jokes.

vii

JESSIE

I like it up here in the dark, smelling the nice turkey cooking downstairs, resting and sleeping. Martha pulled down the shades but she left the little light on down by the floor, the little nightlight I always have. I like it dark but not too dark. I'm trying hard right now, trying to think about only nice things, nice turkey, nice dinner, nice cat, nice Jessie, nice Martha, nice . . . not bad things that happened a long time ago past thinking or caring about because what can you do about them now, you have to let them go, let them go, even if . . . they won't let go pull you down think they're gone can't hurt you anymore pop up like bodies from the bottom of the lake gonna get you . . . No, it's okay now, it's okay.

Oh, I've seen him look at my sister that way before, yes I've seen, more than he thinks, but oh God, let him not do that, please . . . but it was nothing. See, just horsing around . . . nothing . . . tears sliding down my face all of a sudden where'd they come from . . . nothing, see . . . but I have to stop him, hold on to him tight . . . I don't want to be crazy do you think I like it, I want to say . . . please don't do that to me please don't . . . I can see by his face and feel in his hands how sorry he is and I know I should forgive him but I can't I can't I can't.

Sylvester curls up next to me warm and purring, my friend. I stroke his fur and feel his little body heart beating under the fur so fragile if I just rolled on him he would die but he loves me keeps me company purring and purring puts me to sleep sinking down floating a light from the hall where am I going I don't like this dream door opens slowly slowly someone's looking in someone's quietly watching it's me I push the door and it slides away open white room white bed white walls but its dark curtains drawn in the afternoon make it dark is she sleeping I shouldn't be here but she's dying they don't give a shit when you come surprise just passing by thought I'd drop in why even bother you never give up your own mother open the door let your eyes get used to the dark now I can see I see two people in her bed her arms are around him and his face is turned up to hers and he is holding her I can hear them murmuring see their bodies moving rising up under the hospital sheets surprise is right close the door quietly and stand in the hall can't even breathe was it him? It was him walk away like a zombie full of novocaine now she has it all dumb Jessie backed away so meek and scared should've killed them as if she wasn't going to die anyway as if how could he no her her I know how she is gets what she wants always always bitch throws it away when she gets it she'll make him pay I don't have to doesn't work saying that next time he comes near me tries it I shriek at him and fight him off and people come and take him away and leave me alone in this room, my room . . .

I'm awake and sitting up all of a sudden . . . it's too dark in here. I'm all sweaty. Sylvester jumps off the bed, runs to the door. He wants to get out. Don't leave me. Don't be scared. Just a bad dream I had. It was a dream. I scare Sylvester when I'm crazy. He stays by the door watching me.

vii

JULIA

I took off the good suit I'd worn in Chicago and lay back on the bed in my slip. I set the alarm to ring in two hours. I went to sleep quickly and dreamed of Duffy as a young man with all his hair, pursuing me down a pastel Mexican street. He was wearing a serape. When I woke to the alarm I had that horrid stuffed feeling you get only from a nap in the middle of the day. I put on my suit skirt and blouse again and went downstairs.

Martha was alone in the kitchen, her back to me, peeling potatoes over the sink. The old icebox had disappeared. I sat down at the table. "How's Jessie?"

"She's okay. She's sleeping. I don't know what it was."

"Thinking about your mother, perhaps. It was just this time of year."

"Yes, I *know,*" she said, quite harshly, for her. She hated to speak of Anna, even now. Perversely I found myself thinking almost affectionately of Anna at the moment, still missing her in a curious fashion, the way you miss a complicated relentless noise that finally stops. But then I could afford to be tolerant and half fond. Anna wasn't my mother, thank God. Only my baby sister, a creature I'd diapered, fed, tormented. I said, "I've never seen Jessie cry like that, since she's been ill." And, I reflected, I'd never seen Martha cry at all, not since she was an infant in the crib. She used to try to stare her mother down, a tiny little thing, eyes so scornful, lip held tight between her baby teeth, but never would cry. I wondered how much it had cost her to keep so much in. Not a damn thing, you'd be certain, looking at her now. Martha seemed immeasurably sane.

"It happens sometimes," she said, slapping the knife down twice across a potato in her hand, dumping the pieces into a bowl of water beside her. "It just does. Then she sleeps and she's okay again."

December 5

i

ALICE

Over her shoulder Julia said, "You aren't minding too much, are you? Teddy's still worried you are."

I kept on mopping the dishes and stacking them in the drainer. "Look, I told him over and over. I wouldn't go out there again if you paid me. I like it here. Why don't you spit out whatever it is that's really on your mind?"

But you couldn't rush old Julia like that. She didn't like to give you the satisfaction of maybe being right for a change. "Lovely tea," she said, sipping real slow and casual. She always drank some special foreign kind of tea; Lipton's wasn't good enough, had to be Lapsong Hoochy Koochy or some such, smelled like that tarry gunk that came up off the road in the summer, and I told her so.

"Oh, Alice . . ." she said with her little chuckle that made me want to throw the dish mop at her. "By the way, where was Dennis going in such a rush? He practically knocked me down the stairs."

"Martha went off to the library without her books. He wanted to save her a trip. Andrew'd already left for his meeting."

"I hope . . . well, never mind." She settled her robe around her and added a big spoonful of honey to the tea. "Tell me, Alice, do you think I'm *mad* to be doing this? You remember what we used to be like, John and I." So that was it. Getting cold feet, was she?

"Wouldn't make any difference if I did, would it? Think you were '*mad*.'" I made my voice go all stuck-up like hers. "But I don't. You can always come back and moan and groan about how awful it was.

Besides, I always thought it was real romantic, a 'stormy relationship,' like they say. . . ." I was kind of embarrassed I'd let that part slip.

"It wasn't romantic at all," she said, very quick and sharp. "It was ugly, our kind of fighting. But you're right, dear, I probably wouldn't be able to stand myself if I didn't at least *try.*" Was that really what I'd said? Close enough, I suppose. "And we're both older now. Calmer and wiser. But, oh my, all my clothes are so . . . Ohio-looking. I'll have to buy new ones out there. That'll be fun." She put her cup down on the drainboard I'd just wiped clean. "I'm going to do a little more packing and then go to bed early. So do please try to keep everybody quiet down here, won't you?"

"Yes, Your Majesty," I said after her, but she didn't let on she'd heard. I went off to the den to get Jessie, who was busy watching the end of Milton Berle. I put my hand on her head and ruffled her hair a little. "Up to bed right after this." She scrunched down in the chair, shaking her head in a kind of smarty way. She'd been having all good days for almost a week. Wouldn't last, though, we all knew that. "There's nothing you like on later, anyhow, is there?" She slumped away from my hand again. When I left she was already laughing again, watching Uncle Miltie go "MAY-kup" and hit somebody with a big powder puff.

I went upstairs and took a quick shower and put on my robe, got my bottle and my new book and headed back down to the den as soon as I heard Jessie come up. I'd decided to treat myself to a small private toot tonight, but I wasn't about to sit all alone in my room to drink. That would've been too depressing by half. I'd known all along my luck couldn't hold, but now that the pains had started in my other hand, I was scared. I hadn't told anybody yet. I needed to hang on to what I knew for a little while longer till I could get used to it myself.

ii

ANDREW

I left the PTA meeting at about 8:25, hoping Purvis or anybody else who happened to see me would think I'd gone to the men's room.

Instead I went down to the basement, past the deserted cafeteria, which emanated its usual smell of sour milk and chicken croquettes, and out the double doors into the parking lot.

A thin sheet of new ice covered everything, and the sleety wind was whipping my hair around and freezing the tops of my ears. I saw a car, a station wagon, move slowly down the street and turn through the gate into the parking lot. She pulled into a space, blinked her lights once and switched them off. I walked quickly across the lot toward her, skidding along the ice in my thin-soled loafers. I should have worn my galoshes. I looked like a fool.

"Hi. Here I am." She had on a thick plaid wool scarf with a fringe and looked like something out of a wartime fantasy, the brave sexy peasant girl who'd lay down her life for you. She said, "Let's go wherever we're going in your car. I don't want to put too many miles on this one. I told Dennis I was going to the library, but my books aren't really due for another week."

Hmm. If she'd gone so far as to lie to him . . . she might just mean business. But you never could be sure about them, could you? Women. Freud had never solved that riddle, and neither had I. I had no plan if the best I could hope for occurred. We couldn't very well go and park by the Civil War Monument. All my kids would be there, motors racing, heaters roaring behind the fogged-up windows. A motel was out. Too sordid. Too public. (It was hell in a small town in the winter.)

No, we'd have to have a drink somewhere and, uh, talk, first. Then, I suppose, there was always the car, parked in some more discreet, more adult spot, however. Perhaps she'd even find that amusing, after months of proper horizontal screwing with Dennis. I couldn't afford to be particular. For me, it'd be okay anyway, anywhere, in the backseat of a car, in the front seat, in the trunk; in a snowbank like Eskimos; across a desk in my room at school; in the back row of the Rialto; under the counter in her father's store; in the meat locker at Kroger's; on top of the altar in the First Presbyterian Church; in the show window at Krantz Studebaker. . . . I caught her looking at me oddly, and smiled into the dark. I knew beyond the shadow of a doubt, my bedroom being where it was, that Martha had probably never been horny enough to understand.

* * *

We walked carefully across the ice to my car. I took her elbow once, chastely, and she leaned warmly into it and smiled up into my face. "Whew!" she said. "So cold tonight." A cloud of white frosty breath whooshed out as she spoke. Her cheeks were bright pink.

"Here we are." I sounded stodgy and formal, as if I were showing the Queen of England around our humble little American town. Shit. A sweet vision darted through my mind, Martha lolling back across the hood, frozen odalisque, skirt hiked up past naked thighs, my gloved hands sliding up, everything warm under there, warm inside her. Oh, Jesus. Watch it, Buster, or you'll never get to first base with her. Why did we say that? First base. A sportswriter's metaphor. I took the key out of my pocket, hands clumsy with the cold. She was standing by the rear bumper, hands thrust into her sleeves, jogging up and down to keep warm. Just as I managed to wedge the key into the frozen lock I saw her suddenly stand still, head thrown up like a frightened pony's. Then I heard it too. The doomsday roar of Dennis' souped-up engine. Hot damn.

I slid out between the cars, shivering inside my coat, and not just from the cold. I hadn't meant to get her in trouble. I hadn't meant to get me in trouble. We were just going to talk, for Christ's sake. *Look, mister, it was her idea. . . . We're all civilized adults, aren't we, heh heh. Ulp, Feet, do yo' stuff. . . .* He jumped out of the car and took a few awkward sliding steps across the ice toward us. For a minute I almost felt sorry for him. He looked like some poor tenth-century fellow who'd seen a portent, rain of toads or flying cat, something that couldn't be. Then that brutish gape of pain vanished, and his face went flat and tight with anger. I could see at once what was going to happen. Martha moved urgently beside me, her hand flying out to him. "Dennis, don't . . ."

But he did. He took one more slithering step, and then his fist shot up into my face. I felt my nose go mushy, blood running back into my throat and down my lip and chin. I fell, comically, legs windmilling before I went down, splat, right on my ass. My hand went automatically to my face, to my nose; a favorite feature, that nose. It was wet and sticky. Dennis unclenched his fist and stared at it almost in surprise as he picked his way carefully back to his car.

"You *followed* me," Martha said, her voice small and shaky but defiant all the same.

"You forgot something. Here. Take your fucking books." He hauled them out of the car and tossed them down at her feet. They lay tumbled together, four of them in those shiny plastic library covers, pages riffling in the wind.

"It isn't what you think."

". . . care what I goddamn think . . ." His voice was carried away by a sudden heavy gust. He climbed into his car and slammed the door. The wheels spun violently, and the car shuddered back on its haunches like some enraged beast, shot around and away.

I managed to get up onto my knees. Blobs of my blood were plopping on the ice in front of me, dark and lurid and thick. Very satisfying, in a weird way. There was blood down the front of my coat, too. But I felt okay, not dizzy or sick. It didn't even hurt that much yet. Martha knelt down beside me. She pulled out her mittens and started to wipe off my face. "Poor Andrew." She tilted my chin up, examining my face. "I think you'll be all right. He really didn't hit you very hard. Not as hard as he could have. Dennis is so strong."

I considered grabbing her and shaking her till her teeth rattled, but no matter how sorely provoked, I wasn't the type. Violence did not flow naturally and picturesquely from me the way it did from Dennis. I felt like laughing instead, but that probably would hurt. "Martha," I pointed out. "I'm bleeding like a pig. He hit me hard enough."

I gave the old schnozz an experimental touch. Whether by accident, because he couldn't get enough leverage on the ice to really bash me, or by kindly design, he hadn't actually broken it. Still, I'd probably have a black eye tomorrow. Whew! Only a black eye! I could feel it insidiously swelling and coloring up already.

"What do you want to do now?" My lips were stiff and numb, like after the dentist. I didn't have any idea what I wanted to do now. Yes, I did. I wanted to go home and climb into bed, alone, lie there quietly rereading *Middlemarch* or *Barchester Towers* or *Kiss Me, Deadly.* All desire had fled, absolutely.

"Come on," she said, slipping her hand under my arm. "People will be coming out soon."

The key was still in the car door where I'd left it. I turned on the motor so we'd have some heat, and we sat there listening to it for a few minutes, not looking at each other. "It'll be all right," she said suddenly, breathlessly. "I know it will. He has such a quick temper. We ought to give him a little time to cool off." She leaned over, touched my chin with the tips of her fingers again, smiling kindly into my eyes. "He shouldn't have hit you, though. Your poor eye."

"I know. Let's go someplace dark where nobody can see it." We both started to laugh giddily.

iii

ALICE

I poured myself out a half tumbler of whiskey and opened my book. I let the television stay on in case I had trouble getting into the book. The show on was Philco Playhouse, and I couldn't decide from the first ten minutes whether it was going to be good or not. First pages of the book were just okay. A biblical story by Thomas B. Costain. Roman soldiers on the jacket. Everybody was supposed to be reading it and Martha had to wait for two months to get it from the library, which probably meant the rest of the world had finished with it months and months ago.

I was trying to be practical now, toying with a lot of sensible plans about what I could do with myself when I stopped flying since that was what I was going to have to do. Clerking in a store? Not the worst idea in the world. No problem for me to deal with any mean and cranky customers after all the time I'd spent closed up in airplane cockpits with every kind of mean and cranky individual going. And in a store you could throw them out if they pushed you too far which you couldn't in an airplane, though I'd been tempted a few times. I looked down at Thomas B. Costain's photo on the back of the book and thought, how about if I wrote a book myself, for a few laughs. Told all about the old days . . . and who did I think was going to read this book of mine? Maybe eleven or twelve people in the world who weren't called Rice. I filled up my glass again.

I was sitting there, quietly thinking and drinking, one eye on the tube, one on my book, when all of a sudden the front door banged open. I cringed a little for Julia and Jessie upstairs trying to sleep. Then there were some loud fast footsteps and Dennis burst into the room. I said, kind of offhand, "Well, did you catch Martha . . ." He just stared at me, and I could tell something must be awfully wrong, his face looked so white and grim.

"Catch her? You bet I did. . . ." He hooked one foot around the little embroidered hassock and shoved the poor thing halfway across the room. "Catch her is right . . ." He was muttering a lot of stuff I couldn't understand. ". . . the two of them . . . fucking books . . . in his car . . ." He finally threw himself down on the sofa beside me, breathing hard, anger rising up off him like heat.

"Hold on now, hold on." I went to the cupboard for another glass and poured him a hefty shot. "You look like you need this."

"Damn right."

"Now tell me what happened, right from the beginning, so we can try and straighten it all out," I said, in a real soothing kind of voice. Looked to me like he'd gone off the deep end.

"Said she was headed for the library, Martha did . . . you know that part . . ." He knocked back about half the shot and took a deep breath. ". . . uh, went upstairs, found her damn books, figured, you know, nice guy, make that stupid guy, go after her, save her a trip . . ." He shook his head, ran his hand through his hair. "So . . . so I take off like a bat outta hell, but she doesn't stop at the library, no, pulls into the goddamn school lot instead, blinks her lights and there's fucking Andy waiting for her, like it was all planned. . . ."

"Andrew? I don't believe it. Then what?"

"Then, uh, guess I hit him."

"Now that was sensible." My first loyalty was to my niece here. But I loved Dennis too. Oh, far as I knew Martha never did actually cheat on anybody—underneath it all she was straight as an arrow—but she certainly did enjoy provoking the boys she liked. "Very sensible, hitting him when you're mad at her."

"Look, Christ, you don't have to tell me." He put one hand up to his face. "Thought I grew out of all that stuff by now. Shit."

"Did you hurt him bad?"

"Don't think so. I mean, his nose was bleeding like hell, but it wasn't . . . uh, when it's broke it feels horrible and kills your hand. . . ." He lay his head back against the top of the sofa. "I was so goddamn *surprised* . . . still can't believe it. Leaves the goddamn books laying there plain as day, wants me to see, wants me to make a goddamn fool of myself. . . . Did, too. Real good job. Bet they're laughing themselves silly over it now if they're not . . ."

"That's crazy talk, Dennis." I took the glass out of his hand and filled it again, along with my own. No sound of a car on the drive yet. Now if I'd been Martha, I'd have burned up the road coming back here to put things right, but then I'd never been all that smart about men. Sometimes they liked these arrogant careless girls the best.

He glared over at me like he'd been reading my mind. "She won't be coming back here any too quick, you can bank on that. Always got to show me she doesn't care. 'It's not what you think. . . .' Goddamn better not be. . . . But, shit, Alice, I shouldn't've laid all this on you."

"Now, look. I was planning on getting drunk all by myself tonight. I'd be happy to have some company." I figured if he was sitting there getting quietly snockered with me, he wouldn't be out looking for trouble somewhere else. "Say, you didn't actually kill him or anything, did you? I mean, I'm not going to have to hide you when the sheriff comes, am I, 'cause . . ." I thought I'd try to lighten things up a little.

He gave me a gloomy sort of a smile and handed me his glass. "Why the fuck not? But, listen, how come *you* want to get drunk tonight? You got as good a reason as me?"

"I'll tell you, old son. . . ." Figured maybe hearing about my troubles might distract him a little from his own.

"Shit, Alice . . . don't know what I can say . . . sure is a bitch . . . give up something means so much to you . . ."

"Way it goes sometimes, you know."

"Forty-three goddamn years, still can't believe that . . . must've been a little kid when you started . . . I'm serious. Give me that glass now. . . ." We'd been going at it pretty good, the two of us, and his voice was getting a little furry-sounding. He had a hard head, Dennis did, but there weren't too many guys I couldn't leave way behind when it came to putting away the booze. Still no sign of Martha. While I'd been going through my whole song and dance for him I remembered all of a sudden that time way last summer when I saw Andrew and Martha together in town, when she was supposed to be at the dentist. But I filed it back away fast. I couldn't believe Martha'd do a thing like that to her sister, or to Dennis either. Couldn't really feature Andrew and Martha together, come to that.

". . . have to be thinking about quitting myself, soon . . ." Dennis mumbled. "Hell, I'll be thirty next spring."

". . . not so old."

". . . I seen some guys keep at it till they're forty maybe, but Christ, rack yourself up at that age, you don't heal so good, maybe lose your timing, have to fake it, sad to watch those guys. . . . Figure I'll give it a couple more years, quit while I'm ahead. . . ." He added, with a little hard laugh, "I bet all those forty-year-old guys said the same thing once. 'Cause you miss it like a sonofabitch."

"My brother Cliff loved nearly getting killed all the time too. And then he got killed." I didn't have any idea why I'd said that. One of those fool remarks you make, sitting and drinking with somebody, doesn't sound too insulting till it's out of your mouth and floating off like a bomb with a lit fuse.

He gave a snort. "Oh, no, I'm not one of *those* guys, no offense. I'm real simple-minded. Like to win races, like to beat the shit out of everybody, that's all. You'll never see me take a real crazy chance."

"That's a lot of baloney, Dennis. I've seen you pull some stunts."

"Well, yeah, maybe. Sometimes looks crazy . . . doesn't feel like anything at all, sort of, uh . . ." He shrugged. "Seems like a good idea at the time. You know what I mean. Later maybe it hits you, *asshole,* could've got yourself killed doing that. Too late then, though. What the hell . . ."

"And who am I to talk, anyhow. Used to think we were nutty as fruitcakes, going up in those little eggbeaters, nothing but wood and cloth and dope . . . but so help me, I loved it. You were right out in the open air, not closed up in some metal thing like now. You could feel it all happening to ya, practically get drunk on it . . . guess I'm running off at the mouth a little. . . ."

"Uh-uh . . . know just what you mean. Way I got started, my big brother Bobby had this scooter, see . . . I snuck out with it one night and really got her going, sixty-five, seventy maybe, wind in my face, winter, so damn cold, got so excited, next thing I know, wham, right into a goddamn tree. Didn't even see it coming. Nothing left but little bits of metal, a couple of busted-up wheels."

"Lord, you get hurt?"

"Not hitting the tree I didn't." He started to laugh. "But Bobby, he about took me apart. I mean, I was black and blue all over when he finished with me. Then my dad near killed us both when he found out we been fighting . . . so, uh, I mean . . ." He inched himself back a little on the sofa, squirming along on his shoulders like a snake, turning his wrist so he could check his watch.

"Go on," I said real quick. "Go on. . . ." How long did I figure I could keep him off Martha, though, and where was the girl?

"Shit," he said. "Shit, Alice, what the hell am I supposed to think but the worst now? I don't want to do it to her, but she's making me."

"No, no. She's playing at something here, Dennis, take it from me. I know how she is."

"You think I don't? You think I don't know Martha and all her tricks? Leaving those books there where I'm sure to see 'em. That's worse than her maybe fucking him, so don't try and make it look good to me, Alice, I mean, don't."

We had another couple of drinks and started pretending to look at television, nothing but roller derby on now. Dennis' eyes were drooping closed half the time, though every once in a while he'd snap his head up and mumble something. He was good and drunk now, and I hoped that was for the best.

iv

ANDREW

Beanie's was a square concrete bunker on the highway with the regulation martini glass and corny scroll letters spelling "B-A-R" in purple neon on a creaking sign over the entrance. It reminded me of roadhouses just across the New York line where I used to tank up Smith and Holyoke girls in my carefree youth: Order beer and drink out of the bottle, we'd tell each other in the men's room, among other things. Tough guys. I glanced over at Martha. "Are you all right?"

"Oh, yes, um-hmm." I didn't believe her. At first she'd been full of giggles and tremble-voiced jokes, a little hysterical maybe. But now she was fading away from me, brooding about what to say when she got home probably. Dennis wasn't exactly the type who'd pretend to believe any outlandish tale to save everyone's face. Well, it was too late to save my face anyway, heh, heh. Christ, I was probably a little hysterical myself. The inside of my nose felt nasty, stiff and fat with dried blood.

"Don't worry." I nudged her wrist with the edge of my finger, a quick electric touch, though I'd intended it for comfort only. But, yes, desire was returning stealthily, cat feet up my spine. She sat there with a drooping guilty mouth, chin on her hands, shoulders hunched up so her breasts lay round and neat on the table not six inches from my right hand. She was wearing a pale blue cardigan buttoned up the back . . . soft blue wool breasts, matching skin ones underneath. . . . I slid my hand away, unpredictable randy lizard. *Back, back I say* . . . I dropped it safely into my pocket and turned to study the two of us in the splotched mirror beside the booth. My face was grotesquely swollen, hideously discolored. Partly the mirror, I hoped.

I tried to catch her eye, but she wouldn't look at me. She took her straw into her mouth demurely, eyes downcast, tip of her tongue sliding primly out and in. Pretty gesture. Women and straws always drove me wild, did they but know it. Wicked pussycat tongues . . . The unlikely green stuff in her glass sank another quarter inch. But . . . creme de menthe on the rocks in a joint like this? The bartender had to wipe the dust of centuries off the bottle. Did Dennis let her get away with it, ordering such crap? Probably thought it was cute. "And for the little lady . . ." while he scarfed down boilermakers or depth charges or something. At least when he was in a relatively civilized place like Beanie's and couldn't simply swig from a bottle. (My own ideal, of course, was someone on the order of Paul Henreid, invariably snapping out "Champagne cocktail" while tamping a cigarette on a silver case, in even the meanest waterfront dive.)

"I had a black eye once before, when I was in the sixth grade, remember? You weren't that far behind me in school. I was out on the playground, and Billy Bascomb, that big fat kid, the one with one green eye and one blue eye, hit this tremendous line drive, only time he ever hit the ball in his life, and . . . pow! Right in the eye!" I smacked myself, gingerly, on the good eye. I was doing my best to amuse her, you'd have to admit.

"No," she said firmly. "I don't remember that at all."

Then it dawned on me, the simple truth. She was innocent. She didn't have to make up a story. I'd been temporarily befuddled by my own vast array of lusts and guilts. "Look, Martha, there's no reason for you to feel bad. You didn't do anything wrong."

"But he must believe that I would, you know."

"No, I'm sure he doesn't. He's too sensible, underneath it all. . . ." What the fuck was I up to, sitting there defending the bastard, with my face turning purple and my eye swelling shut? But I could see she'd taken it all to heart in some implacable female way, and I felt sorry for her. "Come on, he'll understand when you explain."

She didn't answer, just sat there very closed and still. Maybe some dark primitive part of her was secretly pleased as well. Hitting me wasn't the kind of thing she could do. (Martha never lost her temper, never screeched or smashed things or socked people, never wept or threw up.) Hitting me wasn't the kind of thing I could do either . . .

. . . Which didn't mean I'd not been one to royally screw up my own life through a heedless mad caper or two, in my time. Mine was a slightly different process, that was all. Sparks connected somewhere deep in the murky recesses of Dennis' brain and he bashed somebody. Now, my mistakes, and Lord, there'd been enough of them, I always made slowly, leisurely, gracefully. Some lazy treacherous current would pick me up and carry me for a while. Oh, I might notice I was being taken somewhere I didn't at all want to go, but there was time, still, lots of time. . . . And how pleasant being borne along by that warm kindly flow. When I finally heard the water roaring across the sharp rocks up ahead, realized how close I was to disaster . . . oops, too late. I'd be down there gasping and tumbling among the rapids. . . . Yup, that was the way it always was.

Slowly, slowly, I was sinking, the bog of dread reclaiming me and dragging me down. I wished I could erase it all, the night before Thanksgiving, coming upon Martha there in the warm kitchen, dark November night outside. If only I'd walked around to the front door . . . if I'd stayed in the car listening to the news . . . if I'd come home right after school instead of farting around in the car. I hated this moment so much. I saw myself so clearly now, a corrupt infantile creature, daydreaming, mucking around with other people's lives, hurting them, hurting myself, irresponsible, criminally stupid . . .

"Andrew . . ." She was sucking on the straw in her empty glass, making that hollow raspy noise.

"Yes, sweet, what is it? Want another drink?"

"Nooo. I think we ought to go home. I keep worrying."

I was relieved, disappointed; ashamed. "Okay," I said. "We'll go."

The school lot was deserted and the station wagon sat alone, a crust of new snow on its roof. I parked alongside and went around to open the door for her. She pulled the fringed scarf out and tied it on. Her face was calm and remote in the bluish light, her mouth firm. She let her eyes flick over me as she climbed into her car. "Don't look so worried, Andrew," she said softly. I closed the door on her. A little ledge of the new snow fell off onto my feet. I stood back and let her drive off.

V

ALICE

It must've been close to twelve-thirty when I finally heard wheels crunching along the driveway. A few minutes later Martha came barreling into the den with a look on her face I knew real well, the same fierce keyed-up look she used to get back in the old days when she was planning to take on her mother about something and win. Martha wasn't the kind to bide her time till everything blew over, even when she was in the wrong, especially when she was in the wrong. She stared hard at me, at Dennis lying half passed out on the sofa, and I could see we were in for it. She started shaking him, good and hard. "Wake up, you . . ."

"Why don't you leave him be? He's got kind of a skinful, but that's mostly my fault, maybe your fault too, my girl. No reason why he can't snooze there for a while. Anyhow, you're never going to get him upstairs."

"I don't want to leave him be. And I will . . . get him . . . upstairs." She was working him over good for a little thing like her, thumping on his chest, slapping at his face, shouting in his ear.

He pushed her hands away. ". . . lea'me alone."

"Oh, no . . . I want you *up,* now come on. . . ." She grabbed at his elbows, but he slid away from her like Jell-O. I was damn sorry I'd let him get so drunk. Gave her an advantage she was going to milk for all it was worth.

"What did you do to him, anyway? I've never seen him like this. And he has to drive to Escanaba tomorrow. He's probably forgotten all about that, too busy punching people. . . . You should see poor Andrew's face. . . ."

"I'm not going to say he was right about everything. Even so . . ." Thought maybe I could talk a little sense into her, but she rolled right over me like she didn't hear.

". . . I mean, don't I have the right to have a drink with my own brother-in-law without telling the whole world about it? Well, *don't I*? But of course Dennis thinks he has to know every single little thing I do. . . ." Her voice was sliding up and up, and I could see she was getting into one of her regular *states,* so there'd be no reasoning with her tonight. Once, twice a year maybe, it happened, and you had to leave her alone with it till she calmed down. She was like her mother that way, though you'd sure never catch me telling her that.

Finally Dennis staggered up onto his feet. He kind of swept Martha out of his way, and we could hear him stumbling around in the hall and up the stairs. She stood there a couple of minutes with her hands folded tight together and her head down. Then she flounced off upstairs herself, without another word.

Later on, while I was reading in peace, I heard Andrew tiptoe in. I caught one quick glimpse of his face, a big purple eye, as he went past the door and up the stairs.

December 7

i

MARTHA

The room was slowly filling up with that ghastly early-morning winter light, all bleached out like old bones. I could tell it was going to snow later from the heavy white look of the sky outside the window. I'd heard the radiators clanking and groaning fifteen minutes before, but the room was still cold as a tomb. I hadn't slept a wink all night. Oh, yes, that was supposed to be an illusion, just a neurotic fantasy, not sleeping a wink all night, but I knew better. I'd been lying awake in that bed every single minute since my head first touched the pillow, my eyes open so wide they hurt.

Dennis had dropped his clothes on the floor as usual when he'd staggered in, then flopped down and passed out cold again. Now he was sunk down under the covers, almost invisible except for one long elbow bent across his head, already protecting himself from falling wreckage, you might say, except that he always slept that way, like somebody in an air raid or a mine disaster. Maybe that was what he liked to dream about, cracking timbers, choking dust, *don't-talk-save-your-breath,* tapping out S-O-S on the ceiling or the drainpipe. But if Dennis dreamed, he never told anybody what. I kept a huge catalog in my head, different people I'd known sleeping and dreaming, shifting and sighing their way through the night: on their backs with wide-open fish mouths, curled up like worms, tunneled under the blankets, flung out flat like stars. But nobody on earth could have been carrying around such a picture of me. Nobody could ever have seen me asleep.

I folded back the covers and slid out into the frigid air, feeling around with clumsy cold feet for my slippers. I put on my robe and walked slowly down the ghostly gray dawn-lit hall to the bathroom. I turned on the shower and let the hot water run until the whole room was filled with warm steam. It was almost as good as sleeping, standing like a horse in a downpour, water thundering around me, all other noises and thoughts shut out. Finally I turned off the water and hunched there shivering for a minute, everything cold and silent around me, except for the drip-drip of the leaky faucet. I was all alone in the world with that little echoing angry sound. I couldn't even see my face in the fogged-up mirror. No reflection, like a vampire . . .

I crept back down the hall to our room, and there was Dennis, sitting on the edge of the bed with the blankets still half around him and his hair falling all over his eyes and his chin on his hands, the picture of despair and gloom. But that was the way he looked every morning. He slept like the dead and came awake slow, and *mean.* And today he'd be hung over too. Well. I walked briskly past him to the closet. "Are you still planning to leave this morning? I thought you might have forgotten, the way you were acting last night."

"Didn't forget anything." He ran his hand through his hair and glared up at me.

"Dennis . . ." I felt confused suddenly, angry with him still, but also burning with nerves, desperate and frightened. "I didn't mean to hurt you." I knew as soon as the words were out of my mouth that they were the worst, the very worst, I could have picked.

He made a little sound at the back of his throat, some snarl or growl that would have set me to laughing any other day, and stood up slowly, like Frankenstein. He stalked around the room, dragging on his clothes; sank down on the bed again, shirt flapping half open, staring down at his shoes as if he'd never seen them before; his usual early-morning zombie performance, but ominously silent, no muttering or swearing today. He tied the shoes and hoisted himself to his feet again. "Going up to the attic, get my bag."

His bag . . . he was only supposed to be gone four days. Besides, he usually didn't bother packing, wore his brothers' clothes when he went up north. I could hear his footsteps creaking on the attic floor. So amazing it always was, how quickly your life could shift and tumble down around you, caved in utterly, like a house on stilts. Yesterday at this very minute . . . there we'd been the two of us, locked together slick as porpoises in a roil of blankets, oh, groaning and sighing and carrying on. . . . How I hated that kind of talk, yesterday this, a month ago that . . . (Ten years ago I was twenty-four and I'd never heard of any Dennis, and what did it matter, you see?) There was a thump above me, and I went out of the room and down the stairs fast to get away from the sound.

Once in the kitchen I was totally calm, starting my regular morning routine: bread in the toaster, coffee in the pot, eggs in the pan. I turned on the radio for the weather report. Dennis wouldn't eat oatmeal, but I made some of that too, for somebody. He finally appeared, treading stealthily across the linoleum like some renowned merciless inscrutable Apache. I didn't turn a hair, hummed a tune to myself. He sat down at the far end of the table and I placed a mug of coffee in front of him, cheered up a little by how bad he looked, face all pasty and badly shaven, eyes tiny and bloodshot. Who'd want him if he looked like that all the time? Not me.

Of course he wouldn't touch the coffee until I'd turned around. I had to watch his distorted reflection in the side of the toaster, bulbous forehead and monstrous eye. It occurred to me that if I poisoned him somehow, I could keep him upstairs, helpless in bed, until I decided what I wanted to do with him. However, by sheer force of habit I made his eggs perfect, dry and fluffy yellow, exactly the way he liked them. I saw him recoil slightly at the smell of the hot food, but he started in grimly to eat. I poured myself a cup of coffee and leaned against the stove to drink it, keeping an eye on him so he'd have to go on eating, no matter how queasy he felt. The radio murmured on its shelf over the sink, ". . . expect near-record snowfalls in the Great Lakes region later today . . ."

"You're really going to drive in all that?"

"Why not?"

At the instant he finished he stood up and pushed back his chair. He walked way around the other side of the table as he went out. He wouldn't come anywhere near me now, and I couldn't decide whether to let him go or run after him. When he made a lot of noise being angry, slamming things around, I knew exactly how to deal with him. When he was quiet like this, I didn't have the faintest idea. For a full minute I stood there paralyzed, watching the second hand slowly sweep around the dial of the clock; then I pushed through the swinging door and ran up the stairs and down the hall, all on tiptoe so no one waking up would hear me.

He was standing by the bed, stuffing clothes into his duffel bag, piles and piles of them, it looked like. He glanced at me as if I were a bug flying into the room, his face neutral and set. I went and stood at the end of the bed, hanging on to the footboard. I hated what I was doing and hated him for making me do it. "You can't leave this way, with nobody saying anything."

"What do you want to say!" He kept his head down, playing with the drawstring on the bag. "HEWITT" and a serial number were stenciled across its side as if it belonged to some person I didn't know.

"You're being ridiculous. I mean, it wasn't what you think, what I guess you think, last night . . ."

"Okay. So what was it then? You thought the school was the library because they look so much alike and you never been there before? Come on, Martha, make it good."

My mouth went dry and my legs were starting to shake, but a little red coal of anger was lighting up somewhere too. He wasn't giving me a chance. Everything had closed down in his brain, the same as it did when he decided to drive to Michigan in a blizzard or skid across a track to make up a lap and win some stupid race. I tried to explain it all to him. It was like talking to a hatrack. He wouldn't listen, stared at the wall over my shoulder until my voice sort of ran down and faded away. ". . . I really only needed somebody to talk to, that was what it was . . . and, uh, he is my sister's husband . . ."

He snorted. "Sister's husband, my ass. What was wrong with talking to me? You're living with me, remember? Doesn't mean a hell of a lot to you, though, does it?" He grabbed up a flannel shirt and shoved it down into the bag. "Uh-uhh, not to you . . . bet you just figured I'd do my work a little better, I got to screw you all the time. Probably right, too. Must've been a bunch of happy mechanics around here is all I got to say, plumbers, carpenters, I forget anybody? . . . Oh yeah, maybe the milkman . . ."

"Oh, that's . . . !" My hand flew up and smacked him across the side of the head. And it felt good, too. My arm ached with it all the way up to the shoulder. I thought he might be going to hit me back, he looked so mad. And I almost hoped he would, so we'd be even. (My God, hit a poor little woman? He'd rather die. All his dumb rules . . .) My hand was fairly itching to hit him some more, but I lay it gently against his flaming-red assaulted ear instead. "Oh God, I'm so sorry . . ." He flicked my hand away, shouldered his bag and walked out without another word.

I went to the window and watched his car hurtle down the driveway and disappear beyond the curve in the road under the first aimless cascading flurries of snow. I felt breathless, as if I'd jumped off a bridge, all options gone, the end of everything coming up to flatten me in two seconds. I stood there for I don't know how long, my forehead pressed to the cold windowpane.

I poured myself another cup of coffee and drank it standing up, waiting for Andrew to come down. The brown faded grass in the backyard was slowly being covered by a sparse crust of snow. Farther back, through the bare trees, the hangars looked dilapidated and sad in the blowing white swirls. A few little flakes were ticking against the window and piling up along the frame. Let him go. I'd find somebody else. I always found somebody else. I put my empty cup down in the sink.

The back-stairs door creaked open and Andrew came through. The flesh around his left eye was a huge bright spiral of colors, violet and brown and black and maroon. Looking at it made you want to cringe, but made you want to laugh, too. A black eye was always a joke for some reason. "Andrew, you poor thing."

"Beautiful, isn't it?" He sat down at the table and gave me a cautious and rueful smile. "How are you . . . I mean, er, everything okay, and everything? I was really worried later. Sort of wondering, you know, if he hit *me,* he might . . . well, hurt you too. . . ."

"Oh, you don't know him at all," I cut in, irritated. "Here." I handed him the pitcher of milk for his cereal.

"Thanks. Uh, I saw him go off."

"He went up to Michigan for a couple of days. His nephew's being christened. Really, Andrew, what on earth are you going to tell them at school? That awful eye."

"I ran into a door, what else? It's traditional. No, actually I was racking my brains for a comp topic and this is perfect." He took a spoonful of cornflakes. "A few laughs for everybody."

"Maybe there's something we could do to it. In the movies they always use raw meat."

"A fairly disgusting idea, if you ask me. No, don't worry. It's a little sore, is all. And what I'll really tell them, if it comes to that, is I fell on the ice. True enough, really." He grinned and stood up with his cup still in his hand, buttoning his jacket. "Getting late. I'd better go." He stood by the table regarding me intently for a minute, some kind of uneasy excitement coming through to me from behind that comic-book black-eye face. "You know what? . . . I . . . Jessie spoke to me last night."

"When was this? We got home so late." I wasn't being very nice to him. I couldn't seem to help myself. Nothing was his fault. Everything was my fault. But I was feeling very mean. I wanted to take it out on somebody.

"It was pretty late. She was still awake, though. She asked me where Sylvester was, so I found him and put him in the bed with her." He was staring down at his chest, smoothing and smoothing his tie. "It was so funny, hearing her voice like that, I sort of forgot what it sounded like."

"Oh, Andy . . . I don't know if you should get too encouraged, you know . . . ?"

"No, I'm not, really I'm not. I'm sort of passing it on for what it's worth. I thought she'd been a little better, except for Thanksgiving, and that was, well, Thanksgiving. Who knows, though?"

I felt bad, seeing him with his poor bruised eye and now something else about Jessie to get his hopes up and cause him more pain. We'd been through this so many times before, when it would seem for a while as if she might be better, but nothing much ever came of it. I couldn't imagine what Andrew's daily secret life must be like—he'd never had the chance of a last dramatic fight with Jessie, of harsh ugly words and slapped faces, of walking out, being thrown out, driving off never to return. She was still here and he was still here, like characters out of some terrible old story of living death, the red shoes, the goose girl, all the morbid ones I'd loved as a child. . . . It did scare me, imagining what it must be like for him, so much worse than anything that could happen to me. Today there was that ugly niggle of gratitude as well, knowing I was better off than someone, finding that cheered me up some, to tell the truth, unkind as it was to profit from the miseries of others.

I put my hand on his sleeve. "I'm real sorry about what happened last night, you know, I really am."

He smiled at me again, like one of those Greek statues we studied in school, a perfect, not especially happy smile. "Don't worry about it," he said, and patted my hand. He was so nice, always. Maybe that was half his trouble even, being so nice. Of course, look who was talking. If I'd been him I'd have been furious with me. I'd have wanted to get back somehow. But not nice Andrew. "Bye, bye. I'll see you later." He went out, and I could see his head through the porch window as he wound a blue muffler around and around his neck. Then the outside door slammed and he disappeared.

"Well, you know, dear," Julia was saying as she stirred honey into her tea, "we could always try to get this Smythe creature to take another option, another three months perhaps, to give us a bit more time." I'd decided I might as well tell them everything. They'd find out now anyway, and keeping secrets had already caused me enough trouble. Neither Julia nor Alice was anywhere near as shocked and cut up as I would have expected them to be about the idea of selling off the old field and hangar, not exactly overjoyed, but not prostrate either. Here I'd been trying to protect them and spare them pain, taking on that huge burden all by myself, and all for nothing. A foolish, selfish girl I'd been . . . I kept thinking about Dennis; I couldn't help it, pictures of him sliding across my mind like those little dots from a flashbulb you can never blink away, the look on his face last night in the parking lot, and this morning when I'd smacked him. . . . Oh, I didn't think I could bear it, five days until Sunday, shut up in this house, nothing to do but wait and think and think and wait. I wished I could drive off somewhere and leave it all behind me. Dennis was lucky. . . .

"Are you all right, Martha dear?" Julia tapped my wrist with her long pink nail.

"I'm fine." I slid my hand away without looking at her.

"Now there's one other piece to the puzzle, and this time I'm the one who's been keeping a secret I owed it to you to tell—sorry, Martha," Alice said in a rush. "Don't get too excited now, nothing all that bad. But . . . I went to see Ray, and he took some pictures and it's the arthritis, same as Mom. First we thought I'd only have it in the one hand, but now looks like it's in both of them." She smiled out at us, one of those wide fake smiles. "So I guess that's that. Pretty soon I won't be flying at all anymore." Julia slid her hand around Alice's neck and leaned against her for a minute. Alice turned her face into Julia's, then pulled away and said with a little laugh, "You remember how Mom was, took it right in stride."

"Oh, do I ever. I do hope you're not planning to be like that." Julia cocked her head at me, one eyebrow raised. "You see, dear, your grandmother was always very . . . *stalwart.* It was hard on us all."

"That's not fair, Julia. She wasn't so perfect."

"Well, you were *close* to her. I saw her differently."

"She loved you too. . . . She wanted to, anyhow."

Julia smiled slightly, gazing at the snow swirling outside the long dining room window, slowly stirring her tea. Alice picked up the teapot, filled her own cup and mine as well. The three of us sat there together in the dim room, watching the midday snow, listening to the clock strike in the other room.

"Well," Alice said at last. "Didn't mean to shut everybody up."

"We could always hire someone to fly for us, I suppose," Julia said. "Why don't you teach Dennis?"

"Dennis is afraid to fly," I murmured, disloyal in spite of myself.

"Is he? Well, it's nice to know he's afraid of something. I do hate to think of losing that land, though. Are you *sure* there's not some other way, Martha? Have you really racked your brains? Concentrate, now."

"I *did* rack my brains, Aunt Julia, for hours and hours and hours last summer, before I went to see that awful man. If you think you can do better than that . . ." I stopped. I'd heard my voice rising, getting all thin and shrill. "I didn't mean to sound so . . . It's . . . I wish Dennis hadn't gone off today . . . he took it all wrong . . . last night . . ." I was sorry at once I'd blurted that out. The last thing I wanted was sympathy and advice from people who'd lived a lot longer than I had and knew me better than I knew myself. I wanted to be let alone to suffer.

"You know, dear," Julia began, "I can see how it might irk a man like Dennis to think you'd . . ."

"Oh, Dennis and his pride, I'm sick of it. What about my pride?"

Alice said, "The thing *I* can't exactly figure out is why you'd pick Andrew to talk to of all people. I mean, he's a nice boy, but not the most practical fellow in the world. You could have talked to *me.*"

"I didn't want to worry you, and I thought he'd be sympathetic but not pushy, which is exactly the way he was, and probably . . . I mean I thought Dennis would . . . and anyway . . ." Suddenly I was so irritated with the two of them, sitting there cross-questioning me, making me feel small and foolish. "Oh, honestly, I can see you're both on *his* side."

"No, dear. There aren't any *sides* here. I'm sure Dennis behaved abominably too."

"You were trying to do the right thing," Alice chimed in.

They were peering across at me like twin Rice birds, for once the resemblance between them clear: faded blue eyes and curly hair and little elfish ears. I got to my feet without another word, loaded up the tray with the tea things and took it out to the kitchen, letting the door whoosh shut behind me, trying not to listen to the cautious undertone of their voices in there *discussing* me.

I put the tray on the drainboard with a clatter, marched upstairs and down the hall to our room. In a sort of frenzy I started dragging his things out of dresser drawers and off the floor—shirts, socks, T-shirts, underwear—piling it all together in the middle of the room. He hadn't taken as much with him as I'd thought. I shoved the Millersburg rocker into the closet, way back behind my clothes, whipped out all his clothes, jeans and leather outfits and his one suit, kicking along ahead of me his boots, the bent skid shoe from the accident last summer and a dented helmet I found in there, too, souvenir of another disaster. I heaved everything up on the pile, then crammed it all into three laundry bags, ready for shipment anywhere. Nothing was going to take me by surprise now. He could go to hell for all I cared now. Might as well go to hell as go to Escanaba . . .

But the good feeling faded away before I'd even had a chance to enjoy it. I sat down on the bed because I was shaking all over. The three laundry bags of his stuff looked awful, drastic, forlorn or else just stupid. But it was too late. I was damned if I was going to put everything back.

After dinner my father came out to help me with the dishes, surprise, surprise. Alice had probably put him up to it, hoping he could calm me down, since nobody else could. I'd been so bitchy all day long, getting on everybody's nerves. She'd have told him the whole story, I was sure. I couldn't ever quite figure the two of them out. I mean, were they sleeping together or not? I kept finding them sitting together like little kids who'd been playing something they weren't supposed to and were going to start up again the minute you closed the door. It was getting on my nerves.

"Uh . . . Martha?" my father said, half choking on the word, such a hard one, you know, his own daughter's name. I wasn't being fair, but that was just too bad. He was so scared and anxious with me sometimes he made me feel awful, like an ogress or a crazy woman. It was the way he'd been with my mother, of course . . . couldn't he remember when I was little and cute and helpless? . . . and where had he been then, when I'd needed him? . . . *Oh, Daddy, you'd never fight for me, would you . . . and now look at me . . .* My mind was racketing along every which way; I had to stop it.

"Alice told you everything, didn't she?"

"Uh, what?"

"She did, didn't she? Well, what do you think I ought to do?"

He stood there hanging on to the vegetable dish and the dishcloth for dear life, his mouth twitching and working like an old rubber band. "I don't . . . I don't think I really have a right to say . . ."

"Oh, damn it, Daddy, you have as much right as anybody."

"No, I, uh, it's not my place to . . ."

Of course I'd scared him out of anything halfway useful or sensible he might have been going to say. He'd clam up on me completely now, I knew that. He carefully laid the vegetable dish down on the counter and picked up the meat platter. I kept my back turned to him so I wouldn't have to watch. I could hear the maddening squeak-squeak of the cloth on the platter. He was practically wiping the damn pattern off. I clenched my fists under the dishwater, trying to be patient, trying to be understanding, trying to be a good daughter. I didn't know what to expect from myself anymore. I was by nature a cool person, always calm and collected, and here this morning I'd whomped Dennis; who knows, tonight I might whomp my father, knock the meat platter right out of his hands, smash it into a million pieces on the floor at his feet. . . .

I glanced up at the clock. Almost eight-thirty. For the hundredth time that day I wondered, where would Dennis be at this precise moment? Into my mind jumped a romantic picture of him, a solitary figure gazing moodily over the rail of the ferry at the deep black mysterious waters of the straits . . . I hoped he'd had sense enough to stop if the weather was really bad. I knew how much he liked the idea of driving straight through, always one to relish any painful and ridiculous challenge to his body. . . . Ohio people thought he was crazy to drive six hundred miles in a day, but in Michigan if you grew up in the upper peninsula, you were entitled to be a little wild and strange. The U. P. was legendary, huge gray sky like an empty mirror, endless miles of lapping gray water, wind sighing through the lonely forests, mournful water birds calling for their mates . . . I'd heard all about it. I suppose that might explain Dennis, but what about me? I couldn't help thinking of all the painful and ridiculous things I'd done to myself over the years. Who was I to criticize Dennis? On the other hand . . .

I felt a feathery touch along my top hair. Daddy. His only known caress. He couldn't ever bring himself to try anything more definite. And he always made sure he was standing behind me or off to one side, so it was impossible for me to see his face. I yanked my head down by pure reflex and then, filled with remorse as usual, had to reach over and pat his wrist reassuringly. "I'm sorry, Daddy. I'm in such a horrible mood today, don't mind me. Dennis and I had a big fight this morning, and now he's driving in this snow and I'm worried to distaction."

But it was always a big mistake to tell my father what was really on my mind. He never knew what to make of it or what he was supposed to say back. Usually there'd be this dumb silence, and I'd feel so silly. Like now. He took forever putting the platter down on the counter, as if it suddenly might grow legs and jump out of his hands onto the floor. Then he picked up another dish and started to dry it with the same squeak-squeak. Finally he said, "Dennis is a pretty good driver."

A wave of exasperation flooded over me. I knew he thought Dennis was the worst driver in the Western Hemisphere. "Oh, Daddy . . ." I said in a not very nice voice. It was hopeless.

When I closed the door to our room on little old me and climbed into bed alone, I tried to remember the last time I'd done that. A year ago? Two years? He'd been around a long time, Dennis. I had to stop and think. No, there'd been plenty of weekends when he'd stayed over at racetracks far away. And last summer when he spent a night in the hospital after he broke his ankle. All the other times he'd driven up to see his family. He'd offered to take me along on some of those Escanaba trips, but I always weaseled out of going. I didn't want to meet relatives and be looked over, I guess. With most of the other men in my life the issue never came up, and that was the way I liked it. Now, I probably wouldn't get another chance.

I tried to read for a while, a mystery story, one of the famous unreturned books, all battered and stained from its experiences. I couldn't really concentrate. Even though I was lying in the middle of the bed—to get used to the idea again—I kept rolling over onto one side or the other where the dents were. I turned out the light and then tossed and turned in the dark for half an hour before I decided to go downstairs for a glass of milk.

Jessie's door was open a crack, and I pushed it open a little more and peeked in. Faint moonlight shone through the frosty window, and I could barely make out the shape of her little body in the whitish glow. I was quietly pulling the door closed behind me when I heard her say, ever so softly, "Martha . . . ?"

Andrew was right, even that faint rusty whisper of my name had a power—so unfamiliar now, my own sister's voice coming out of the silvery-lit bed in the dark. It made me shiver a little, as if a cat or flower had suddenly started to speak. "Yes, dear, it's me. Go on back to sleep." I tiptoed slowly down the hall and climbed into my bed again.

January 10, 1953

i

MARTHA

I stood on the landing for a minute, looking out across the bare trees to the naked spot where the old hangar had been. The raw earth there was crawling with yellow contraptions moving like huge insects: graders, diggers, cranes, what-have-you. The hangar itself was now only a pile of worn maroon rubble. I could barely read the faded letters *FA* and *FL* and *CIR* on one last relatively intact section of roof.

In the middle of December Mr. Hutchens had asked Mr. Smythe if he would consider taking another six-month option, or even a three-month option, but he'd refused. We had to sell or go bankrupt, that was what it boiled down to. The only part of the back forty acres we'd managed to hang on to was the stream. Mr. Smythe turned up his nose at it, and we did need it since we had no fire pond.

Under the bright winter sky the five planes sitting together on the strip, wings gleaming in the sun, had an ironic prosperous look. But if you got up close you'd see they were old and shabby and not long for this world, like all the Rice enterprises at the moment. Before the builders razed the hangar we'd had to empty it out and find space for everything somewhere else, trying to save as much of the historical old junk as we could: trunks and scrapbooks and logbooks and funny old flying clothes, even a ratty wicker balloon gondola and my grandmother's moth-eaten tights. Right now Dennis and Alice and Buddy were out on the strip making chalk diagrams and trying to figure out how to fit all five planes into the two remaining hangars. I leaned against the windowsill, watching Dennis push one of the Jennies around. He was wearing his ratty navy peacoat and a blue wool hat pulled down nearly to his eyebrows. The only chance I had these days to take a good look at him was when he was off in the distance somewhere and couldn't catch me at it.

He'd come back from Michigan exactly when he'd said he would—Dennis' promises were written in blood, in case I'd forgotten. He'd staggered in at precisely three minutes to midnight that Sunday, walked past me up the stairs, fell into bed and slept till noon Monday. On Thursday he actually deigned to speak to me. (He said, "Pass the bread, please, Martha.") Oh, you might look at us together and not think anything was wrong, but everything was wrong, everything.

I knew what I was up against, too, did I ever. Dennis the monster-stoic, better than any Christian martyr or Spartan child. Last summer he'd lain back, face ashen, not moving a muscle or uttering a sound, while two friends lifted the smashed bike off his leg. (I could still hear that horrid faint crunch of broken bone.) And now when I tried to talk to him, he gave me that same wooden Indian look, oh, noble in its way I grant you, but also ridiculous, a waste of my time.

I had another little problem too. I'd missed three periods, and I couldn't pretend any longer not to know the reason why. There was a little worm growing inside me, a tadpole, cells piling on by the minute while I breathed and slept and ate and looked out the window spying on Dennis. It probably even had fingernails by now. Thinking about it made my blood run cold. Me, a mother. And I knew enough about Dennis to be sure that once he found out, he'd make it a point to marry me even if he hated the very sight of me by then. He'd endure that obligation down to his toes and into the roots of his hair. (I spent a lot of time these days recalling wistfully certain men I'd known in the past, frivolous despicable types who'd disappear in a cloud of dust if you merely whispered . . . *I'm a little late this month, dear* . . . But here I was, stuck with Dennis.)

Of course I could have done what nice girls were supposed to do when they got in trouble—disappear for a few months, come home all thin and innocent, baby safely adopted somewhere, your reputation intact. But where would I go? How would my family manage without me while I was gone? The whole place fell to pieces if I went off for so much as a day. Besides, even though I knew I didn't want the child, no, not at all, I also knew I didn't not want it. It would be a

Rice child, with all the genes of my tribe, and I couldn't bear to cast it out into the world to be brought up by strangers.

I felt the same mixed way about Dennis. I didn't want him around anymore, the way he was acting, and I didn't exactly not want him around either. Sometimes I'd catch myself recalling the way it used to be between us, and I'd feel that old fatal yearning, never mind what he'd said, what I'd done, what I'd said, what he'd done . . . he only despised me now, it was written all over his face, and somehow I couldn't bring myself to try to change his mind. Oh, I'd been terrible, lied to him, betrayed him, *struck* him, and I was sorry, but that was all in the past. I didn't want to be bothered with it anymore. Of course mine was the shallow and practical position, the woman's position, not the resolute moral position upon which civilizations had been built, wars had been fought, dynasties had crumbled, the position he was bound to take as a wronged *man.* Yawn.

I went into the bathroom and checked the full-length mirror again, sideways and frontwards. Nothing was showing yet. I wasn't getting sick in the mornings either, so I could keep my secret. Not for much longer, though. I had no plan for the future. I put on some new lipstick and strolled down to the kitchen to make lunch. As I was hauling the carcass of Friday's roast out of the fridge to start slicing it for sandwiches, I heard Buddy and Dennis outside, and heavy footsteps tramping up the back steps. I smiled at Buddy, making a point of not looking at Dennis because I knew he'd be making a point of not looking at me. "Isn't Alice going to eat?"

"She said to tell you she'd be in later," Buddy answered. He was used to doing most of the talking by now, Dennis' mouthpiece.

"You want some mustard on your roast beef, Buddy?" He made a face and shook his head. "And you, Dennis?" I said politely.

"No mustard for me, thank you, Martha." He slid like a snake around behind me and sat down next to Buddy. He never touched me anymore except purely by accident.

"What did you decide to do with the Jennies?" I asked, to preserve a semblance of normal conversation, for Buddy's sake. Dennis and I, left to our own devices, could keep a good chilly silence going for hours on end. However, I didn't think it was right to expose this poor child to such a spectacle and sour him forever on romance.

"We were thinking we could squeeze one of them into the school hangar, and then keep switching around, so a different airplane was outside every day."

"Sounds like a good idea." I handed them the plates with their sandwiches and a slice of pickle each. "Now, do you need anything else?"

"No, thank you, Martha." Dennis tipped his chair back and opened the refrigerator. He took out the carton of milk, meanwhile talking to Buddy in a low voice as if I weren't there.

I escaped into the dining room to wait till they were finished. Sometimes being near Dennis these days was like being between grinding stones, and I couldn't stand it for more than a few minutes. I sat down at the table and started thumbing through the newspaper that was lying there. Upstairs Jessie was playing her new record of the *American in Paris* ballet for about the umpteenth time that day. I scanned the editorials and cranky letters and Today's Chuckle page, flipped to the next page and saw at the bottom a drawing of a woman in an enormous ballooning smock printed with Teddy bears and drums. A tiny stork in a top hat was flying over her carrying a ribbon in his beak that said, ". . . for Ladies-in-Waiting . . ." I closed the paper at once and picked up the envelopes lying underneath it, two letters from California, one from Teddy, one from Julia, giving completely different versons of their Christmas holidays; a circular from Daddy's store; the phone bill; the gas bill. At least I didn't have to quake with terror every time I saw a window envelope anymore. We had money in the bank again. For the time being. From out back came the obnoxious crunching and groaning sound of a grader demolishing some further section of the Fabulous Flying Circus.

ii

ANDREW

Caught off-guard, without its usual sheen of liveliness, Martha's face looked worn and sad. She lifted her head and smiled at me. "I was going to make some lunch for you in a while. What do you feel like having, soup maybe? Leftover roast beef? If they don't finish it . . ." She jerked her head toward the kitchen.

"Soup, I guess. I don't know."

"She really loves that album, doesn't she?"

"God, yes . . ." I sat down across from her and picked up a section of the newspaper. I didn't particularly feel like going into the kitchen while Dennis was there. Actually, he'd apologized to me, quite handsomely as a matter of fact, a few days after The Incident, when my eye had faded to mere sulphurous yellow, chartreuse and sunset pink. He came upon me in the den where I was quietly watching Ernie Kovacs, clamped his big hand down on my shoulder and said, "I want to talk to you. . . ." I bet I jumped a foot. He looked like some huge ungainly bird ("Nearly Extinct Species"), looming over me with his long nose and fierce little eyes. But I couldn't even enjoy being snide. When he released my shoulder and backed away a little, I could see he was horribly embarrassed, mortified, in fact. "Sometimes I just don't use my goddamn brain," he said, frowning so hard his eyebrows practically met across his nose. "Seems like I was way out of line, and, I mean, uh, anyway . . . I'm sorry."

I replied, "Quite all right, old man," or something, one of those British movie lines, suitably gracious and urbane, and returned to the Kapusta Kid. My part was easy (except for the eye). But I didn't think he'd forgiven her yet. Nothing but silence from their room these nights. Somebody was making somebody pay.

"Oh, and here." Martha handed me a blue airmail envelope. "From Julia. You saw Uncle Teddy's letter, didn't you? I think he was exaggerating a little. Read it and see what you think."

According to Teddy, Julia was not happy in California; Duffy wasn't treating her well; he'd run off with a starlet on Christmas Day; he'd left her alone on her birthday; he'd done this, he'd done that. I'd taken it all with a grain of salt. The Julia I knew could look after herself, even if, like Martha, she had terrible taste in men. "You know, I was't exactly impressed with that guy when he was here. He seemed a little, well, crude, for her or something."

"Alice says she was crazy about him once. They used to fight all the time, though. Ask Alice, she knows all the stories. Get her to tell you about the time Aunt Julia sent a big cactus to a girl friend of his, had it delivered to her in a restaurant where she and Duffy were eating . . . ."

"A cactus? I don't get it."

"It was a big, big one. You know, like a huge . . ."

"Oh, yeah . . ." I cut in quickly. These Rice girls could always embarrass me, so serene and blunt, always ready to call a whachamacallit a youknowwhat. I couldn't do it, couldn't name my own organ out loud to a woman. *Cock. Prick.* The words sounded ugly. All of a sudden, sitting there blushing under Martha's cool and curious gaze, I remembered the first time I ever made love to her sister, trying so hard not to frighten or hurt, moving with such aching slowness over this fragile child, when she gave a little raunchy sigh, opened her tight wet self, drew me right in. I was so damn young myself. Twenty-three. It hurt to think about that; it hurt to think about being twenty-three, which was why I didn't much.

I picked up Julia's letter, unfolded the thin airmail sheets. Behind me in the kitchen, I heard chairs scraping back, the voices of Dennis and Buddy diminishing outside. Martha got to her feet and stretched. So she'd been listening too. "Okay," she said. "You must be starved by now."

Jessie and I sat in her room at a child's miniature table, part of a set the girls had had when they were small. Jessie still fit into the matching little chair, and if I sat sideways and stretched my legs out straight I could be reasonably comfortable in mine. The phonograph was playing at medium volume. Gene Kelly's husky voice on "Love Is Here to Stay." Silence. Soft thump of another record dropping, the French guy singing "I'll Build a Stairway to Paradise." I caught myself starting to mouth the words along with him. Christ, I knew the whole damn album by heart.

Jessie wasn't exactly playing with her food anymore, not the way she used to. But she still had some kind of a thing about eating, would make up weird little routines for herself that drove me crazy. Today, for instance, she'd eat a level spoonful of tomato soup and then take a precise quarter-bite of a saltine and then another spoonful of soup and another quarter-bite of saltine. I was fascinated and exasperated watching her. She looked over at me and smiled. "It's good."

"Um-hmm, it certainly is."

Being with her wasn't like being with an adult woman or like being with the Jessie she'd been before, leaving food aside. She scared me a little. She scared me a lot. I was so afraid of rushing her, damaging my chances, damaging her chances, far more than I'd been, all needlessly, when she was seventeen.

According to the doctor, talking again (she'd been doing it since December, since the night Dennis punched me, in fact) was only a first step toward . . . well, he used a whole killer paragraph of opaque jargon. Jesus, doctors. But it was essentially the same tired old theory he'd given out, stroking his beard, years ago. She'd been worn out by the stresses of wartime: flying the dangerous planes, forcing herself to excel for the good of the Women's Corps; then the accident that killed her best friend, her mother's illness and death. He'd seen it all before, he said, that utter exhaustion, that retreat into silence and dependency, especially among women, sensitive, fearful types with great stores of will and too much respect for duty. I'd never thought of Jessie as fearful, or even particularly sensitive, but what the hell, it was a theory. I had a friend from college, one of those tediously rowdy fraternity guys, always slapping you on the back singing *drink-chug-a-lug,* who'd come home from the tank corps and become a Trappist monk. And another, a suave Brahmin type, who even now would throw himself flat in a gutter if he heard the click of a Zippo lighter on a dark street. Everybody had some way of being haunted.

Including me. I'd never even made it overseas, but I had my own bad memories stored away—kids' faces mostly, scared shitless before they were shipped out; or remembered later when I heard news of their fates on the seas or in the jungles. I felt enough complicity to make that painful, and a lot of times I'd wished I had the guts to be a C.O. My parents were Quakers, so I had the correct pacifist credentials, but I didn't really have the correct principles, when you came right down to it. What I did have was merely your normal cringe for the flesh, my own, anybody's. The killing was really okay with me, but not the maiming and crushing, the ripping and shredding and flaying, the blowing to bits, the burning alive, the mowing down in a hail of bullets. I didn't want to do it and I didn't want it done to me . . . but then I was pretty lazy, too. I ended up letting myself be drafted and hoping for the best. Sometimes I imagined that Jessie was a way I, the noncombatant, had been given to pay for what I had missed. Along with all the other things.

Jessie scraped her bowl clean—it came to one last complete spoonful—finished the last quarter of the last saltine, and sat back with a little prim smile. I moved the bowl an inch, like a magician, and revealed a hidden saltine. "Oops, you missed one." I meant to make a joke, but I could see I'd really upset her. A horrible grimace crossed her face, and she snatched up the extra cracker and held it in front of her, eyeing it balefully.

"It's okay, honey, I was only teasing." I pulled gently at a piece of hair over her ear. But she sat there intently scrutinizing that damned cracker. Finally I snapped at it like a dog, chomped it down whole, and got her to smile at last.

"It didn't come out right."

"I know, but I fixed it. Rrowf!" I barked at her and nuzzled her neck and produced a faint, soft, startled sound, almost a giggle. "Listen, I only have a couple of papers left to grade. Then I thought we could, what do you think, go for a walk? Would you like that?" Physical exercise was supposed to be good for her, too. No sex, though. That was out of the question for now. The doctor'd taken me aside discreetly, even kindly. Well, Jesus, of course. It was like walking on eggs; every day you held your breath. Anything, whatever it was, I'd do it, not do it.

"I'm going to play my record again."

"Okay, but better yet, why don't you pick out a new record? Surprise me." I'd bought her dozens of records for Christmas, all kinds of stuff—classical, pop crap, jazz, show tunes—it was a celebration, but so far all she'd ever play was that one album, the sound track from the movie *An American in Paris.* Originally, I'd liked it myself, moderately. But by now I thought I might run amok if I heard those adorable little French kids sing, *"Parlez à nous en anglais, Jeemy?"* one more time. *Amok,* a lovely word. But no, I wouldn't. You can get used to anything. Who knew that better than I did?

She turned over the same old stack (someday they'd wear out, praise the Lord), flicked the changer switch and slid down uneasily beside the pile of other albums, still in their cellophane wrappers. Jessie herself was wrapped all in gray today, skirt, sweater, knee socks, a pretty pale wraith. I pushed the soup dishes out of the way and started on my pile of test papers, red pencil moving down the pages with a will of its own, always amazing me, circling errors, correcting spelling, writing out rude comments, as if by remote control. ". . . Lord Byrone . . ." I read, ". . . was in love with his sister and so was William Wadsworth . . ." Oh, God. And more of the same. Only three more papers to go. The sun moved out beyond the roof and gleamed sharply through Jessie's window at me. I put up my hand to shade my eyes. I heard a rustle of cloth.

Jessie had taken off her gray sweater and was holding it crumpled up against her waist. She'd taken her bra off too. She had pretty, small breasts, like the ones in old Flemish paintings, perfect little oranges, impossibly round when the nipples were erect, like now. I stared, unnerved, but also excited, Christ. I twitched the curtain along its rod to keep the sun off her face too. She kept her eyes lowered, twisting the sweater in her hand, wouldn't look at me. A sudden idiotic memory leaped to mind: an old *National Geographic* we'd sneaked peeks at as kids, Greek slave girl, half stripped on the block, naked breasts soft and vulnerable, mortified downcast face. ". . . He probably said not to . . ." she whispered. ". . . he probably told you I'm too crazy to fuck . . . didn't he?"

"Oh, sweet. Nobody could tell me that. . . ." I reached for her hand. Well, what else was I supposed to do?

"I'm sorry, Andy."

"What for . . . what do you have to be sorry for . . . ?"

"I'll be nice now . . . I promise. . . ."

She leaned over me, sliding her arms around my neck, dragging those soft little breasts and tight nipples across my face, my eyes, my mouth. I was helpless, crammed into the tiny chair, breathing hard. "Don't, uh, wait . . ." I laughed shakily. "Not so fast . . . you'll lose me . . ." She laughed too, breath warm on my face. ". . . not here, anyway. Let's get in the bed. . . ."

I tried to stop once, I was so afraid. She grabbed at me, frantic, ". . . no, please, please . . . it's all right . . ." The last record on the stack played itself again and again. "I'll Build a Stairway to Paradise," natch. I came too fast the first time. Couldn't help it. Later she went all slack and heavy under me, turned her face away, and I felt terrible. "Are you okay . . . what is it?" There were tears coming out of her eyes, rolling back into her hair, her ears. "I won't . . ." I tried to disengage myself gently, but she hung on, her strong little pilot's hands tight across my back.

January 20

i

ALICE

When Julia finally came on the line her voice was kind of echoey and static-y, so I couldn't tell much about the mood she was in. We'd had that Lieutenant Driscoll of hers calling up in the middle of the night and scaring us all.

"Hope it was okay to give him the number out there. . . ."

"Of course, of course," she said, very testy. "A little boy's been kidnapped. Somebody sent the mother a piece of his ear in a Kroger's shopping bag. But I don't have time to go into it all now. Just tell me if you can meet me in Cleveland."

"Won't be a problem. . . . Are you okay?" But she'd already hung up. Typical.

There was a new framed clipping up on the wall by the phone. It was from the town paper and dated January 6, 1953. *HISTORIC BUILDING RAZED Old Rice Airfield and Hangar Sold.* Under the headline were a couple of photographs, one a Fourth of July show from back in the twenties, mostly a bunch of heads looking up at a dot in the sky, me or Teddy; and another of the knocked-down hangar the way it looked now. Martha'd bought a dime-store frame for it and hung it up there the day after the paper came out.

Right underneath the new thing was an old picture of Cliff and me standing by that French job of his, the airplane he ordered right before he got killed. I was in such a morbid sort of mood these days I'd find myself thinking Cliff'd been *lucky*, dying when he did so he didn't have to go through the whole business of getting old and useless. It'd come to that.

I'd pull all kinds of tricks on myself, trying to be sensible about it. Look, I'd say to myself, *look*. You're only but sixty-three. Chances are you'll live another twenty years, easy, nearly a whole lifetime for Cliff. You going to spend every single day, that's about six thousand of them, feeling sorry for yourself? After all, my grandma lived to be ninety-two, bright as a bird. And my great-granddad was ninety-four when he got himself thrown by a fractious horse and broke his neck. He was pretty fractious himself, they used to say. No reason I couldn't be the same way. . . .

No matter how I tried to sweet-talk myself, though, I still felt real depressed most of the time, had to force myself to get out of bed in the morning, force myself to eat and talk to people and act halfway normal. Maybe it was only natural to feel depressed right now, never mind my particular problems. This wasn't exactly a cheerful time in any of our lives. We'd had the worst Christmas I could remember, all of us missing Teddy and Julia and brooding about how we were going to feel when the men came to tear up our land. Little Jessie acting so much happier'd been about the only bright spot.

The door creaked open behind me and Martha said, "Wasn't that the phone? I thought it might be Timmy Driscoll again. That was a real horrible story he told Dennis last night."

"No, it was her nibs herself. She's coming back tomorrow. Wants me to fly up to Cleveland to pick her up, unless she can get a connecting to Akron." Martha and I exchanged looks. We were worried about Julia because of all the gossip from Teddy. "I couldn't tell . . ." I said.

"Maybe we're all wrong. There wasn't anything really terrible in that letter."

"No, but, well, I know Teddy'd be loyal to Duffy if he possibly could, and if it was anybody except his sister, so if *he* said . . . and you know John always did used to have a roving eye. Never bothered her then. He'd run off for a weekend or something with some little cutie, and she'd go off with somebody too, to show him. Now, I don't know . . ."

"She's very beautiful still."

"Ye-es, but it's a little easier for the men when you get to be our age and that's a fact." My eyes slid back to the wall of photos and junk, and there was Julia when she was about twenty, looking very damn beautiful indeed. And next to her Vern with Anna, also gorgeous enough to knock your eyes right out of your head. Not much difference between Vern in the picture and Vern today. He'd gone bald early and then hardly changed a bit over the years.

"Which one are you looking at?" Martha said, slipping her arm through mine.

"Right now, Julia. Before I was looking at that one there, me and my brother, your uncle Cliff. Also at your mom and dad."

"I hate that one. I really hate it, those fake happy looks. They make me *sick*!" She said it so loud I had to turn and stare at her. She added, shamefaced, "Well, you know how things really were between them. That's why I hate those smiles. It's too bad it wasn't always you and him. You're so different from her. Even Aunt Julia is. I don't see how that can happen. Such a bad person in a family of normal people."

Of course I was kind of taken aback to hear her drop that out so casual about her dad and me. But I was almost more surprised to hear her talk about her mother at all. Usually she acted as if she'd never had a mother and that "Anna" we all talked about sometimes was a complete stranger to her. I said, "Well, she wasn't really a *bad* person. She could be a lot of fun, back when we were kids. But even then she was a handful, made herself pretty miserable sometimes, never knew how to let up on anything even when she wanted to. She made a lot of other people miserable too, I guess."

"You don't have to tell *me* . . . by the way, I'm sorry I let that drop, about you and Daddy. I don't care, you know. I even think it's nice. I only wanted to show off that I knew. Pretty childish of me, don't you think?"

"Doesn't have to be any big secret. Think your dad would like it better if nobody knew for a while, though."

"Oh, I bet he would! I just *bet.* He'd put you in a closet and throw away the key if he could. He'd put you in *jail* if he had to, because that's the way he was with Mother. Hated her to have friends, even women; honestly, he'd go and hide, actually *hide* when people came to visit, even you and Teddy or Julia. I can remember it real well. . . . He'd go running down to the basement and she'd be beside herself, screaming and yelling, 'Come up here, you coward, you worm. . . !' And we only made them worse, Jessie and me. We made her worse.

. . . Oh, it makes me sick thinking about it!" She kind of shook herself all over. "Sorry . . ."

"No, get it off your chest." Guess I'd been staring at her like she was a talking dog or something. I'd never seen her in this kind of a mood. Seemed like everybody was turning nutty on us. There was something she'd said I wanted to get at, though, a real important point I had to make. "I think you're wrong about your dad and me, and him keeping it a secret and all. His problem is he's afraid of people laughing at us, two old codgers getting romantic. . . ."

Even while I was saying that, I was thinking with kind of a jolt that . . . maybe she was right. Took me by surprise. One of those little clicks in your head, and all of a sudden everything looks different, but makes a horrible kind of sense. Vern *was* like that, he was. The idea that he might want to treat me the way he'd treated Anna, keep me all to himself, was flattering as sin, I had to admit. It scared me too. I didn't want to be just another Anna to him. I always liked to think I was different from her, and being different made me proud. I didn't want to be hoarded away, if that was what he'd do with anybody. A crazy kind of logic, but I couldn't help thinking that way.

And then I had an uglier thought. Maybe he'd even be pleased if I turned out to be crippled and couldn't make my own way anymore. I'd be all his then, easy as pie, wouldn't have to ask me for any fool promises. . . . My mind backed up on me again there. It was the first time I'd ever considered he might have had something to do with *that.* Always before, in my head, it'd been his mother, that mean old dinosaur, who'd ruined Anna's life, making her quit flying like that. . . . The minute I had the thought, I felt bad and wanted to erase it. I felt like I'd been real disloyal to Vern, and it'd count somehow against me. Told myself, old girl, you're really losing your marbles now. It's your hands supposed to be going stiff on you, not your brain.

Martha was watching me, biting her lip. I guess my face must've looked funny, and she probably got the wrong idea. "I'm sorry, that wasn't a nice thing to say about my own father. And to you especially. But that's why it's always such a big mistake for me to ever start talking about Mother and Daddy. I get too mean and catty and say stupid things and hurt people. . . . Oh, *damn* it!" She bent down all of a sudden, peering under the desk. "Look at all that dust!"

She flounced off and left me standing there with my mouth hanging open. In a minute she was back, trundling the vacuum behind her, kicking at it when it got stuck on the rug. She'd really worked herself up into a fine boiling temper, poor girl. As she yanked the canister past the sofa Reggie jumped out, fur standing up all down his back. "Get out of here, you horrible animal!" She made a disgusting sort of kid's face and kicked at him. I was about to sneak away before she could kick me too, but she said in a calmer voice, "Are you going to town later? Because if you are you can get me a gallon of milk. Make it two damn gallons." What next?

Vern's head kind of reared up when I asked him about Anna and how she came to let herself be talked into making that promise. I guess you couldn't exactly blame him, since I'd sprung it on him out of the blue after all these years. I'd been trying to soften myself up, just in case, remembering things like my old pal Mattie Moisant and how her family made her stop flying after a couple of bad accidents. If you loved somebody you might not like being scared for them all the time, and with kids it would be a whole lot worse . . . I could see that.

He was sloshing his coffee around and around and it was taking him a long time to answer, but finally he said, "Yes, it was Mom who first suggested it. She thought a woman with children ought to be ready to make a sacrifice." He sneaked a look across at me and then squeezed his eyes shut and screwed up his mouth over his coffee cup. "It was Mom's idea, but . . . uh, I pretty much had to go along with it."

"She never did like Anna, did she? Figured she could scare her off that way, I suppose." He nodded and gulped down some coffee real fast. "I don't get it. What was the point? I'm talking about for you. You knew what it meant to her."

He stared down at the table, playing with the spoon in the saucer. I was forcing myself to do this, to go on asking questions, as if it didn't have anything to do with me. I wasn't taking any pleasure in it. ". . . I couldn't have kept her, just me . . ." he said. "If she was going off all the time . . . she was so pretty . . ." He was practically whispering now. ". . . a way to be sure . . . I wouldn't . . . lose her."

"But supposing you never had any kids? I still don't get it." But I was beginning to. I guess I'd been pretty thick not to figure it out before. He sure didn't want to say what was coming next, so I said it for him. "She already was pregnant, wasn't she? Wasn't she?"

He jerked his head up and down, his eyes closed tight. "I never told

Mom that part. I told . . ." He had to gulp and clear his throat. "I told Anna I couldn't marry her . . . marry anyone Mom didn't give her blessing to . . . no matter what . . . Martha was such a tiny little thing, nobody ever guessed."

All the coffee I'd gulped down was making me queasy myself. "You really had her over a barrel, didn't you?" The truth of this hadn't sunk in yet, even though I could talk so calm and collected, as if I thought it was funny, like some lamebrained prank of Teddy's.

He picked up his cup and his hand was shaking so bad he had to put it right down again. "I . . . I guess that was probably, uh, probably the worst thing I ever did."

"I guess it damn well was. But you remember this: She didn't have to go along with it. A promise like that doesn't count anyway. It's worth . . . *shit.* Besides, she was a grown woman. She had a family that loved her *no matter what.* . . ." I'd heard my voice change in the middle of that, getting harder and meaner. I couldn't keep on trying to be fair to him, trying to see his side of things and all that. Even if Anna wasn't around anymore, Martha and Jessie were around, still suffering for what he'd done to her. But the main thing eating at me was this, a deep-down selfish point: I knew what *I* was going through right now, having to give up doing what I loved more than anything in the world. And I knew what Julia'd gone through twelve years ago. But that was different. Julia and I'd had to accept what happened to us because it was nature, our bodies failing us as bodies always will. But Anna at twenty-four, healthy and strong . . . "Why?" I said. "Why the hell did she ever stick to it?" I was asking myself really.

"I don't *knowww.*" I could see he wanted me to shut up now. He was shaking his head like he had a toothache. "I don't *know.*"

"To spite your mother maybe?"

"To spite *me, me.* For letting it happen to her. It was *me.*"

"Vengeance, you mean?" As soon as I said it I thought it was maybe too grand a word and I was getting a little carried away, but he jumped on it as soon as he heard it.

"Yes. That's exactly what it was. You didn't really know her, how she could be. Like iron . . ."

"No, I still don't see . . . Well, yes, maybe I do." I remembered Anna and Teddy and Cliff having a contest once, hanging upside down by their knees on a branch of one of the old maple trees like three bats, trying to see how long you could hang there. The boys got bored and sore and dropped down after a while, so Anna won easy, but that wasn't enough for her. She wanted to see how long you could do it; winning wasn't the point. So she hung there all afternoon and on into the evening, missing her supper, on into the dead of night. She tried to fight my dad off when he climbed up finally to carry her down. She was stiff as a board, and he had to lay her on the bed sideways with her legs still bent. The doctor said she'd just about killed off some muscles there, gave herself gangrene almost. But she was still mad she'd been pulled down. Wouldn't speak to my dad for a week after. That was Anna all over. Hanging out there twelve hours after Teddy and Cliff gave up. And it was only supposed to be a game. "Yes, maybe I see. . . . Anybody else, no, but Anna . . ."

"Martha's turning out just like her," he said. "A cold woman, hard."

I kept him fixed with my eye. "She's obstinate as a mule. But I wouldn't call her hard. Or cold."

"Yes, she is. And Jessie's like me. She shrivels up and lets bad things happen."

"No . . . no . . . don't think that now." I said it in spite of myself. He looked awful, greenish-white, sick. And I'd done it to him, crushed him right down. No, he'd done it. He wasn't innocent.

"My daughters . . . my pretty daughters . . . I ruined them. I let her ruin them."

I didn't say anything to that. Now I was getting truly disgusted. It seemed to me his daughters were the best things he had to show for himself, even poor Jessie, and it was hardening my heart against him to hear him carry on that way.

We paid for the coffee and walked back down to the store together, not saying much of anything, bundled up to our ears in our heavy winter clothes. It was a raw clear night, the stars coming out real bright already, looking awfully lonely and cold. I couldn't figure out if I'd done what I'd done because it had to be done or destroyed my last affair, the last bit of that kind of love I was ever likely to have, out of pure stubbornness. Anna was dead, after all. It was all in the past. I could have let the sleeping dogs lie. Maybe I was an old fool.

I could tell by the way he was fiddling and fiddling with the lock on the shop door that he wanted me to go away, disappear off the face of the earth for making him suffer the way I could see he was. Sick of the sight of me. Sick of the sight of himself too, maybe. I knew he'd hole up in there, go without dinner, sleep on that ratty old cot without even a blanket on this cold night. He was like some old R.C. saint, the kind who like to get grilled over a slow fire for their sins. He gave me one terrible look and closed the door on me.

I worried at it in my head on the way home. What I'd asked him for was only the truth. But I knew as well as anybody that a lot of awful things had been done in the name of *truth.* No, truth wasn't worth all the suffering. But I guess blood was, when you came right down to it. Anna was my sister, and he'd ruined her, tangled her up in her own nature so tight she couldn't get loose, and that was what seemed so low.

January 29

i

JULIA

Cold air was whistling in across my neck through the slit of open window that could not be closed. Dennis would insist on using his car, heavier in the rear, better traction, etcetera, comfort be damned. I shivered and put my hands into the sleeves of my coat. To think that just over a week ago I'd been sitting on a balcony in the sunshine, preposterous California foliage everywhere. And yet I was rather glad to be home, all things considered.

Of course I could tell everyone had been worried to death about me, out there in the clutches of the ogre Duffy. All the tactful scrutiny. I supposed I had Teddy to thank for it. Actually I hadn't been at all nonplussed by John's behavior. In fact, when he'd absconded with his dreary chiquitas (two fairly depraved-looking Mexican girls, manicurists, I believe. They'd spent the week in Tijuana, in itself a feat. I couldn't bear the place for more than forty-five minutes), I'd been . . . relieved. *Relieved.* Oh, where was the Julia Mott of yore? Evidently become a phlegmatic old person to whom all that rough strife was a deadly bore. However . . . what was it about sex and smoking? Stop for years, forget you ever wanted to do such a silly thing, then presto, you were hooked again. I supposed I'd have to seek out some old party with a cardigan and a pipe. . . .

"I'll give you some more heat," Dennis said. "You got that damn window right on your neck." He took a pair of pliers from the dashboard and delicately adjusted the knobless heat control. Truly a luxury vehicle, this. But a blissful rush of warm air soon was streaming across my feet. "Okay?" He dumped the pliers back on the dashboard.

"Umm. Lovely."

"So you found that kid's body?" he said gloomily, after a long knotty silence.

"Body is not quite the word for what was found. 'Remains' would be more accurate and tasteful, I think."

He made a face. "Christ. Don't tell me about it. That stuff makes me sick." He swept off his blue wool cap and dropped it onto the seat beside him, running his hand through his hair, glaring out at the road ahead.

"You're looking a bit morose these days, Dennis, if you don't mind my saying so. Is anything wrong?"

"What could be wrong?" He rolled down his window to signal a truck, letting in a blast of cold air. The truck groaned by up the grade, and he closed the window again. "Rough day to drive."

"I know how Martha can be sometimes. I love her, but she can be damn difficult."

He shot me a hard look out of the corner of his eye. I'd only offended him. "I got no complaints."

"I don't mean to pump you, dear. But I left in the middle of all that business with Andrew. And I'm always curious about those things, shamefully, I can't help it. I want to know what happened."

A grudging laugh. "Yeah, but nothing happened. I made a big fat mistake."

"I hear he had a gorgeous shiner."

"Jesus, what do you think I am?" he burst out. "Bad enough I hit the guy in the first place. I felt like a shit. Martha thought I was a shit. Still thinks so." He lifted his hands off the wheel in a sudden dismissing gesture. "Look, I don't want to talk about it, okay?"

"Of course, dear. I won't press you."

Another long, prickly silence. Naturally the car had no such thing as a radio. I was dying to hear a news broadcast about the Ryan boy. My left foot was well and truly scorched by now. I took the pliers from the dash and adjusted the heat control for myself, then slid back against the cold window and recrossed my stiff legs. I felt as if I'd been traveling all day, which was not surprising, since I'd left

Moundsville at nine and sat in a stuffy bus all morning and it was now nearly 2:30.

A minute or two later Dennis spoke, all in a rush. "See, when I first met her I thought she was, well, what she looks like, little girl, soft, kind of figured on getting my own way a lot. . . . Took me a while to catch on . . . little girl's hard-nosed as me, worse maybe . . . got to back off . . ."

"Not what you bargained for, hmm?"

He gave me The Look again. "Didn't say that, did I? No, keeps me busy, gotta watch her every minute, give an inch, she'll take a mile . . . no fun if it's easy . . . guess you know what I mean, uh, what I hear . . ."

I gave him a Look of my own. "That was the old me, Dennis. The new me has decided easy things can be quite wonderful. That's middle age for you. But yes, I do, know what you mean." For pure devilment I added, out of the corner of my mouth, ". . . says he likes a woman with *spunk* . . ."

"Look, you started this, Julia, so don't give me a hard time, okay?" He guided the car off the icy road into a truck stop. "I could use some coffee." He squinted out the back window, slung the car at top speed into a tiny space between two huge rigs, let the motor die. Then he sat there, hands stuffed into the pockets of his coat. "Listen, there's this one other little problem . . . see, uh, I think Martha's pregnant . . . not that she'd tell me."

I gaped at him. "No, it can't be." Martha was too careful. "Then how do you know?"

He leaned over to pick up his cap and I could see he was practically blushing, Dennis of all people. "Look, I got two sisters, I mean, and I lived with girls enough, so, I know what's, uh, supposed to happen . . . three months it doesn't . . . not fucking blind."

"She hasn't said anything?"

"Not one goddamn word." He yanked at the door handle, muttering things under his breath. ". . . 'ckin' idiot . . . go and open your big mouth . . ." He slammed out of the car, stalked around in front and flung open my door. Watching him made me grateful not to be his age, for once. All that pain, all that energy . . . But this was indeed a jolt. I'd need time to sort it out. Keeping it to herself for three whole months, that was Martha all over.

* * *

It was warm and stuffy in the diner, the windows befogged, herds of people chattering, coughing, breathing into steaming cups. The tea was wretched, catnip-tasting stuff, but I drank it anyway. "You know, Dennis," I began, "Martha's been through a lot in her life, suffered more than you think. Her sister . . ." But I could tell he wasn't listening. His face was closed up tight, polite and watchful. Of course, now he was sorry he'd squealed. Men.

"Look, I might be wrong," he said, staring past me. "In fact, I probably am."

"Well, just don't think the worst of her."

"Hell, no. Whole thing's her business anyhow, she wants to tell me, she doesn't want to tell me. You going to have anything else?"

"One of those nice apples, I think. I'll take it along in the car. But you mustn't blame yourself for speaking out, if all this has been preying on your mind." I did hope I wasn't going to turn into one of those meddling old women, some dreadful Spring Byington sort of creature, full of heartwarming advice for young lovers. A perverse form of sublimation, no doubt.

He didn't answer right away, leaning back in the booth, eyes narrowed. Then he relented. "Yeah, well, sorry I blew up at you. Mad at myself mostly. I got no right to talk about that. Been on my mind so much. Sometimes I want to grab her, shake her till she tells me what I know anyhow. Don't make sense."

"Why won't she tell you? That part doesn't make sense to me."

"How the hell do I know? Doesn't want a kid, doesn't want *my* kid, doesn't want me around here anymore. I mean, I got no idea. What am I supposed to do, anyhow? Wait for her dad to get out the shotgun? He doesn't even have to, that's the stupid part. Not on my account he doesn't."

"Perhaps you ought to make that clear to her. For what it's worth, I hear she was quite distraught when you went to Michigan in December. She was afraid you'd gone for good. Of course, that's only my sister's version, so . . ."

"I'm sorry, but it's bullshit. She had all my stuff packed up, like she was hoping I wouldn't come back. Now, I know you mean well and everything, Julia, but . . . Let her come and tell me, I'll leave in a minute, that's what she wants. I mean, hell . . . not going down on my knees to beg her, though, one way or the other."

I gave up. I sheerly gave up. "Dennis, please, don't ever let me hear you say that I *mean well* again. You make me feel like an old biddy." I reached for my coat.

The steps down to the parking lot were glassy with ice. I clutched at Dennis' arm for balance. On the third step from the bottom I felt a tremor at my feet. My knees buckled; the bag holding the apple fell out of my hand and rolled away. I sat down suddenly. My face and neck were blazing hot. Flames were crackling somewhere. I looked around me, lifting my head, pulling off my gloves to lay my cold hands against my face. *No. Please, no.*

Dennis leaned over me, touching my shoulder. "Now, how'd you do that? I thought you had ahold of me. You okay?"

"I don't . . . Let me sit for a minute." He went to retrieve the little bag. I hugged my arms against me, watching him. *Dennis. No.* I closed my eyes for a minute. Gray shapes, colored dots moving. But what could I tell him? Nothing. What could I ever tell anybody? I opened my eyes and looked up at him. "Maybe I'm coming down with something. Maybe it's the flu."

"Lot of it going around. Come on. Let's get you home." I felt the coarse wool of his coat brush my cheek as I stood up. It smelled of motor oil, axle grease, one of those garage smells. I swallowed and my throat was sore. Maybe it really was the flu.

February 17

i

ANDREW

I opened the journal and riffled through until I came to some blank pages. I wrote the date and big numbers 1-9-5-3 across the top margin. I was using my old fat green Waterman pen, gift from my mother when I went off to college years ago. I lay the pen down and sat back in the chair, staring out at the pale blue sky behind the white grid of the window frame. I'd moved most of my clothes and things back down to Jessie's room, but I was still keeping my books in here. My old monk's cell. I wanted to write something about Jessie, but I didn't know where to begin. I wanted to write about Anna too. Even though I knew I'd said it all before, somewhere.

Whatever anyone else might think, I could see for myself that, underneath it all, Jessie was no better than she'd been before. Maybe she was even worse. But what did I know? Maybe all she needed was time. I kept on hoping. Nothing else to do. I was in this thing for good, for the duration, for some mysterious expanse of hours and days not yet revealed to me. Karma, kismet; so merciful, those ideas. Everything was *out of your hands.* The moving finger had writ, and you could lie back and give in to whatever it was. I'd never had any trouble doing that, had I? Anna knew. *Anna.*

The thing was, I never asked for what happened with her . . . but I didn't bother to resist either. How could I? She was a terror to me, a woman dying in bitterness, life wasted, body wasting . . . I was her last chance and I knew it. And I could see myself there in her melting flesh and dry bones. Frailty, remorse, awful hunger, terrible ecstasy, everything slipped away at last. She needed and I succumbed. . . . Rationalizing? Maybe. Who knows? Who even cares? My Anna had a power, she did; something burned in her, hot and fierce enough to sear your soul. You could say it ruined my life, or you could say it was the most splendid goddamn thing. . . .

But she exhausted me finally. Guilt began to rise, belated, you'd say, but bitter as bile. Okay, Jessie couldn't know, but that just made it worse for me. Husband and mother, who closer, draining ourselves away from her, leaving her white and empty, shucked clean, and she didn't *know.* That ugliness . . . Then in the end it was she, Anna, who stopped the thing. The last time I came to see her she wouldn't even speak to me. Turned her face to the wall the minute she saw me come through the door. Well, but I was going to be around next week, wasn't I, picking my nose and scratching my ass, next week, next month, next year, while she . . . she hated me for that, and who could blame her? Anna always hated better than she loved. She told me that once, and it was true. That was her finest, fiercest passion. So I kissed that beautiful feverish face, on its mouth, its ear, its closed eyes. I wanted to give her what she wouldn't take. I wanted to woo her, please her, still. But she lay there unmoving, like a woman of stone. I had to leave her like that, almost beginning to hate her back a little. Maybe that was what she wanted from me all along.

I picked up the pen and wrote fast, letting it flow out of my head, down my arm and through the pen. "I am . . ." I wrote. Uh, uh, *I am* . . . what? Close your brain down, tap into the deep well . . . which teacher told me that . . . describe a dream, any dream. Okay. "I am . . . sliding . . . sliding . . . sliding down a long smooth . . . cold slab of . . . stone . . . sliding toward dark water far far below . . . sliding faster and faster . . . but . . . I can keep on sliding forever . . . wind slapping at my face . . . sky and trees and rocks whizzing by . . . so free and yet so helpless . . . dark lake below . . . looming up so close I can see . . . little waves on the oily black surface . . . deep, deep the lake is . . ." The pen stuck on the paper and blotted; my mind went blank. I waited. Nothing. No more signals coming through today. Sorry, kid.

I didn't want to read what I'd written. I could read it later, spring it on myself as a test. I liked to write that way. I picked up the cap to the pen and screwed it on. It made a clean hollow sound, the cap of the pen closing down over the point. I lay the pen carefully across the open book.

I went down to Julia's room. Jessie was sitting beside the bed, her hands neatly folded, a small careful smile on her face. Julia was sitting back against the pillows with a new *Vogue* open across her knees. She looked up as I came in.

"How are you feeling now?" I said, sitting down on the edge of the bed. Jessie pulled my arm around in front of her, plucking at my sleeve.

"Better, thank you, dear." Julia's voice sounded hoarse and actressy from her cold. "Jessie brought me up a nice cup of tea with honey."

"And bourbon," Jessie added. "Alice put in some bourbon."

"No wonder you feel better." I blew gently against Jessie's neck. "Want to come for a walk with me?" She nodded, leaning back against me, hair soft against my chin. "Go and get your coat then." She pushed my arm open like a gate and slid away, gone almost before you saw her move. Julia was studying me across her magazine. She put one hand on my knee, holding it there till I met her eye.

"You look tired, Andrew. I'm worried about you."

"I'm okay." I was tired, though. I'd never been so tired in all my life. I folded my hands and put them down between my thighs. I couldn't think of anything to say. Usually I loved to chat with Julia. Now I couldn't seem to find the energy to put two words together. I'd snap out of it. It was just reaction still, the strain. I smiled at her. I knew she wouldn't push.

"She seems fragile still."

I nodded. "Yes. She is."

"You're good with her, I must say. . . ." She glanced past me and went quiet, still smiling. Jessie was standing there in her green hooded coat with the dogleash snap closings. Her pride and joy. She'd sent away for it from *Seventeen* magazine.

"Where's your coat, Andy?"

"I'm going to get it right now."

* * *

We walked along the road to the airstrip, boots crunching through a thin sheet of ice into brown springlike mud underneath. A crowd of sparrows was gathered in one of the trees beside the road, making a racket, a friendly jumbled sort of noise, a miniature town of birds. We turned off onto the path beside the stream. Off in the distance we could see Dennis pushing one of the old biplanes out of the hangar onto the strip beside the Cub.

"It's the J-3's turn inside," she said. "The Jenny has to come out for a while. That's fair."

"Do you think I should go see if Dennis needs help? You can take your walk by yourself, can't you?" She liked to be gently teased and threatened.

"No. Stay with me." Her hand in its wool mitten slid up under my coat. A tiny gust of cold air crept inside with it, like a little shiver of pleasure from the rough wool moving up and down along my rib cage. It was cold today, but in that mild damp way of late winter. The temperature would drop again later, and there would be biting cold and frost tonight. That was the pattern of these days.

"Maybe we'll see a crocus somewhere," I said. "It's almost time for them, isn't it? Or a jack-in-the-pulpit."

"Too early."

Off to our right the construction machines sat silent, temporarily abandoned in their huge crosshatches of muddy ruts. There was only a thin coating of ice over the stream. The water was moving swiftly along beneath it, breaking through in places, brownish foamy stuff bubbling out free. A sparrow dived down onto the path and hopped along at our feet. Even Jessie's size-five boots were about three times as big as he was, but he strutted along, little smartass, wrapped up in his tiny bird life. He cocked one eye at us, then pecked down at something he found in the mud, some invisible bit of bark or leaf or dead bug.

Jessie pulled a handful of seeds out of her pocket, and suddenly scores of birds flew down around us in a soft flutter of wings and cheeping murmurs. She threw out another handful from the other pocket.

"Where did you get those?"

"I don't know. Had them."

* * *

The birds disappeared in ones, twos, threes, darting back up into the branches. Jessie turned to me, lifting her face, nuzzling it against my chest, her arms around my waist. I leaned back against the tree, slid her hat back so I could stroke her hair, all gilded by the pale winter sun. I could feel the sharp edges of the bark catching in my hair. Jessie shifted against me, pulled her arms away, stuffed her hands down into her pockets, her face gone grim and melancholy all of a sudden.

"What is it?" I said. "Jess . . ." A quick little uproar of cheeping and muttering from the birds at the sound of my voice, but she didn't move or speak. I closed my eyes, letting the slow peaceful minutes pass. I said again, softly, whispering near her forehead and lifting her hair, "Jess . . . are you in there?" She nodded. "Do you want us to go back now? Are you tired?" She nodded again. "All right, then, we'll go." She cowered down, walking huddled inside my arm, hiding her face, cloud across her sun. I could never figure out what set off her sudden glooms, a dozen times a day. They never lasted long. Her wool cap was sliding off her head, all askew. I took it off and stuffed it into my pocket.

The hangars cast long afternoon shadows across the path. Dennis was nowhere in sight, but the biplane and the Cub were still standing together on the strip. Jessie bounced along beside me, sprightly and bumptious, snapped out of her mood. "Let's go this way," she said. "By the airplanes." Our muddy feet left tracks on the gray speckled surface of the runway. She strode over to the Piper and began to unlatch its doors.

"What are you doing, Jessie?" I growled in my ogre voice. "What are you doing over there?"

"I want to see . . . This dumb old thing. We used to have a real nice trainer. That Aeronca. Stupid Martha sold it."

She unlatched the door, and the lower half flopped down with a clang against the side of the little plane. "Do you remember the first time I ever took you up? You were sooo fucking scared." She was on tiptoe, craning her neck to see down into the cockpit. She stuck one arm in, feeling around for something.

"Now, wait a minute. You thought I was *scared*? Just because I turned green and threw up?" In point of fact, I'd done nothing of the kind. I'd been scared all right, for the first two seconds. This ninety-pound teenager at the wheel or the stick or whatever they called it. But then I'd relaxed, and she'd given me a smooth ride, no tricks, no showing off, nonchalant and professional. I was mighty impressed. A crisp fall day it had been. I could still remember how the trees looked, brown and gold and green, sliding under the wing the first time we banked, and my stomach gently lurching, the smell of burning leaves drifting across the strip as we glided down to land. . . .

She came up close to me, grabbing my hands. "We could go for a ride."

"No, not, uh . . . No. You don't really want to, do you?"

"Oh, please Andy." She gave me a quick sharp glance. "You don't believe I can. I know that look on people. Crazy Jess . . . It's stupid."

"Oh, I don't think you're . . ." I did, but what the hell. "I mean, okay, we'll . . . if you . . . if the plane's . . ." What was the matter with me? I was as crazy as she was.

"It's okay, I checked already. Here's the log." She pulled out a flimsy black leather notebook. That was what she'd been looking for inside. "Go on, get in."

I clambered awkwardly up. "I forgot what a bitch it is to get into this thing."

She stood by the propeller watching. "Well, do you remember what to do now?"

"I think so." My voice suddenly sounded very shaky. "Do you? I mean, really?"

"Sure," she said, and laughed.

ii

DENNIS

She left a sandwich sitting in the middle of the table for me. A note on top of the sandwich. "Dennis, here is your lunch." A goddamn note. I wished to Christ she'd lay off me for a while. Leave me a fucking note, needle me a little more.

I ate standing up so I could get back outside fast. Not fast enough, though. Footsteps coming. Before I could make a move she came in, caught me standing there like a goddamn idiot with half a ham sandwich in my hand. She was wearing her old black skirt, stretched real tight across the front. She didn't give a shit. So what if I saw. Just another guy, but this one knocked her up . . . that was the way it was, might as well clear out right now. Yeah, sure. A lot of big talk from you, Hewitt, don't see a whole lot of action.

"You found your lunch all right," she said, like she'd hidden it so good she was surprised.

"Yeah." What the fuck, think it took a genius?

"Don't you want some milk to go with it? You *are* allowed to sit down, you know." She was using that fake nice voice of hers, made me want to smack her. "You're certainly eating late today."

"Got busy."

She came up a little closer, yanked my gloves out of my pocket. "What on earth . . ." Sounded like she was ready to burst out laughing any second.

"You've seen them before." Real old pair of racing gauntlets. Made you look like Captain fucking Marvel. Protected your wrists, though. Good in the cold, too. I pulled them away from her, started putting them on. Something to do. She was making me feel real stupid.

"How fancy. I bet some girl gave them to you back in your show-off days."

"Bought them myself." She knew as well as I did. Just trying to get a rise out of me, but I wasn't going to bite. Got to do better than that, kiddo. She stood there staring at me, no smile, no nothing. Hard to figure out how we'd let things get so bad between us. Plenty left on my side, she'd give me half a chance. But no, not her . . . Something caught at my ear, something I shouldn't've been hearing. I went over to the window to listen better. Yeah. "Who the hell took the J-3 up?"

"How should I know? Alice and Buddy probably."

"Uh-uh. Not today." I went out on the porch and listened a couple more minutes. Shit. I didn't like what I was hearing. Not one damn bit. I went down the steps into the yard. She came out right behind me in only her sweater and skirt. "Get back inside," I told her. The sound of that engine was making me nervous. Course she'd rather freeze to death than do anything sensible if it was me telling her to do it. Alice came around the side of the garage.

"Engine's running pretty rough."

"Don't I know it. That Buddy up there by any chance?"

She shook her head. "Got to be Jessie. I saw her and Andrew go along that way about an hour ago.'

"So did I." I felt something twang in my chest. I didn't want it to be Jessie. Didn't think she was up to flying anything yet. Alice kind of leaned around Martha, gave me a real worried look. Both of us thinking the same thing. Airplane came out over the house again. If it was Jessie, she looked okay, flying straight and level, no problems there, but low, too goddamn low. Made me sick to see her so low with that rough-running engine. But she sure wasn't flying like she thought she was in trouble. And that frigging engine was coughing and spitting like a bandit, getting worse by the second. "Listen to that mother . . ."

Three of us started to walk across the yard, sort of following under the big circle Jessie was flying. "What is *wrong*?" Martha said. She had to kind of run to keep up with Alice and me. "I wish you'd tell me."

"Don't know for sure . . . sounds like she might have some ice in there. Whaddaya think?" Alice said, real careful. Martha was watching and listening so close. Didn't want to scare her. Both of us knew for sure what would happen, Jessie let her carb ice up on her. Keep losing power, engine'd quit, she'd stall and that'd be it, flying so goddamn low. Ought to have her head examined. Oh yeah, real funny. Supposed to be a good pilot before she cracked up. You don't forget that stuff. And Christ, she could put the frigging thing down anytime she pleased.

"Heat control was stuck again the other day. You got it in the log."

"I saw. Shouldn't be sticking now. . . . Why doesn't she bring it in, she's got a problem? Why the fuck doesn't she just . . . ?"

"Maybe she will, now, maybe she will," Alice said. I could see she was trying to stay calm. Airplane roared over our heads another time, couple hundred feet lower. Jesus H. Christ. I was good and scared now. Something bad was going to happen. Feel it in my bones. Hated like hell standing there waiting for it. Sickening goddamn noise . . .

Caught myself, mind playing tricks, a lot of old bad stuff coming up. Jap in the crippled plane, flying low and slow. Bastard rams it right into the stack. Everything blows up, roaring and burning, and I'm laying there all of a sudden, my insides coming out in my hand like big worms, bits and pieces of guys all over the place. Ship goes dead in the water, gives a lurch to starboard, feel it under my back, *finished she is, like me . . . oh Jesus* and I'm crying and trying to move, like a baby . . . oh shit, I could still hear that motherfucker making up his stupid Jap mind, hitting that lousy engine one more time, hear it coming in so low and slow and . . . hold on, now. Hold on. Had to try . . . shove the whole business back down where it belonged. Last thing I needed right now. Last thing I wanted on my mind . . .

Looked down and saw I'd grabbed ahold of Martha. "Listen," I told her. "I don't want you out here right now." I said it nice too. "Do me a favor and go back in the house. . . ." Probably the house wasn't even so safe. Thing could come down anyplace. But the house was a hell of a lot safer than out here. Where I wanted to be, I'd tell you that. Inside something, under the bed, down in a hole. Be okay if I didn't have to see it coming at me.

"Oh, let go of me. . . ." She picked my hand off her like it was some big germ.

Made me so mad, old red curtain came right down. Always like I was blind or something. Grabbed her and spun her around hard. "You goddamn do what I tell you, carrying my kid!" was what came out. Stupid thing to say. Wasn't any invisible kid I was worried about. Order her around, she'd do the fucking other thing to spite you anyway. Didn't I know it? But I was going nuts out there, sitting goddamn duck, waiting for the sky to fall on me. "You hear that?" I gave her a shove. "Go on. Move!" Her eyes flashed up and she opened her mouth to spit something back. Never got the chance. Everything went real quiet. No more engine noise. Another noise, a real horrible slow crunching, loud like thunder, ground shaking under our feet.

Over through the trees I could see the tail of the J-3 sticking up out of the school hangar. A lot of black smoke. I waited for the explosion; didn't come. Wondered if there was half a chance . . . started running like hell.

Hangar door was stuck, warped shut by the heat. Something was burning right by the door. Barrel of gas I kept to soak stuff in. There was already a ton of smoke around and it was hard to see anything. I got the door open just enough to slide through. Airplane was back in the corner, shoved down at a godawful angle. Looked like the engine was rammed into the cockpit, nose all bent up like an accordion. Just that little fire by the door making all that smoke so far. Damn lucky. But gas was leaking and dripping along the wing right over my head. Wouldn't be long. Oh, shit. Jessie was lying all bent up on the floor. Heard goddamn Alice right behind me. Hoped she'd kept Martha back. Shouted at her to take Jessie and get the hell out. Andy was slumped down in the cockpit, alive or dead I couldn't tell. Bottom door was buckled shut, top one torn off like a piece of tin can. A lot of damn gas leaking. Smell it and see it. Last place on earth to be, those tanks blew. Take your pick, blow up with them or fry nice and slow. I started pulling at the bottom door, so hot I couldn't hardly hold it, even with the gloves. Andy six inches away, could've been a mile in the smoke. Flames crawling up the wall toward that weird sticking-up tail, crackling right in my ear. Yanked one more time and the door popped open. Had to shove hard to get it to swing all the way down. Reached in and got my arms around him to pull. "Don't," he said in a high kind of voice, like a shriek. Then I saw how he was pinned, legs all crushed by the engine. No way to get him out of there unless you cut him in half. Kept staring at me, eyes big and wild, didn't say another word. Hand it to the bastard. Me in there, probably be screaming like a banshee. Couldn't make myself look at his legs again. Flashed on me what I had to do.

"Please," he whispered. He kept squirming away from his legs. I was looking around for something, anything. Trying not to see that gas dripping everywhere like crazy rain. Found my big wrench laying over by the wall. Hot when I picked it up. He saw, threw his hands up across his head. Reflex, must've been, because he didn't really fight me. Brought the wrench down hard once, only hit his hands. Blood on them. Felt so damn clumsy. Next time I had to let the wrench sink into his skull. Seemed like everything was happening slow, but it must've been happening fast. His head kind of tipped down onto his chest finally. I hoped to Christ I'd done it. Couldn't hold the wrench anymore. Flames were licking along the floor, trail of gas like a fuse. Had to get out of there fast. Wind was blowing just right, door hadn't caught. Lucky for me. Better believe it. Threw my shoulder against it, didn't fucking budge. Tried again, holding my breath, busted through.

Cold air hit me in the face, cold air burning in my lungs. Running blind in the smoke, heard myself breathing so hard. Braced myself, then it came, knocked me flat on my face in the road. Big roar, flash bright as day. Rest of the airplanes went up, one by one. Blam,

Blam . . . Fourth of goddamn July. Siren screaming in the distance, four blasts, our road.

I got myself back on my feet, came up by the women. Could tell Jessie was dead, head bent sideways like that, neck must be broke. Better off than him, though, Christ. Soon as I quit running, I started shaking all over. Didn't want the women to see. Martha was kneeling by Jessie. Not a mark on her, no blood or anything. She was wearing a green coat with a hood, the hood part all ripped back. "You okay?" Alice said. I nodded. "Andrew . . . ?"

I shook my head was all. Couldn't believe I'd done what I'd done. Didn't want to, more like. Julia was standing out there too all of a sudden. Had a bathrobe on. I was still shaking like a leaf. Saw the pumper truck come in, spin its wheels on a patch of ice, head off down the road, right into the fire, it looked like. A lot of cars rolled in behind it, guys parking every which way on the grass and running back to the fire. One car swerved in and stopped on a dime beside me. I knew the guy, couldn't think of his damn name. "My God, Denny . . ." He was staring past me, at Jessie. "But listen, you got to tell me where your water is."

"Stream back there . . ."

"Not froze up, I hope. Wind's blowing away from the house. Just pray it don't turn." He hit his accelerator and spun off fast to catch the pumper.

I went back to Martha. There was this orange light shining over everything from the fire. It looked real weird. "I have to take Jessie inside." She was talking in a regular everyday voice, but she sounded far away. "Dennis . . . It's all damp here. I don't want her on the ground."

"I know." I pulled her up on her feet and held on to her for a minute. "You go inside. I'll do this."

iii

MARTHA

The four of us sat around the dining room table, Alice and Julia, Dennis and me. Half-empty glasses and coffee cups, plates holding sandwich crusts and crumpled paper napkins littered the table. The volunteers had struggled for hours through the night and into the early morning. At first they thought they might be able to salvage something from the fire, a hangar wall, the barest, blackened shell of a rooftree. But then, around eleven, the wind shifted, and they gave up trying to do anything but put the fire out, before a stray spark could leap to the house. Even so, one of the trees in the row behind the house had caught and gone up like a torch, a flickering crackling head of orange hair.

At about one o'clock it started to snow, soft flakes blowing into the light cast out by the dining room window, and billowing away into the dark. The ambulance had taken Jessie away but would have to come back tomorrow for Andrew because everything was too hot to touch still. My father was upstairs sleeping. Dennis had put Jessie onto the plaid sofa in the den, and my father had sat by her like an old hound dog, throwing himself awkwardly across her feet when they wanted to take her away. Finally the doctor gave him something to calm him down. The doctor wanted to give me something too, but I wouldn't let him. I had to make sandwiches and coffee for all those men who'd been working so hard, fighting the fire, fighting the low water pressure and the cold and the wind and then the snow. I'd seen their shapes like good demons against the terrible yellow light of the fire every time I looked out the kitchen window. Dennis was out there helping, and Buddy and his father and brother came, about half an hour after the other volunteers. Somebody had called them up because they lived too far away to hear the siren.

I didn't know why we should all still be sitting here at whatever ungodly hour it was, except that maybe everybody else felt the same way I did. Once you gave up and went to bed, the next thing would be getting up in the morning and finding out it was all real, everything that happened was real. Right now, sitting at that littered table under the garish overhead light was like the end of a party almost. Or like a dream you had sometime last week, different times and moods and people jumbled together, the point of it all kind of shifting and uncertain. We all looked strange too, distorted, the way even the most familiar people look in dreams.

Aunt Alice had gauze wrapped around her hands where she'd burned herself pulling Jessie out. Dennis had been wearing those silly gloves, of course, so he hadn't been burned. I was sorry now I'd teased him about them before, whenever it was, this afternoon, not that that had anything to do with anything. But I didn't want to start thinking about all those things, wishing I had or hadn't said this, that or the other to Andrew, to my sister . . . I wanted to hold all that off as long as I could. I had to . . . Julia was coughing and blowing her nose every other minute. She was wearing someone's coat over her nightgown and her hair was all awry. Dennis and Alice were smudged and sooty and had had their poor eyelashes singed right off. I'd had to phone my uncle out in Los Angeles. I hated calling people up with bad news. Poor Teddy'd sounded so awful when I told him. "He said he'd be on the first flight he could get tomorrow morning. . . ."

"This morning," Julia said in her croaking voice.

"He'll call from Cleveland or Akron . . . when he gets in."

"I'll drive in, pick him up," Dennis said. We'd had this same identical conversation half a dozen times, it seemed like. Everybody wanted to say the same things over and over again.

Alice kept shaking her head. "Still don't understand . . ." She had just enough of her fingers sticking out of the gauze to hold on to a spoon and stir her coffee. "Can't figure it all out . . . why would she . . . ?" We'd had this conversation before too.

"I saw from upstairs," Julia said. "Engine quit on her. Looked like she was going to bring it in, rolling into a final. She tried to sideslip, and of course she stalled it. Just mushing along by then anyway . . . But why on earth did she wait so long?"

"Shit," Dennis said. "That's what I'd like to know."

"Doesn't figure, doesn't figure at all . . ."

I shut out the voices. I was watching Dennis across the table. For hours, underneath everything else, all the chaos in my mind, I'd been hearing what he said to me right before the accident. I knew I'd have to get it all straight with him, the baby business. I couldn't make myself believe in any of it now. A baby living inside me seemed no more possible than Jessie lying dead on the plaid sofa or Andrew in pieces outside. I willed Dennis to look at me. I was beginning to feel obsessed. I had to talk to him about everything, *right now.* If I didn't, who knows, something else terrible might happen and I'd never get the chance. I couldn't wait a minute longer. But he was staring down at his hands, not receiving my message. The clock struck in the other room, four times, four o'clock. Something clicked against the window, a branch or stone blown there with the snow.

Julia said slowly, "I saw this months ago . . ." She took a Kleenex from the pocket of the coat. "Of course I didn't know what it meant, not until now. . . ."

"What the fuck are you talking about?" Dennis said, very agitated all of a sudden, jarred out of his lethargy. "What did you see?" His voice was as hoarse as Julia's, from breathing so much smoke.

"A sort of building, it was all black and charred, and white, too, that was the snow . . . it was hot and cold at the same time, there was an awful feeling of dying in a not pleasant way . . . really, I don't think it's anything I want to talk about right now. But I imagined for a while it might be you, Dennis . . . I wasn't sure." She added, with a gentle bitter smile, "It didn't do anybody any good, did it?"

"Well, at least . . ." Alice started to say something, then stopped. "I was trying to say at least it was quick, for both of them."

"Yes . . . there's that."

Dennis' coffee cup clattered, and he put his hand down over the top of it to quiet it. "Anybody want anything from the kitchen?" He pushed his chair away and stood up. The three of us shook our heads. "Back in a minute . . ." I couldn't figure out what he was up to.

I picked up some dirty cups and saucers on a tray and followed him into the kitchen. He was sitting there in half-darkness, with only the flickering blue fluorescent stove light on. I put the cups down and leaned over him. "You knew . . . ?" I started right in.

"Knew what? Oh . . . that? Sure." He closed his eyes and slumped back in the chair like an old rag doll. "I mean, sure, after a while I did."

"I probably should have told you."

"Yeah." He didn't even sound angry, just tired to death. I wasn't tired that way; I was jittery and dizzy with extra energy from somewhere.

"I guess I was afraid you'd feel, well, trapped, or something." That wasn't really true. I couldn't begin to explain it to him. What would be the point?

"Not me that feels trapped, is it, Martha?" he said very softly.

I pretended not to hear. "But you don't have to, you know, do anything . . . I can take care of it all myself, I really can."

He cut in on me again, still talking very low. "Don't you get it? I know I don't have to. I want to. I'm happy about it even, so stop worrying. . . ."

I wheeled around, squeezed my hands around the cool enamel edge of the sink. *Happy* about it? Who was he to be *happy* about it? All I could see in the dark window was a reflection of the kitchen, eerie and blue-lit, some luminous evil place, a dreadful cave out of a nightmare, a spaceship adrift in the void. . . . He wrapped his arms around me and dragged me back into his lap. He didn't say a word, hung on to me so tightly I could hardly breathe. I could feel the pulse in his neck, smell the ashy wet smoke in his hair. "Let me go, Dennis." I had to struggle up and peel his arms away. "Please, just let me go."

March 27

i

ALICE

The oil in the pan was sizzling to beat the band, and there I was, holding up a pinky-white chicken leg, all tricked out in a ruffly apron of Martha's, waiting for her to tell me what to do next.

"Go on . . . dip it in the milk, then in the flour, you remember . . . that's fine. Now lay it in the pan. . . ." I picked the gloppy leg out of the flour by its ankle, dropped it into the pan, hot fat spitting out everywhere. That spooked me a little, but Martha kept talking to me patiently, like I was a balky old horse. "Come on now, try another piece. You're doing just fine."

I picked up a wing, slopped on the milk and flour, flipped it into the pan. "Now, you don't want to throw it in like it was a bomb. Just lay it down neatly, like this." Of course there was hardly any of that nasty sizzling from her piece. No glop dripping all over the stove either. I heaved a big sigh and tried again. "See . . . you can do it when you put your mind to it. Now, all you have to do is . . ." She stopped all of a sudden, like she'd forgotten what she wanted to say, forgotten she was even talking to me. Happened to her a lot these days. She'd drift off on you in the middle of a sentence, like she'd gone to sleep with her eyes open. She stood there stock still, arms at her sides, her blue and white stork-printed smock floating up in the breeze from the window over the sink.

More than a breeze was coming through that open window. The cussed sounds were with you all the livelong day, whining saws and drills, pounding hammers, groaning cement mixers. We'd have to wait another month before the trees had enough leaves to blot out the sight of those runty half-built houses and half-paved roads. And blot out the ugly blackened stretch of ground where the other hangars had been, too.

The charred-up mess of rubble from the fire was long gone. Dennis had borrowed Otto's tractor and hauled every stick of it off to the dump. Then he'd built a makeshift shelter for the only airplane we had left, the Jenny that by dumb luck had been sitting out on the strip the day of the accident. Too bad it couldn't have been one of the business airplanes, but not much point moaning about that in the light of the rest. At least I had something with two wings and an engine to give Buddy his lessons in. My last student. But I was pretty resigned to all that now. I'd even managed to bring myself around to feeling lucky it turned out to be a kid like Buddy. Nice way to finish up. But then I'd always been a Pollyanna type, more like my mom than I liked to admit.

I made a little throat-clearing noise to get Martha's attention. She turned around slowly, blinking at me, frowning down at the sizzling pan. ". . . Oh, yes, sorry . . . just finish browning the chicken . . . bake it for an hour or so . . . that's all . . ." Right at that instant the Harley started up in the garage, an earsplitting roar, and she had to shout the rest at me, ". . . bake it at, um, three twenty-five . . ." She was heading off toward the door, planning to leave me to finish up. I wanted her to stay and watch me, like a little kid. It wasn't easy, learning a new job at my age, I could tell you.

"You planning on coming down to Coshocton with us Saturday?" I said, trying to stall her off a while.

"Oh, I don't know . . . it'll be cold at that track."

"Nope. Supposed to be a warm snap . . . Dennis wants you to go."

"Does he?"

"Sure, I can tell he does."

But she'd started edging toward the door again. She looked like a little sailboat, gliding along so slow with her smock billowing out behind her. "Maybe . . . I'll have to see how I feel . . . I'm going upstairs now."

"Wait a minute. What about all this chicken here?"

"Oh, you'll be okay. Put a few potatoes in too. . . ." Her voice trailed away up the stairs.

Nobody had been able to figure out if she was acting the way she was on account of her condition, or because of what had happened to Jessie and Andrew. She'd seemed perfectly okay right afterwards, when the rest of us were still moping around, showing our rough edges, Dennis so jumpy and mean-tempered, Julia extra *nice* which was worse, me so washed out and gloomy I could barely move out of my chair. It seemed like there was such a lot of empty space in the house, especially after Teddy went back to California. But Martha plowed on through the days, same as always. Amazing, people said, her bearing up so well. And she was amazing, too, coping with the houseful that came from all over for the funeral, flying people from the old days, students of Andrew's, Jessie's WASP pals, town folks, neighbors, all of them yammering and crying at her about her sister, so young, so sad, terrible tragedy . . . and she stood in the middle of it like a stone in a stream, like it didn't have anything to do with her at all.

When the house was empty again, she set herself to sorting out all of Andrew and Jessie's stuff, deciding what to keep, what to give away, boxing and labeling it like she was sending it to Alaska instead of up to the attic or out to the Goodwill. But nobody else had the heart to do it. Then as soon as that was finished she started to sort of fade away on us.

Oh, she still cooked the meals, did the laundry, saw to it the dust didn't get too deep on the floor, but she did it all slapdash and lackadaisical, like she didn't take pride anymore. After a while I decided maybe I'd better lift a little of the load off her shoulders. The days had been getting pretty long and empty for me. I was ready for something new. Okay, we hadn't had a whole lot of business before the fire, but there was a big difference between sitting around the house knowing you *might* have a job to do tomorrow and sitting around knowing there wasn't going to be anything much for you to do maybe ever again. So there I was cooking up chicken for dinner like some beat-up version of Betty Crocker, me, who failed Home Ec in high school. Life sure had some strange surprises in store for you.

I finished browning the chicken pieces, though with a few of them you'd have to have said *blacking* them, because I'd get to daydreaming and forget about them. But I just scraped off the burned parts. They said carbon was good for you anyway. The minute I closed the oven on them the racket started up again out in the garage, a smaller motor this time, more of a put-put-putter, somebody's outboard maybe, now that it was getting nice enough to take a boat out on the lake. But the whole garage and half the front yard were always filled these days with sick machines people brought to Dennis to be fixed; cars, motorcycles, power mowers, Gravely tractors, outboards, you name it. And that didn't count the big stuff he worked on out in people's barns, tractors and potato harvesters and combines and corn pickers.

Of course, Dennis had always been what you'd call a hard worker, but since the accident he was almost fanatical, going at it eighteen hours a day. Came inside to eat, sometimes; came inside to sleep. And if Martha was getting bigger and slower and vaguer every day, poor Dennis was sharpening himself right down to the bone, and with such a fine edge to him he'd flare up if you so much as looked at him cross-eyed. Now we all knew something had been wrong between the two of them for a long time. The accident hadn't changed that a bit, though you'd expect a sad time of loss might bring people together. And there was always that other delicate little question in the air: when were they going to . . . well, we did wonder . . . get married? Martha would frown or stare off into space if you brought the subject up to her. And when I screwed up the courage to ask Dennis, he didn't even bother to get mad. He shrugged and said in that flat voice of his, "What do you want me to do? Drag her off or something? Uh-uh . . ."

It sure looked like that's what he was going to have to do, what somebody was going to have to do. I couldn't figure out what she was waiting for, what she wanted from him, or even if she knew, herself, anymore. I recalled how she'd once told me I saw his side too much of the time, so I was keeping my mouth shut. Let them work it out for themselves, if they weren't going to take any advice from me. I did worry about a child coming into the world with that bad label attached to it, *il-le-gi-ti-mate;* then I'd think, whatever it turned out to be, girl or boy, blond like Martha, brown-haired like Dennis or with an auburn mop like a regular Rice, it was doomed from the start to be a pigheaded little individual and wouldn't need my sympathy. Probably the other way around.

I opened the oven to take a peek at the chicken and was surprised to see how nice it looked, brown and crisp and juicy, like something people might really want to eat. Now for the potatoes. I was getting to be a pro at this. I slung the string bag of them up onto the counter and then had to stop and think, how many would I need? That was the kind of stuff that came so hard, at first, remembering to put up two less potatoes for supper, all the other ordinary little signs that kept jumping out at you to remind you two people were gone.

You'd have thought Julia and Teddy and I could be tougher about it than most, since we'd been through it so many times in the old days, losing people in freakish accidents that never should have happened. But with Cliff, with Jimmy, with most of the other kids we'd known, you had to figure they'd gotten what they deserved, not in any bad sense, only because they took their chances clear-eyed. This thing with Jessie was different, a terrible mistake, one Rice disaster you wouldn't find hung on any wall. Couldn't take any of that weird sort of pride in this one. We were never going to know for sure what had happened up there, and it could drive you crazy thinking about it.

I counted out four potatoes, then added an extra one in case Vern decided to put in an appearance. I didn't think he would, but there was always that outside chance. People in town said he was living like a hermit in the back of the store, eating off a loaf of stale bread and a bar of American cheese, drinking milk right out of the carton, or else picking up hamburgers at the new drive-in; not shaving, wearing clothes that looked like he'd slept in them, letting himself go every way he could think of. Everybody was real sympathetic, giving him a lot of respect for taking Jessie's death so hard.

I thought there was more to it than that. I was pretty certain that when I'd pushed him to the wall in January I'd made what he'd done to Anna come real to him for the first time, and it was that, along with Jessie, was making him want to suffer and pine that way. I knew I ought to feel sorry for him, but I couldn't. All my sympathy, all my love for him, sorry to say, had drained away somewhere, and some kind of wall had gone up between past time and now. Not one minute I'd spent with him, out of the whole long four years, seemed real to me, but far away and small like I was looking through the wrong end of a telescope. I'd known way back in January I wasn't ever going to feel the same about him, and I'd only turned out to be right. Now I was shut of him, and I had Anna to thank for it. Left to my own devices I was never any good at cutting loose.

I had one other bone to pick with Vern at the moment, and that was the way he was treating poor Martha. In a way it was almost funny. He and Anna'd been in the same fix as Dennis and Martha once upon a time, and here was Vern snubbing his own daughter in the street, like one of the old biddies. That was about the limit, as far as I was concerned. I dropped that fifth potato right back in the bag.

Before I went up for my two quick ones before dinner, I remembered to poke some holes in the potatoes. The first time I ever made supper I put them in right out of the sack. And then, don't you know, half an hour later, four explosions, baked potato all over the oven. Julia'd pretty nearly choked herself laughing. Nobody else thought it was too funny, me included. Still, it was hard enough to get a smile out of even Julia these days, so I'd let her enjoy herself a little at my expense.

April

i

MARTHA

Hours might drift away from me every day, in a fuzzy sort of daze, like half-sleep, but I still couldn't sleep at night. I lay awake, staring at moonlit ceilings, watching dawns slide over the windowsill and creep slowly across the floor, gazing jealously at Dennis while he slept, or while he dreamed, yes, dreamed. Always the same one, too. I'd crouch over him sometimes waiting for it to start, the way you'd wait for one of those horrible German clocks to strike, the kind with all the dancing mechanical figures. . . .

I didn't want to think about Dennis and his dream. I didn't want to think about the whatchamacallit, the tadpole, kicking and turning inside me. I didn't want to think about any of it, any painful or ugly or frightening thing.

I remembered the little plane circling and circling, the ratchety sound of the engine that made Dennis so frantic, the lurch and shudder as it stalled and fell out of the air like a dead bird. I remembered kneeling beside Jessie, touching her cold cheek, the ground shaking under my knees, flames shooting up to the sky . . . was Dennis in there? No, he was standing right next to me. . . .

First he'd roll over on his back and throw his arms across his face. Then he'd say, "Kill me," or, " Don't kill me," as if the dreaming part of him couldn't make up its mind. He never shouted or thrashed around the way you might expect, which made it worse somehow. It mortified me to think I'd brought him to such a state, begging to be put out of his misery, begging for mercy. *Kill me.* I was his misery. Martha the Bitch. *Don't kill me. . . .*

It rained all the time now, every day, warm rain, cold rain, drizzle, torrent. It was April. One day I took the Shaker rocker out of the closet where I'd hidden it back in December. All that seemed so far away now, comical and ancient. Dennis knocking Andrew down in the school parking lot, me slapping Dennis' face, corny old scenes. He came in and took it as a sign, me sitting in his chair, but I stared him down and his face closed up tight again. Sylvester crept in behind him and crawled under the bed, still searching for Jessie. I heard Dennis clattering down the stairs.

I liked to sit there rocking away the dismal afternoons, watching the rain. Pregnant women always liked to sit in rocking chairs. It was hateful to be typical. At least I didn't have cravings, never sent Dennis off in the middle of the night for adorable snacks, never gave him any of the normal little joys . . . *Oh, look, darling, look, see the baby kick,* no, none of that. By myself I watched my skin stretch and dent in that creepy sort of way. Something angry was inside, a little prisoner wanting out of its cage, like me.

Except for poor Sylvester, there wasn't much of Jessie's left. I'd seen to that, burrowing through her closet and drawers and trunks in a frenzy, like a crazy raccoon. I threw it all out: her ratty old angora sweater; her balding doll Catherinanna; a scrapbook of raggedy pictures cut from magazines—kittens, bowls of flowers, smiling ladies in Bab-O ads; worn-down lipsticks in purplish old-fashioned shades; dried-up corsages nothing but powdery florist's wire now; sexy letters from boys; letters from me when she was in Texas, on that thin wartime paper; tacky cereal box rings; an ID bracelet with a broken clasp; somebody's lighter with an air corps crest. I thew it all out. But I kept Andrew's room like a museum, everything exactly the way he left it, everything except that picture (Jessie and Mother and me a hundred years ago, a horrible thing) because Andrew didn't belong to me. I had no right to rummage through his clothes, his books, his letters and papers and doodles and bills, his mateless cufflinks and all the other odds and ends of his life. There was no one to send it to. Andrew had been all alone in the world. Lucky Andrew.

I didn't want to think about any of it. I tiptoed around in my mind, trying not to shake loose what I knew must be lurking there. I caught flashes of it disappearing around a corner, a twinkle at the edge of my vision, a claw or wild white eye, a sudden blink of terror, blink of memory . . . my mother's face when she was angry, my own face in a gray mirror, Jessie's dead face . . . images breaking apart like shadows in the water. . . .

I brought that picture back here and hid it in my bottom drawer. You'd think it might have made me cry, but no, nothing made me cry. I wanted to smash it to bits instead, break that glass, tear open that face, her face. It was just an old picture, mother and two little girls, mother, no, no mother to me. I wanted to smash her for what she did to Jessie . . . for what she did to me, yes, to me. My heart began to pound, my head began to throb as if it would burst. It was too late. She was dead. I had to stand back, breathe deep, damp the thing like ashes. Grief was what I was supposed to feel, grief, sorrow, remorse, pity, guilt, instead of this . . . whatever it was, this . . . fury.

Last night I actually had a dream of my own (you see, you do sleep, you silly girl). I opened a closet, as long and dim as the back hall. A shaft of light flew in like an arrow, and there, piled against the wall, were dozens of cartons crammed full of Jessie's stuff, all her stuff, the cartons I gave away. There they were. Somebody'd rescued them. Then the light went out and the door closed, and I was standing there alone again.

May 2

i

JULIA

Alice had produced a very tasty egg salad for lunch, along with a cold buttermilk soup, also acceptable. I had to admit it, she was developing the knack. She and Dennis and I were sitting on the front porch afterwards, Alice and I with tall glasses of iced tea and fresh mint (Alice gone overboard), Dennis with a bottle of beer. He'd mown the front lawn that morning, and the smell of cut grass came up across the porch deliciously in the heat. It was a freak day for early May, hazy and sticky as July, a day to lie back in a chair on one's porch and drink iced tea.

Then I heard footsteps and the creak of the screen door. Martha. Alice grimaced faintly at me, the way she might have when we were children caught in some forbidden activity, tasting the gin, putting doll clothes on the cat, a quick glance of apprehension and resignation. One did have to steel oneself to cope with Martha these days.

She sauntered out between us, carrying a glass of milk, yards of cloth fluttering around her fore and aft. Her skin was pink and glowing, her blond hair, longer than usual, curling softly around her ears. Pregnancy became her, in purely physical terms at least. She steadied herself on a porch pillar and lowered herself carefully down on the top step.

"Sit here," Dennis and Alice said at once.

"No, I'm fine." She didn't look at all fine, but no one dared challenge her. She held her head high, like some empress in confinement, disdainful, fastidious, surrounded by imbeciles and upstarts.

Oh, she did make me want to slap her sometimes, baby and all. She took a delicate kittenlike sip at the milk, averted her face.

"Well, so how about it, Mr. Hewitt?" Alice said into the little uncomfortable pocket of silence. "A dollars says anybody but Native Dancer. Two bucks on that whatsitsface, Black Star."

"Don't like to take your money, Alice."

"Is it going to be on television, the Derby?" Martha asked, with faint imperious interest.

"Yeah. Five o'clock." Dennis slowly lifted the bottle of beer and set it on the arm of his chair. One booted foot was propped against the porch railing so he could teeter his chair back and forth, watching Martha through his knees. Three fingers on his right hand were immobilized by tongue-depressor casts, which was why he was free to while away a Saturday afternoon with us. Motorcycle mayhem was not responsible for this injury, but a paltry accident in the garage, a can of spackle falling off a shelf onto his hand. We'd all been enormously relieved this morning when he'd discovered the lawnmower and a task he could perform with one hand. Poor Dennis was not one to take kindly to idleness, a grave flaw in his character. I pitied them, all those puritan strugglers, my mother, Anna, Alice, the Martha of old, who couldn't bear to be deprived of their toil. I adored being deprived of toil myself. But no, what had I been like thirteen years ago? Furious, a fly in a bottle . . . until I got used to it. . . .

A battered pickup roared into sight around the curve in the road and stopped with a screech and rattle at our mailbox. Young Buddy leaned out, collected the mail, then swung the truck in next to an old green Hudson parked there waiting for Dennis' professional attention. "Well, hi, Buddy," Martha called out to him, quite pleasantly. Of course, he was not a member of her wicked and obtuse family. "You look all excited."

"Yeah, I guess I am." He smiled hugely at her, blushed and sat down a step below her. Buddy had a bit of a crush on Martha these days. He handed her the stack of mail, which she immediately passed to me over her shoulder without giving it a single glance.

I began sorting through and handing out. A letter addressed to Dennis in a semiliterate scrawl from an APO box. A sale catalog from the Western Auto store in Dover, also to Dennis. *The New Republic,* that commie rag, for me. Postcard from the library for Martha; her reserve book was in. A card for all of us from Teddy. My heart jumped, just a fraction, for there under Teddy's signature was a sentence in Duffy's bold hand. I passed the card to Alice. Next, a long white envelope from the insurance compay. I held it in my hand for a moment, debating, then leaned forward, tapped it lightly against Martha's shoulder. "You really should be the one to open this, dear."

As soon as she saw what it was, she drew her shoulder delicately away. "No, I don't want to."

"All right, but it's not . . . it's only money, you know . . . I hope." I slit open the evelope quickly. They were all watching me, even Martha. "How much?" Alice piped up. I held the check by its corners and passed it slowly across her face. "My God," she said, and grinned. It was, indeed, quite a sum. I flashed it over at Dennis. He whistled.

"With that kind of money we could all go off to Tahiti for a year. Wear sarongs." Imagine Alice in a sarong, I ask you. "Watch the volcanoes, swim, eat fish, that's the life."

"Too boring. All those hot places are. Not for men, I suppose, brown-skin girls and so on. But essentially boring. Somewhere else, though, where?"

"Alaska. Up in the Yukon."

"Ugh. That's even worse. Really, Dennis, you can do better than that." I was trying to decide where my own fantasy would take me. What fabulous place, of all the fabulous places in the whole world? A gentle memory passed slowly through my brain, unaccompanied by grief or horror; Andrew whispering, a droll aside, "Gee, how about Luray Caverns . . . or Keansburg . . . maybe Cedar Point . . . ?" His guide to third-rate resorts. I did miss him, poor boy. I said, out loud, "For me, the Hungarian plain. Dashing fierce men in high boots riding little shaggy ponies, zithers, slivovitz . . ."

Martha had managed to heave herself to her feet, her face twisted with effort and distress. "How can . . . oh, you all . . . I can't bear it . . . I'm going upstairs." She was shaking her head in disapproval, moving her arms briskly, as if she were swimming away from trash in the water. Dennis reached out instinctively, as if to stop her, and she knocked quite sharply against his damaged hand, paddled grandly on.

"Shit." He yanked the hand back in and held it against his chest.

"She didn't mean to, Denny," Buddy said owlishly, man to man. "She'll come around anyhow, I know she will."

Dennis gave him a baleful stare. "Why don't you keep that mouth of yours shut when you don't know what you're talking about, *little boy.*"

"I believe she will, that's all," Buddy replied, with commendable dignity. "You don't understand her. . . . Martha is a fine woman." He blushed again, and turned to Alice. "What I came over for in the first place was to tell you some good news. Well, sort of good news."

"And what might that be? I could use some *sort of* good news."

"I told my dad about the lessons. More like, he found out."

Dennis laughed. "Went and took the hide right off you, I bet. What my dad would've done, caught me fooling him."

Buddy lifted his chin, ignoring this. "See, I always told him I came over here to help Denny and stuff, but I left out the lessons part. That really burned him up, me telling him only half the story kind of, but once we finished with that . . ."

Dennis unbent one leg and nudged at Buddy's shoulder with the toe of his boot. "What'd he say about the lessons, huh?"

Buddy shot him a rather small cool smile. "He said it was my money and he didn't want to tell me how to spend it. He said he'd be coming over to talk to you sometime, Miz Rice, see if I'm as good as I told him I was."

"Sounds like a pretty fair man. Well, I'll sure tell him. Come on, now, let me get my jacket and we'll go out back. Ought to be able to knock off a couple of hours today. Every little bit helps." She went inside, and we could hear her rummaging around in the closet by the door.

"Well, Buddy," I said. "What do *you* think we should do with all this money?"

"Buy a new airplane," he replied at once. "That's what. Then I'll fly it for ya. Won't take me long to put together my two hundred hours. Wait and see."

"What will your father say to that?"

"I can still be a farmer, and a flier too. Why not?"

Alice came out, shrugging into her flying jacket. "Why not is right. Well, come on, Smilin' Jack, I'm strictly a passenger today."

The two of them went off together around the house. Buddy had eked out another inch in the past few months and now was almost as tall as Alice. They both walked the same way, too, an officious half swagger, listing to port.

* * *

Dennis said, "I shouldn't've blown up at him. Not his fault."

"You're quite right." He was still nervously rocking his chair back and forth on its rear legs. "What do you think, though? Was it tacky for us to talk about this money the way we did? Martha obviously thinks so."

"I don't know what's eating her, I really don't. Thought it was me for a while. Thought it was the kid. Now I don't know. The money? Like you said, that's all it is. Difference does it make? Shit . . ." The chair teetered back, balanced precariously, slapped down. He was frowning out across the lawn, his face gloomy and preoccupied.

I said cautiously, not particularly wishing to have my head bitten off the way Buddy's had been, "You know, for what it's worth, I think the child may be right. She may very well come around . . . but whether she'll ever actually *marry,* you or anybody . . . she seems to be blocked entirely on that subject. For good reason, I might add."

"Look, don't even say that to me, maybe she won't. That I don't want to hear."

"Does it matter so much to you, making it legal? I mean, *really,* Dennis."

"Don't give a flying fuck about legal. But, uh, she won't, I'd be hanging around is all. You see what I mean? Besides, I want my kid to have my name, that so terrible?"

I took a deep breath, hoped steam was not shooting from my ears. "It is her child too, I believe."

He turned to me wide-eyed. "I ever say it wasn't?" He had the baffled air of an embattled but perfectly reasonable man, which I supposed, up to a point, he was. I had to admit he was right about Martha. If she couldn't bring herself to marry him, it wouldn't do at all for him to stay on.

"What will happen then, if . . ."

The chair clattered down again. "Told you. Don't even want to think about that. I can't . . . got to wait it out." He sighed, ran his hand through his hair, leaned his arms down on the railing, turned his wrist to check his watch, kicked at the pillar. "Don't know what fucking else I can do," he said finally, and jerked himself upright in the chair. I watched him amble out across the lawn and lift the hood of the Hudson. He stared thoughtfully down into its innards, touching things experimentally with his left hand.

* * *

On the front of the postcard was a picture of Graumann's Chinese Theatre. Teddy, or someone, had drawn in several extra sets of footprints, big and small, with numerous extra toes. I ran my fingertip across the deeply indented letters made by Duffy's heavy hand and pen. All he'd written was, "Love to you, D." The card was addressed "Rice Family."

I remembered now, sitting there, Duffy crying when he got off the airplane for Jessie's funeral, crying throughout the service and the wake. He had no shame that way, one of the things I'd always adored about him. He cried in the movies, the way women did, the way women were supposed to. He cried at weddings, funerals, graduations. He cried when he saw a dead dog in the road. He cried when we parted and he cried when we got back together again. The man was miraculous, a human flood. And then the whole catalog of other ready excesses, mighty blasts of rage, roars of pleasure, laughter that fairly shook the earth. Every single emotion enormous, right up on the surface, the next moment all of it blown away and forgotten. That I hadn't adored a bit. He always lost track of what we'd said or done one day, so we'd have to say it or do it all over again the next. Constant evaporation, ropes of sand, driving me mad. Living with him was like living in a vacuum, in the eye of a hurricane, on a mountain, an island. I couldn't stand it then, couldn't stand it now. . . . Sad, really.

But still . . . there we'd been, the two of us, sneaking out after Jessie's wake, parking like two teenagers behind the Monument, clutching at each other, performing the usual ridiculous gyrations. And me now, mooning like a Brontë heroine over a piece of cardboard with three words scrawled on it. *Peace,* I'd decided. And *Peace* it would be. Nevertheless . . . what I really needed was some utopian system, a week in space with Duffy, three weeks off, another week with Duffy, and so on and so on. I tapped the postcard against my chin, looking at the dowdy familiar objects around me, the poky old porch with its peeling paint, tired green wicker chairs, creaking steps. Up on the ceiling among the gray wasps' nests, caught on a nail, a faded scrap of Cliff's checkered shirt, tossed up by Teddy some forty years ago, ancient prank. Scraps of my life, my kin, all around. I squinted out across the brown fields and hills with their new dabs of green, and up into the bland May sky. I knew I couldn't face California again. Podiatrists dressed like movie producers. Tans. Houses perched over canyons. Chose not to, rather. Not even for Duffy.

Above my head I heard the clackety motor of the Jenny and saw its cruciform shadow loom suddenly across the lawn. Dennis shaded his eyes and peered into the sky. Buddy dipped one wing at him and soared up gracefully in a steep climbing bank, racket of the engine diminishing along with the airplane over the fields. Dennis caught me watching him and smiled. "Smartass kid." He brought the hood of the Hudson gently down with his good hand. I stuffed the postcard back where I'd found it, in a slot of wicker under Alice's chair.

May 23

1

MARTHA

A light breeze came through the window and the rocker started moving by itself the way it had back in October, in the tent in Millersburg, the very day I got pregnant, *maybe.* Oh, there was a system all right, that perfect twenty-eight-day thing with the five danger days in the middle, ha, ha, ha, but it was mostly theoretical, no matter what those little pamphlets about *Becoming a Woman* said. Dr. Bodenweber told me the same thing Aunt Julia's doctor told me when I was twenty; might as well wear your damn diaphragm every minute until you were fifty. At least, if you were, uh, liked to be, uh, well . . . He was so embarrassed I had to help him out. ". . . spontaneous, you mean?" He'd been very nice to me even though everybody in town knew I wasn't married yet, and he wasn't even the right kind of doctor. I didn't have the energy to look for anybody else.

I was pushing people's tolerance of Rice eccentricity to the limits, of course, but there hadn't been a really juicy scandal around town for quite a while, so I figured in the long run they'd be grateful to me. I was providing so much nice gossip, along with a nice clear moral lesson to use when they lectured their daughters on the wages of sin and pleasure.

I could see the toll it was taking on poor Dennis, though. I mean, he'd never been exactly what you'd call clumsy, and now not a day went by when he didn't drop a can of whatsit and break his silly hand, poke himself in the eye with his screwdriver, cut his thumb to the bone on a new razor blade. And he hadn't been to a race in weeks.

(He'd told me once how stupid a guy had to be, take a bike on a track, only half his mind on his business, a goddamn menace.) I was grateful to him for that at least, for not plowing through the dust like a madman every Saturday, trying to get himself crippled or killed to make me feel more guilty than I did already.

I knew I was being unfair, to him, to everybody, but I'd gotten used to that, the way I'd gotten used to sleeping all afternoon, eating food I'd never seen before the instant it was served, being treated like a lunatic by my entire family, what was left of it. I was a puzzle and a burden to them all. I was a puzzle and a burden to myself. Yes, I caught them at it, exchanging glances behind my back, rolling their eyes, shaking their heads, mouthing things at me so carefully and tactfully, in case I might have a tantrum or a fit or something.

And of course what they wanted me to do was only the most natural and reasonable thing in the world to do. What harm would there be for the poor little tyke to have an official male parent, after all? I could go into town with a ring on my finger and nobody staring pruny-faced at my big stomach or, later on, at the little bastard thing. My father might even speak kindly to me again . . . Then my palms would begin to sweat at the thought of those awful words, *till death . . . I promise . . . I do. . . .*

It wasn't Dennis I was afraid of. It wasn't the child. It was everything. I was merely following a sensible animal instinct, eluding the clang of some heavy cage door, the soft tangle of some sinister net across my shoulders, the end of whatever I knew about myself . . . . I kept hoping for a single perfect moment to arrive, when I'd know exactly what to do, when it would all simply fall into place by magic, without a flicker of conscious thought. If I did think about it too much, I got scared the way I did when I looked out the window of a tall building, the same sudden, dizzy, sinking, suffocating panic, as if I might fly out screaming, sucked into hideous space. . . . I had to close my eyes, hold my breath until I could get down to safe calm earth again.

I heard footsteps in the hall and lay back pretending to be asleep, my eyes opened the merest crack. Dennis tiptoed across the room and carefully opened his top drawer, peering around behind him like a burglar. Then he crept over to the bed and opened the drawer in the bedside table, stealthily rummaged in there for a minute, stood up again, rubbing the back of his neck. I let my eyes droop slowly open. "Dennis . . . ?"

He gave a start. "Jesus. I thought you were asleep."

"I was, but that's okay. What are you looking for?"

"I can look for it later. Go back to sleep." He moved away.

"No . . . Dennis, stay a minute. Talk to me."

He sat down gingerly on the edge of the bed. "Talk about what?" He kept his eyes fixed on the wall behind me. His voice had that sullen edge to it, his polite *fuck you* voice.

But I was going to be the soul of patience, calm and mature, ready to make amends. "You must be uncomfortable sitting there all twisted around like that. Why don't you lie down for a minute? I can't sit up, so why don't you lie down? You look tired anyway." I smiled at him. It had been such a long time since we'd done anything but sleep in that bed, even a smile seemed like some luscious outrage. "What are you up to today? Start with that."

"I been working on your dad's car."

"Daddy was here today? And he didn't even come up."

"He left it last week. Haven't seen him since."

"Did he say anything . . . about . . . you know?" My father took Dennis aside every chance he got to grill him about when we were going to . . . *set the date.* Those were the only words he could bring himself to use to cover the situation, *set the date.* That made me want to laugh and laugh, but Dennis didn't find it one bit funny. The way he saw things, I was humiliating him, grinding his honor in the dust, shaming him in the eyes of other men, even miserable specimens like my father.

"Uh-uh. Didn't give him the chance." He made a bored face at the ceiling, cast an obvious look at the clock, shifted his legs impatiently. *All right for you, Dennis.* I wanted to be good, but I could only take so much, after all. I said softly, as a gust of wind floated in across the bed and made the rocker move again in its ghostly way, "Oh, look at the chair, just like that day, remember?"

"What day? Oh. Yeah," he said, so curt and disdainful I couldn't bear it, not one more second. *All right for you.*

I glared down at him. "Why don't you tell me about those stupid dreams you pretend to have all the time? You're not fooling me a bit, you know. Very, very childish."

"What the hell are you talking about?" He tried to sit up again, but I shoved him back down. I had a lot of leverage these days, like a walrus.

"I know how horrible I am, how horrible it must be . . ."

"Wait a minute . . . you're crazy, what dream?"

". . . living with me. I know how . . . awful . . . I mean, I know . . ." I stopped suddenly, gagging. I was going to choke. I hadn't planned this part. I was going to explode. ". . . kill me, kill me . . . you said . . . I'm not that bad, I'm not . . ." I hugged my arms around myself, holding me tight, rocking back and forth. A noise started coming out of me, hurting my throat, an ugly animal noise tearing, ripping loose. I crouched sideways, butting at him, thumping my head against his chest, howling and choking and gurgling. He put up his arms, trying to fend me off. "Cut it out, Martha, Jesus . . ." He sounded scared silly. Well, so was I. One of his shirt buttons nicked my eyelid, a key in his pocket scraped my cheek. But I couldn't stop. "Don't . . . don't hurt yourself . . ." He finally got a grip on me, seized me in some rigid necklock so I couldn't move. I went limp against him, gasping in air like a runner, aflow with tears and mucus, melting, dripping, floating on myself, the sea of Martha, I'd drown us both.

Everything hurt, my chest, my throat, my nose, and my eyes were practically stuck shut, but I felt wonderful, clean and empty, embarrassed in a luxurious, almost sexual way, as if I'd done something wicked and exquisite to surprise myself. Dennis' shirt was damp against my face. When I raised my head I saw he was asleep, his face flopped over on his pillow, peaceful and remote. I'd actually put him to sleep. I lifted my heavy head up to the other pillow and fell quickly asleep myself.

When I woke up he was lying on his side watching me. "You feel better?" No I did not feel better. Now I felt only mortified at the spectacle I'd made of myself. And I had a headache. The bitch was back. He tried again, his voice tentative and courteous, "You had me worried there. . . ."

I turned my head away, gazed out the window at the patterns of dark leaves, the patches of blue sky. "Worried? Well, I *am* sorry."

"Now *look* . . ." Trust him to rise, or sink, to the occasion. His hand flashed out and clamped tightly around my chin, swiveling it around toward him. "You can talk to me now, lady."

"I can't very well, with you squeezing my face like that."

He slid his hand up across my ear and left it there, heavy against the side of my head. "Okay, but I mean it, Martha. Don't want any more of this shit."

I opened my mouth to say something else fresh, but his face was about two inches away, and his eyes were fixed on mine, very perplexed and weary. I could see he was fed up this time, and I knew he had a right to be. I lowered my eyes. "It's . . . you see how I am . . . and I'll be worse . . . I'll turn into a monster. You'll end up despising me, wait and see. . . ."

"I couldn't despise you. Not you."

"I might make you."

He sighed deeply. "Well, shit, okay, means that much to you. You going to spend the rest of your life trying?" He was moving his thumb absentmindedly along the edge of my ear. "Being stupid, Martha. You know that."

"No. I'm being smart, and you ought to listen to me."

"Christ . . ." He let his head slide down along his arm and closed his eyes. He stayed that way, without moving or speaking, for minute after minute, but I could tell from the angle of his head and the line of his mouth that he wasn't about to fall asleep on me this time.

"What are you thinking about now? I can tell it's not me anymore. I'm sure I'm too boring to keep on your mind for very long." I nudged at him with my shoulder.

He rolled over onto his back and opened his eyes. His face had a wary unhappy look. "I was thinking about what you said before, that, uh, dream. Were you serious?"

"You think I made it up just to get at you?"

"No, come on. But . . . hell, I hate the idea, saying things I can't remember. It's like Julia's stuff, gives me the creeps."

"Well, I can't help it, that's what you said. A lot of times, too. I felt so guilty. . . ."

"Yeah, but it wasn't even about you, that's the thing."

"What was it about then?"

"Must've been . . . Doesn't matter. Not about you, though."

All of a sudden my mind tuned back like a radio to the night after the accident, Alice's voice saying *quick at least,* the clatter of Dennis' cup. I did know him so well by now. "Something about Andrew, isn't it?"

His head jerked up. "Jesus Christ. How did you . . . ?"

"I didn't. It just flew into my head. What about him? You'd better tell me."

He heaved himself around, leaning on one elbow, plucking at the tufts in the bedspread as if they were little weeds. At first I thought he wasn't going to answer. Then he said slowly, "Look, I don't want to go into it. No point . . . over and done with."

"Dennis, I'll go crazy not knowing."

"May be sorry you. . . ." He stopped again, and looked up at me with an odd stiff smile. "Kind of hard to talk about."

"Is it something that awful?"

"Yeah . . . no, I mean I don't know what you'd call it . . . see, there wasn't, uh . . . it could've been so slow, Christ, the worst way, and he wanted me to, he really did . . . poor bastard was pinned in there so bad . . ."

Gradually it dawned on me what he was trying to tell me. My hands began to shake with horror, and an awful wave of selfish relief washed over me. I saw it all so vividly in my mind, the two of them alone and desperate in that fiery place, no options for Andrew, dying one terrible way or another; no options at all for Dennis if the time ran out. "But, Den, he would have suffered so. It was brave to do what you did. You had to . . ." I wasn't going to ask him *how,* but I wanted to know, a sudden bald rush of curiosity and shame. "You had to," I said again, leaning closer, watching him. He was still picking at the bedspread, his face averted.

"Meant to put it out of my mind for good."

"I don't see how you could."

"Maybe not," he said, opening and closing his hand on the spread. "You know, I was thinking the whole time, glad it's him, not me . . . what the fuck, nice guy, huh?"

"I was thinking the same thing, but . . . well, that doesn't mean . . ."

"Sure . . . *sure.*" He made a face. "Normal, right? Got that all worked out . . . still, as soon, uh, you know, forget about it . . ."

"Poor Andrew . . . poor Dennis . . ."

He muttered something I couldn't quite hear. Darkness had crept in quickly as we talked, the way it always did at this hour, even in summer. The room faced north, and once the sun passed over the house the light faded very fast. The birds were begining to bustle and flutter along the eaves, settling down for evening. I couldn't tell if he'd fallen asleep again or not. "It must be almost time for dinner." I blew across his face. His eyelids twitched, but he didn't say anything, wouldn't give anything away. He was waiting for me to do that part, of course. "I'm kind of . . . I mean, there's time . . . we could . . . Den? . . . no, you don't want to, I can tell . . ."

"Don't want to what? Oh . . . nah, gave it up." But in a minute he rolled off the bed and I heard the rustle of his clothes, the clatter of his boots one after the other, the thunk of his heavy belt hitting the floor. The bed shook again as he knelt beside me. He started to unbutton the stork smock, working fast with his big fingers, folding it back, peeling me like a huge banana while I braced myself against his warm bony white flank. ". . . hate this thing . . ." He threw the smock on the floor, half-mumbling to himself like a crazy man. ". . . been so long . . . bet I forgot what you look like . . . Jesus, they got even bigger . . ." His head disappeared behind my pale mountain of stomach and I felt his tongue slipping neatly inside me, finding the center right away, sucking hard. Before I could begin to be surprised, he had me, breath sliding right out of me, head pressed back into the pillow, held there by a mighty force like gravity, so I looked like one of those jet pilots in the newsreels probably, face all stretched and stripped. I couldn't breathe. "Too much . . . too much . . . I can't . . ."

But he kept at me till I flopped loose, shuddered and lay still like the murder victim. I pulled on his hair and he started kissing all along the vast tight drum of skin. That was the main obstacle now, not any plaster contraption attached to him, just my grotesquely swollen inflated self. He kissed my vast pooling breasts, my face, my hair, my eyes my mouth my ears, oh every crease and lobe and hollow, so intent and hungry, just picking my carcass clean. I squirmed under him, preening, nipping at his shoulders, licking his chin, whispering mean little things in his ear. "Thought you didn't like to do that, put your mouth there . . ." He didn't answer and I knew the truth. I could still taste my stickiness on him. Just showing off, he'd been, giving me a special treat, holding back all this time. I let my hand drift down his smooth concave belly, past the ridge of scar. And there he was, hard as anything, poor man, right there trembling in my hand. I felt his whole long body quiver against me the minute I touched him. I was stroking him gently with my thumb, meaning no harm, and he went all slack at first, then was struggling up, wanting to climb on and do it that way no matter how big I was, but I elbowed him down, walrus leverage again. ". . . no . . . just let me . . . I want to be nice to you for a change . . ." He lay back, watching me through his slit eyes, gripping my arm hard. "Well, be careful with that thing . . . ah Christ . . . nice to me, she says . . ."

By the time we were finished, went to sleep for a while, woke up, got dressed and came downstairs, it was very late. Alice and Julia were sitting in the den eating ice cream and watching *Your Show of Shows.* Alice naturally had to wink at Dennis in a way that fairly curdled my blood, but at least she'd thought to put our dinner over hot water on the stove. We sat down at the kitchen table with our plates, ravenous. It was my good old chicken and mushroom casserole that I'd shown Alice how to make, months ago. No, I stopped to think, not all that long, not even two months, six weeks maybe. But I felt as if I'd been locked away in a time machine, coming out blinking and surprised and grateful for every silly little normal thing. What a mess the kitchen was. Someone had left the peanut butter out on the windowsill next to a crusty box of laundry soap.

"Old Alice makes this a lot," Dennis said, digging in. He glanced over at me, deadpan. "Like yours better." He wasn't a complete fool.

Halfway through eating I had to stop, swallow, put down my fork, panic setting in again. "Do you really want to do this thing?" I said very quietly, almost hoping he wouldn't hear.

He heard all right and rounded on me, pushed beyond all limits. "You know real well what I want, but there's no damn gun stuck in your back, so decide what the hell *you* want and let me know sometime, okay?"

"Now, don't start up again." I put my hand on his arm. "I was just sort of asking. I really have decided. We could even do it tomorrow. Oh, no, wait, that's Sunday. Monday, but that's the holiday."

"You can do it any damn day."

"Oh, good. Monday then, I guess."

June 12 and 13

i

JULIA

Finally I called an old friend of mine in Columbus, an urbane and civilized man, and he agreed to perform the ceremony. That seemed a more discreet procedure at this stage than enlisting the services of some benighted local minister. I'd also called Teddy and told him to make a reservation and to come *no matter what.* If Martha knew he'd committed himself to the trip she'd be less likely to back out again. I hoped. I didn't intend to coerce the poor girl, but it did seem clear to me, to all of us, by now, that she wanted to be married far more than she wanted not to be married. Dennis had almost managed to spirit her away to a justice of the peace on Memorial Day, but at the last minute she'd reneged—holiday traffic, a seedy office with a wife in curlers as witness, some dubiously official notary public cum veterinarian. But now, a U.S district court judge and her uncle flying in I hoped would do the trick.

Alice and I sat on the front porch Friday evening waiting for the station wagon to return from the Canton airport bearing Dennis and Teddy. Martha had fallen asleep in the big chair in the den, much to our relief. We were, both of us, drinking stiff bourbons and soda. "Did Vern actually promise he'd come tomorrow?"

"He said he'd see."

"That means he won't, I suppose. Really, I'm disappointed in him. I never thought he'd be so hard on Martha."

"Well . . ." she said. "It may not be that. Maybe he's harking back some."

"To his own unfortunate *splicing,* you mean?"

"Could be."

"But Martha's all he has left. And he seems to like Dennis as much as he likes anybody. And besides, people always forget these things after a while, these, quote, scandals. . . ."

"Well . . ." she said again, softly. "You know, he's an odd duck, Vern."

"Umm, yes, I suppose so . . . by the way, did Teddy say anything *odd* when you talked to him yesterday?"

"Now you mention it, yes, he did. Something about an 'appropriate surprise.' Maybe he hired that blimp with the flashing lights. You know Teddy."

"Yes, that's what I'm afraid of. 'Good Luck Dennis and Martha' written in orange smoke, some dreadful thing."

"Want another shot in there?" The fingernails on the hand pouring the Jack Daniel's were extremely grubby. Now that Martha had recaptured the kitchen, Alice had taken to the outdoors. Even as we spoke, a pile of seed catalogs sprawled across her lap and a slight aroma of fertilizer clung to her boots. She was planning to grow vegetables and flowers in the backyard and sell them at a roadside stand Dennis had promised to build for her.

"Alice, those nails are truly a disgrace. You do have pretty hands, you know, if you'd take care of them."

"Can't be helped," she said briskly. "Just good brown earth, nothing to be ashamed of, plus a little manure, maybe. . . ."

"Oh, *please,* do spare me the details."

We heard a car coming about a mile down the road. Alice squinted off into the murky purplish twilight. A light mist had fallen already, sinking into the hollows of the rolling fields across the road.

"Is that them?"

"Yup, looks like it." The station wagon swerved into sight through the mist, swung around onto the driveway. Alice and I walked together across the damp grass, and she whispered, "There's three people in that car. The extra one's a *woman.*"

"Do you suppose that's the surprise?"

"Lord knows what."

Teddy sprang out of the car, kissed us one by one, then leaped skittishly away. Dennis was leaning on his half-open door, watching what happened next with a sly grin on his face. Teddy opened the back door with a flourish, and a woman climbed awkwardly out. She was small, dark-haired, younger than we, but surely no less than forty, and . . . nearly as massively pregnant as Martha. Suddenly I remembered—yes, I'd seen her with Teddy in a restaurant in L.A. at Christmastime. "Why, hello, uh . . ." I cast about for her name.

"This is Marion," Teddy said. "My, um, wife . . ."

"Your *what*?" Alice started to laugh, a truly dreadful cackle. Before I could myself come up with a precisely suitable phrase, if there were such a thing, Teddy said, "We were married last week, in Laguna Beach. Duffy stood up for us."

Alice continued to chuckle and giggle, nearly beside herself. "Looks like nobody in this family'll ever get married till they absolutely have to. . . ." she choked out, wiping away tears.

"Except me," I shot back out of the corner of my mouth. I had *not* been pregnant when I got married. I was far too efficient for that, but I wondered what Alice had ferreted out about Vern and Anna that she wasn't telling. . . . I leaned forward and kissed Marion's tan cheek. "Sorry about this hilarity. Please do come in, and be welcome. When you see my niece, who is to be married tomorrow, I think you'll understand our . . . amusement." At least I hoped she would. If she didn't, she was going to be in trouble anyway.

Teddy looked extraordinarily pleased with himself, deeply embarrassed, as shy and randy as a boy. His face had turned a rosy pink I hadn't seen since he was fourteen and his voice was changing. A fifty-six-year-old prospective new father. Nothing quite so silly or so self-satisfied, I suppose. And why not? He slid his arm around Marion's hips, bent to kiss her ear. "Don't mind my terrible family," he whispered loudly.

I smiled encouragingly at them both and murmured something, ". . . blah, blah, blah . . . pleasant trip . . ." and so forth.

Martha said, in a sleepy, irritable voice, from the porch. "Well, you're here at last." She shuffled toward us across the lawn, blinking, hugging an old sweater around her. She stopped dead in her tracks when she spotted Marion. It was a delicious moment, like that wonderful Marx Brothers routine of nightshirts in the mirror, the two big-bellied, besmocked women, mouths agape. "My goodness," Martha said in her *deceptively mild* voice. "Whoever is this?"

"Your new auntie," Alice said. "And inside her, your new little cousin."

"Really, Alice, no need to be crude."

"Cousin?"

The men struggled by with the luggage, quite a lot of it, I noticed. Dennis said. "It's the truth. We figured it out in the car."

"Here goes," Teddy said. "Your kid will be my grandnephew . . ."

"Or grandniece . . ." I put in.

"Right, right. And our kid'll be your kid's second cousin and Martha's first cousin. I think that's it."

"Wait till you start in on my family," Dennis said. "This kid's already got, uh, wait . . . well, hell, about ten first cousins at least, maybe two on the way . . . Nothing else to do up there in the winter."

Martha was staring at Marion with that little glint in her eye, that sharp assessing woman's look. Marion ducked her head shyly. "When's yours due?" she asked.

"July tenth, the doctor says, but what does he know? Just look at me."

"So that's what you meant," I said to Teddy. " 'An appropriate surprise,' you sly old thing . . . Now, tell me, when do you have to go back? I hope you can stay a few days."

"Um, but we're not going back. We sort of decided we'd like to stay here. It's a better place for kids. We were both getting pretty sick of California anyway. That's what brought us together, sort of. Marion's an Ohio girl. She's from Piqua, you know."

This time I was the one with the dreadful cackle, thinking of the two grubby drooling tots soon to be crawling across the porch, two mothers hanging diapers on the line, two women in the kitchen . . . oh, dear. But, if I remembered rightly from my one encounter with Marion and all previous encounters with Teddy's women, it was safe to assume she was blessedly undomestic, a room-service and take-out-Chinese girl from the word go. No trouble there, at least.

"Besides," Teddy said. "I can't work for Duff anymore, much as I love the guy. I can't take orders from him, if you know what I mean. Friend is one thing, boss is another."

"I can quite imagine," I said, assuming a straight face. "And how is the old terror?"

We did present a rather astounding picture the next day in Jonathan's chambers. Teddy and Marion in those shiny California peacock getups, the geriatric *primiparas.* Alice in a blue shirtwaist and disreputable sneakers. Martha in a new smock, pale green with pink rabbits, quite vile. Dennis, who did possess a certain spidery elegance in his normal clothes, merely awkward and common in a stiff brown suit.

I was in mauve silk and looked just fine, thank you, making up for all the rest. I wondered as Jonathan read out the words, if he was recalling, as I was, one very long hot afternoon on a deserted stretch of dunes near Montauk, years ago. He'd been a law student then and I a wicked old woman of thirty-five. His pale blue eye met mine, slid away, returned. He smiled.

Vern was taken ill during the ceremony and had to lie down in the back of the car while the rest of us lapped up quite a bit of the excellent champagne provided by Jonathan, stylish and generous as I remembered him. There was more champagne, Teddy's, waiting at home. In the evening we all felt somewhat let down, sitting quietly together in the den, nursing our separate faint champagne hangovers, watching *Gunga Din* on the snowy channel.

ii

MARTHA

When the commercial came on Dennis put down his glass, yanked off his tie and draped it over the arm of the sofa. I was trying to remember how many times I'd ever seen him in a regular white shirt, a suit and tie. Twice, counting today. He looked alien and mysterious to me, a homely man in cheap clothes sitting beside me. He must belong somewhere else, in one of my raunchy fantasies . . . in a bus station, maybe, getting ready to try to pick me up, take me to his seedy room, watch me in a cracked mirror while he had his way with me . . . didn't I wish. But those days were gone forever. No more fantasies and surprises, no more adventures, and this was no stranger sitting here beside me, it was, guess who . . .

Back in high school girls would write their names with boys' names, trying them all out, Mrs. So-and-so So-and-so . . . but I'd never done it, never once. And now here I was, Mrs. . . . I couldn't bring myself to say it yet, even to myself. The old panic was beginning to rise in me again like water filling up a jar. Was I going to have to spend the whole rest of my life like this, scared silly? No, I'd get used to it sooner or later. Everybody did. You could get used to anything if you put your mind to it.

"You okay?" Dennis ran his thumb across the palm of my hand, the left one with the new ring, his ring. I didn't answer. He turned his head, staring down at me warily. Wouldn't it be funny if he changed his mind now, after all we'd been through (all I'd put him through)?

"I'm just fine," I said. "Besides, I can always . . . men like divorced women, don't they, they think they're easy. I'd have some fun again. . . ."

He put my hand down calmly, the way you'd lay aside a book you were reading, though imagine Dennis reading a book, and picked up his glass again. "Sometimes you should just shut up, Martha, you know that?" He sounded merely annoyed. Obviously I was losing my touch. I sighed and closed my eyes. "Now she falls asleep on me," he said, his eyes on the screen.

"No. I'm too tired and too fat to sleep." I leaned awkwardly against him, no longer a walrus—a blimp, a great whale.

"Feels like you weigh a ton."

"I probably do."

July 4

i

ALICE

Buddy and I walked out across the strip, and that very minute the sun came out from behind the clouds, shining off the wings of the new Cessna 195. It looked pretty as a picture sitting there, exactly like the ads in the flying magazines. Teddy'd brought it in from Wichita on Thursday, excited as a kid himself. There were all kinds of gimmicks on the thing, adjustable seats like in a car, a little fold-up step by the cabin door. I could see Buddy sort of hanging back as we got up close. Guess he was wishing for a minute she was the old Jenny, because he knew her and all her tricks.

"Go on, climb in. Let's try her out." As soon as I opened the door that sharp new-metal new-car smell came out of the cabin at us.

"You're going to take her first, though, aren't you?" He hoisted himself up onto the little step. "I mean, this is a real big airplane."

"Only looks big. Now don't go all chicken-hearted on me." I pushed him into the left-hand seat and stretched out on the bench thing behind it. "Look at these fancy cushions back here. Think I'll lie down and get comfortable."

"I wish you'd sit up here, so's you can help me out if I mess up."

"You're not going to mess up. A few new wrinkles, you'll get used to 'em. Right now, uh, there, you need to taxi her in a kind of S pattern, so you can see what's coming at you, with this high nose. Doesn't matter here, but you're bound to be someplace someday when it will."

"Okay," he said. "Yeah, I see what you mean. Wow." I could tell the jitters were wearing off. The new engine sounded big and powerful as we started our roll.

"I'm going to sit here and act like a customer now." I folded my arms and crossed my legs. "You can pretend I'm Mrs. Lah-Di-Dah."

"You going to make a pass at me then?"

"She didn't . . . !"

"Tried it with Denny too, he said."

"Here and I thought she was only after the older fellows like Teddy. . . . Give her full throttle for a minute, right . . . now ease off . . . good."

"Felt like I was using an awful lot of right rudder then. . . ."

"That's the way she flies. Different, that's all. You'll get used to it." He was doing okay, though, more than okay for a kid of eighteen in an airplane he'd never set eyes on before.

As we climbed out I caught a quick glimpse of the picnic table with a paper tablecloth fluttering off one edge; then down below, as we banked, the scorched place where the two hangars had been and the new hangar going up, all raw wood and rafters; then beyond that across the brook the new-laid empty roads of the development with all the little claptrappy houses scattered around like cigar boxes somebody'd put out with the trash. We were going to have to plant something there, to hide them from the house. Couldn't hide them from up here, though, could you? Just too bad.